THE DEVIL'S MARK

THE DEVIL'S MARK

TONY ACREE
LYNN TINCHER

ISBN:

Hydra Publications

Goshen, Kentucky

www.hydrapublications.com

Lynn Tincher Dedication

Dedicated to my husband Eric and to my kids, Emily, Aaron and Becca and my grandkids Max, Eli, Benny, Auggie, and Audrey! I love you all. Most importantly, to my mom, Shirley.

Tony Acree Dedication

In memory of my brother, Wild Bill. I lost a brother, a friend and Victor's biggest fan. We miss you.

Chapter One

It was the mark of the devil carved into a man's chest that made Detective Paige Aldridge offer a rue smile. The blood was dry, meaning he'd been dead at least for a little while. Another murder victim. She was happy this one was not connected to the Demon, Leraje, with whom Paige had been battling for the last few months. This was something different. It even felt like another world. Paige didn't want to think the Devil's Mark Killer was anything beyond a satanic worshipping serial killer and not the real deal. However, she put nothing too far out of her mind. She'd seen enough to know better. And she had one of her feelings.

On her knees beside the victim, Paige knelt in three inches of snow. She ignored the shivers as she looked up at Officer Tom Miller, who was hovering over her and rifling through the victim's wallet. Tom was her personal police bodyguard following a recent attempt on her life. "Do you have an ID?" she asked.

"Yep. This one is Brian McIver from High Street. Aged forty-two." Tom said as he examined the driver's license.

"There's credit cards and cash still in here. Other than being a victim, I'll bet there's no connection to the others. But I'll run it anyway. How long?" he asked the CSI agent, Tamara Evans, who was busy zipping up evidence bags.

"About twenty-four hours," Tamara replied. "He was most likely killed yesterday. Give or take a few hours. I'll know more soon enough."

Paige nodded. With a blue gloved hand, she carefully turned the victim's head to examine him further. This was the fifth victim with an inverted pentagram carved into the skin. The Devil's Mark. The killer had been busy. The victim's hands had apparently been bound at one time as there were rope burn marks around his wrists. However, there was no sign of rope or cuffs or anything of the sort nearby. The snow had just fallen over the last few hours. This made investigating the scene nearly impossible. This was the same MO as the other victims. No sign of robbery. No sign of abuse. Just bound, murdered, and mutilated. Only there was always one more thing...

"Thanks," Paige said as she carefully turned the victim's head the other direction and noticed his face had turned purple and his eyes looked a little bugged out. "Looks to have choked as well. How much ya wanna bet I find an upside-down crucifix shoved down his throat?"

"I'd bet on you," Tom tried to laugh but it faded away.

Tamara walked toward the CSI van. Tom took the opportunity and leaned down so only Paige could hear him. "Get anything yet?"

"No. Not yet. I've been in and out of the Collective Conscious looking for the killer all month. I've not gleaned a thing. Not even from the victims. Not even today," Paige said as she pried the victim's frozen mouth open with a pen from her pocket. She glanced over her shoulder to make sure no one was watching. She had to be careful not to disturb the body even more, but she just wanted a peek inside. Sure enough, the end of a three-inch-long crucifix was visible and lodged top side down in his throat. "I need to be sure to get this from Evidence once the autopsy is done. I want to find who's buying these things." Paige groaned as she stood up. "I'm not giving up. I'll keep looking. I'll find them."

Tom touched her shoulder, "I don't doubt that. Not even for a second."

"I wish I had as much faith in myself. I would have found my sister." Paige's voice drifted away.

After the initial investigation was over, Paige stood and watched as the paramedics carefully strapped the body onto a gurney and then pushed it into the ambulance. Watching their breath form a mist in front of them fascinated her for some reason. She imagined Brian McIver's last breath in the cold. The crucifix had been shoved in violently after the victim had been strangled. The thought depressed her. She had to find the killer. Five victims. All males. No apparent connection to each other, that is, other than being murdered by a serial killer with the same MO. *Why the Devil's mark? What's going on? What are we missing?* Paige said quietly, under her breath. After looking around to make sure no one was watching, she leaned against her car, closed her eyes, and tapped into the Collective Conscious.

Paige was called a Reader and able to read everyone's thoughts that flowed through the Collective Conscious. At times, if she wanted, she could manipulate other's thoughts. Only thoughts and images could be read and only as people thought about them. They didn't stay in the Collective Conscious, waiting to be discovered. They only passed through quickly, never to return unless someone thought of them again. Feelings could not be read unless the words were formed in the thinker's mind like "Man, I feel sick" or "I'm so in love with her." After training with the FBI and a mystical boost from a fellow Reader, Visette, Paige had become excellent at accessing the Collective Conscious at will.

She was one of six Readers and a strong one at that. She knew of four Readers already but was currently looking for the last. Paige needed each to fight the demon, Leraje, who was trying to take each of their powers for his own.

But she couldn't think about that now. She needed to find the serial killer before he struck again. *In the moment, Paige,* she whispered to herself. *Live in the moment.* She settled into her thoughts and returned to the Collective Conscious. She looked for someone who would be thinking about any of the murders, a crucifix or the mark. Even though she shuddered at the thought, she looked for someone thinking about carving the pentagram into someone's skin. Again today, she came up empty.

———

As Tom stood by the ambulance, he looked to his left toward Paige. It was his job to keep an eye on her, and the other Readers, as much as possible. He and Agent Riggs from the FBI were the two Keepers of the Secrets about the Readers and their abilities. Although Agent Riggs was missing, Tom did his best to keep an eye on Paige as they searched for Junna, Paige's sister, and one more unknown Reader. He worried about Paige. Even as strong as she was, she was becoming extremely stressed out and he wondered how much more she could take. Being assigned by the Chief of Detectives to be her bodyguard was a blessing.

———

Paige drew in a deep breath and listened to the thousands of thoughts which moved through. She tried to visualize them as she looked for someone who might be thinking of the murders or planning the next one. Again, she even looked for someone just looking at a crucifix. Anything that might be connected.

After several moments, as Paige drifted from thought to thought, she gleaned an image. It was faint at first, but as the image became clearer, she could see another inverted cross. It too was in someone's mouth. She was onto something. She tried to see more of the surroundings to determine if maybe another murder was in progress or if the killer was just remembering, thinking about what he had done.

———

A strange light suddenly emanated from the slits in Paige's nearly closed eyes. Tom wondered if anyone else noticed it. It was faint, but obvious. He knew she was on to something. Something big. A strange sense of relief consumed him. Tom quickly talked to the other investigators at the scene as he tried to draw everyone to the other side of the ambulance to keep them from noticing what Paige was doing. He wished she had just climbed into her car. It would make his job of keeping her talents hidden much easier. The ambulance suddenly drove away, leaving her exposed to those that stood by.

What to do? Tom thought and then pretended to see something in the snow. Anything to keep them away from Paige. "Hey, there's something over there," he pointed in the opposite direction. As the other officers left to go look, he took one more glance at Paige. She had slid down and sat in the snow against her car. Her head lowered now so no one could see her eyes. Relieved, Tom said, "Sorry. I thought I saw a rope in the snow. Must have been my imagination."

———

Paige watched images fly by like an old-timey picture show in the Collective Conscious. She could see a pair of hands prying open the mouth of a woman. Another victim. The first female victim that she knew of. The hands forcing open the jaw of the victim appeared to be male. Big hands. Paige took a deep breath. *Where are you? Who are you?* She whispered in her thoughts and sent them toward the man. She could see as if through his eyes as he looked around at their surroundings. They were in an alley. Paige could barely make out a street sign. Frankfort Avenue. Okay, Paige knew the area. She could find the body. She had only to scour the alleys along Frankfort. The man then slowly looked down at the victim. Paige could see the top of what looked like an inverted pentagram scratched into her chest, just above her blouse. The blood was fresh and bright red. The stain on her blouse was still growing slightly. Two murders in two days. He was stepping it up.

The woman was blonde, pretty, and not someone Paige recognized. She watched as the man brushed the woman's hair with his hand and trailed his finger down her cheek. *Come on now. Show me who you are.* Paige said to the man. He then slowly stood up and removed a wallet from his jeans pocket. He flipped the wallet open and glanced at his driver's license. After a moment he slipped it back into his pocket. Paige had the name of the Devil's Mark Killer. Victor Riley McCain.

Chapter Two

"What the hell are you doing?"

Victor Riley McCain glanced at the wallet in his hand, shrugged a large shoulder and slipped the wallet into his pocket, then spoke to the woman standing in front of him. "I'm such a pretty man, I wanted to see if my DMV photo lived up to the real thing."

Detective Linda Coffey rolled her eyes and shook her head. "You're a house with feet, you know that, right?"

At six-foot-six inches tall and around two-hundred and seventy pounds, Victor believed he resembled the remark. "And yet you love me anyway."

"I often wonder why." Of medium height with longish brown hair and liquid brown eyes, she wrapped her arms around herself and stamped her feet in the snow, trying to keep warm. She nodded with her chin to the dead body between them. "With the pentagram crap, does this seem like the work of Satan and his minions to you?"

"Hell if I know. Pun intended."

"I thought if anyone would know, it would be The Hand of God, God's bounty hunter."

"What can I tell you? This job doesn't come with a How to Guide listing the top fifty known evil dumb ass moves."

Around the globe were a handful of men and women fighting the good fight, tracking down and killing the things which go bump in the night on behalf of God Almighty. Victor became one of them as penance for his part in the death of his predecessor, causing him to lose his chance at Heaven in the process. It remained a matter of debate which direction his eternal soul would take when his ticket to the hereafter got punched to the hereafter.

They returned their gaze to the dead woman who appeared to be in her mid-twenties, dressed for work in an office considering she wore a white blouse, black slacks, low heeled black shoes, and a chestnut brown winter coat. Victor bent down to examine the coat closer where a patch appeared darker than the rest. He used a meaty finger to move the coat a bit to the side to expose a large tear in the woman's blouse turned red from the loss of blood.

Detective Coffey leaned over at the waist and let out a huge breath, pushing out her cheeks. "Guess we know how she died."

"Yes'em. Knife wound. Up and under her rib cage and quite likely directly into her heart. A hard way to die."

He stood up and glanced around. The body lay behind a beat-up green dumpster in an alley off Frankfort Avenue which ran behind a series of buildings. Each business featured a rear door with a red sign above it. The Giancarlo Altezzoso Gallery hung above the far door. Coltrane's Military Surplus in the middle and, over the closest door, the sign Peas & Shallots.

Linda followed his gaze and said, "The food's not half bad,

as long as you like overpriced food, with small portions which take up about a quarter of your plate and are usually served cold with a ton of garlic."

Victor laughed. "Where I come from, we call something like that Weight Watchers. Of our three choices this early in the morning, I'm thinking art gallery. How'd you end up here, anyway? I thought you were still on a desk. And this lady can't have been dead for more than an hour or two."

"I got an anonymous call on my personal cell, and they dropped your name, saying you might be interested in this one. I thought it might be a hoax and decided to drive out and take a look. I told you about the other murderers. From what I've heard through the blue grapevine is this one is very similar, other than the fact it's a woman, not a man. I'm hoping they'll let me back in the game with this one. "

Victor met Linda when she was investigating two murders they thought had been committed by Victor's brother Mikey. Turns out they were right, but proving it was something altogether different. During the investigation her partner, Sam Wallace, was murdered and Linda suspended because of actions she took during the investigation. Many in the department believed Victor was helping his brother and because of her association with him blamed Linda for the death of Detective Wallace. The case was officially still open, though Victor and Linda knew Mikey was out of the ballgame having been buried at the bottom of a bridge pillar in the Ohio River. And in a strange turn of events, they had been dating ever since.

"I don't know. This sounds incredibly fishy to me. It would have to be somebody who knew you and me and my connection to all things Satanish. Were you able to track down the phone number?"

Linda nodded, "It's a burner phone. I tried calling it, but it seems they removed the battery. It goes straight to a voicemail that has not been set up."

Victor slid on gloves, then stuffed his hands into the pockets of his black bomber jacket and glanced around the scene. "Who's running the other investigations?"

"A detective named Paige Aldridge. I don't know much about her other than she's young and gets results. She's an up and comer. She solved the Ian Messing case a few months ago. Why don't you see what you can find out on your end, and I'll give her a call. "

"Will do. But I've got a bad feeling about this. You need to be careful. There are plenty who would like to hang you out to dry." He walked a few steps then turned around. "The next time you call me for a date, how about we go someplace better than this?"

"Peas and Shallots?"

"Beef and bourbon. The last time I ate peas I think I was six years old."

"I can meet you tonight at The Raven and you can have Guinness and lamb shank instead of beef."

"Done deal."

Victor walked away thinking, *Dying behind a gourmet restaurant. I will have to add it to my list of nightmares.*

Chapter Three

After investigating the scene of the murder of the female victim, Paige sat at her desk staring at her computer while researching anything she could find on Victor McCain. There was not much. She did locate an address and scribbled it down on a small notebook she kept in her jacket pocket. *What is going on in your mind, Mr. McCain? What is your next move?* she whispered to herself, hoping to glean something and half expecting him to flat out answer.

She put her forehead in her hands and took a deep breath. Oh how she wished Jay was conscious and not laying in a hospital bed. She really needed his help. Jay was her partner not only on the force, but in life; until he lost it and tried to kill her. Paige shot him in self-defense, and he had been unconscious ever since. Somehow, she knew it wasn't really Jay in his head. Something else took control of his mind and made him try to kill her. It had to. Jay loved her, after all.

Paige leaned back in her chair and spun around stopping only to pick up a pencil and the phone receiver. Drumming the pencil on her desk, she dialed the evidence room.

"Hey Mariah, any chance I could get a good look at the crucifix in the McIver case?" Paige asked the second Mariah picked up the phone.

"Sure, I have it. What are you looking for?" Mariah asked.

"I just want to see if it's like the others. You know, looking for any detail that might lead me to who purchased them."

"Well, it does look just like the others, but you are welcome to come and take a peek."

"Thanks, lady, I owe you one." Paige quickly hung up the phone and ran down the hall. After sprinting down three flights of stairs, she opened the door to the evidence room and slammed into someone's chest.

"Whoa there, missy." Tom said breathlessly. "I was just going to open the door for you. Mariah said you were coming."

"Yeah, sorry. Didn't mean to plow you over. Did you find anything?"

"No, nothing new," he said, as he walked Paige over to the table where Mariah had the crucifix in a bag under a bright light.

Paige lifted the bag and turned the crucifix over several times. Blood slightly covered the inside of the bag from where the victim's mouth had been bleeding. Some of it had dried on the metal and some on the bag. "What about the one from the female victim, Brenda Mazza?"

Mariah turned and grabbed a second bag and handed it to her. "Same thing."

"Hmmm," Paige grunted as she compared the two. She carefully turned each one around to examine them under the light, careful not to disturb either of them. Identical. Nothing from what she could see through the blood to indicate a maker or a made in China or anything unusual.

"There has to be someone, somewhere, who thinks it's odd to sell these things in high quantities."

"Unless he ordered them online or something," Tom said as Paige nodded. He lowered his voice and asked, "Any luck on finding Mr. McCain?"

"Not a lot. He seems pretty low profile, however, I do have an address. Wanna watch his house with me tonight? That is, if it's a good address. Maybe he'll be home this evening."

"Can't think of anything better thing I need to be doing." Tom chuckled. "Want me to grab a pizza?"

"Sounds great. Meet here at about seven? Then we can just head over together?"

"Um-hmm," Tom replied as he looked closer at the evidence. "Wait, did either of you see this?"

"What?" Mariah asked.

"Here, look." Tom pointed at the clasp on the chain as Paige squeezed in beside him for a closer look. "Looks like a long brown hair. See, it's wound around it, just there."

"I'll look at it. I was just getting into this case and hadn't really looked closely yet," Mariah said defensively as she carefully took the bag from Tom. "I'll let you know what Doc says. It may belong to the victim. I know he will want to run some tests right away."

"Thanks, Mariah," Paige smiled. "You or Doc give me a buzz as soon as you hear anything."

Paige turned to run out the door and yelled, "See you at seven."

Chapter Four

Victor pushed the call button on the steering wheel of his Ford Flex and told the voice he wanted to call Kurt Pervis. While the magic of Bluetooth connected his call, he thought about the dead body. He didn't tell Linda how much the whole situation bothered him. The circle of people who knew what he did for a living was incredibly small and any of them would contact him directly instead of Linda. He knew Linda kept what he did a secret and would not have told anyone.

His thoughts were interrupted when Kurt answered. "What's up, Big Guy?"

Kurt Pervis was the best hacker in the business and over the last couple of years he had grown into much more. A man possessed of surfer-boy good looks, he helped Victor attack the Church of the Light Reclaimed, a radical group of Satanists, first through cyberspace, then directly on missions.

"Kurt, I'm headed your way. I need you to access the Louisville Metro Police database. There've been a string of murders and the lead investigator is Paige Aldridge. There are possible satanic connections and I need to know what she knows."

"Do you ever do anything that doesn't have Satan involved? Dude, you need a career change."

"Underwear supermodel?"

Kurt made a gagging sound. "I think I barfed up my breakfast. See you soon."

He hung up and Victor turned up the satellite radio. Eric Church was singing about Damn Rock and Roll, and he began to sing along, drumming the fingers of his right hand on the dashboard while he drove.

The hacker extraordinaire lived on Smyrna Lane off the Gene Snyder Freeway and Victor got caught by the light at the end of the ramp. He settled into his seat and closed his eyes and imagined the post-dinner workout he would put Linda through when someone slammed into the rear of the Ford, the impact throwing him deep into his seat, the seat belt tightening around him. His eyes flew open in time to see his car shoved into the middle of the intersection.

A middle-aged woman driving a Nissan Pathfinder cruising down Smyrna with the green light, T-boned Victor's car, her eyes wide, a scream on her lips he couldn't hear. The impact crushed in the side of his door, throwing him sideways, and his airbag exploded as the Ford was thrown into a slide.

Victor felt disoriented from the crashes and fumbled the gear shift into park. It required two attempts to click the release on his seat belt. He glanced first at the woman in the Nissan but couldn't see her over the caved-in hood and the airbag filling up her window. He blinked a couple of times and then checked the rearview mirror to see who hit him from behind.

Two men got out of a large Chevy Silverado 1500 twin cab, and he knew his day was about to get worse. The main clue? The two men wore masks over their faces, and each carried a baseball bat. The driver was of average height and packed enough weight around his middle to give Santa a run for his money. The passenger was a few inches taller with shoulders the size of a small mountain.

Victor slid a hand under his seat to grab a gun he kept there only to fail. The gun had been jarred loose by the force of the accident. Shoulders got to his passenger door and yanked it open. He reached in and tried to snag Victor's arm and snarled, "Come here, asshole."

Victor leaned in the guy's direction, letting him take hold of his arm. The man grinned until Victor shot his hand out and clutched a handful of the man's jacket. The smile faded when he pulled hard and fast, slamming the man's head into the top of the door jam. Victor heard a satisfying thunk as the ski mask provided little protection from the metal frame of the Ford.

He shoved the man away and moved into the passenger seat. Fat Man knocked the other guy out of the way and launched a mighty two-handed swing with his bat in Victor's direction. Barry Bonds the guy was not. Victor should have been an easy target for anyone with any training, yet he hesitated enough for Victor to pull the armrest of the door and clip the bat on its incoming trajectory.

Fat Man tried to pull the door open, and Victor let him, once again using the bad guy's momentum against him. Victor shoved the door with his shoulder forcing the bad guy off balance. It was all the advantage he needed. The Hand of God exploded out of his car and this time when Fat Man wound up for his two-handed swing, Victor stepped closer. The one place you do not want to be when attacked by a man with a bat is at the end of the barrel. Louisville Slugger puts the emblem to mark the sweet spot for a reason. Try to catch the end of a bat in full swing and you might as well book your trip to either the hospital or the morgue.

Where you want to be is close to the hand holding the bat. It stops the momentum and reduces the energy of the swing. Victor lifted his left arm and caught the swing as it started, then clamped down hard, trapping both of Fat Man's arms under his. The man started to say something but never finished as Victor slammed a ferocious headbutt into the man's nose. He both felt and heard the nose shatter into a pulpy mess.

The man screamed in pain and Victor bent and lifted the man by the crotch, swiveled and slammed him down hard onto the roof of the Ford, creating a huge dent. He thought, *What the hell? What's one more dent?*

Fat Man slid off the roof and onto the pavement, not moving. Shoulders managed to get on all fours and tried to stand. Victor lifted him by the arm and the man actually said, "Thank you."

Victor smiled and replied, "You're welcome." Then hit him hard in the gut with a right uppercut which sent the man down again, this time for good.

Who says you cannot keep a bad man down?

Chapter Five

Paige sat in her car, waiting for Tom. Her stomach growled at the thought of pizza and a stakeout. She took a small set of binoculars out of her pocket and placed them on her dash. "Come on, Tom," she whispered as she watched the cars pass the police department. Anxious to get to the address, she started to text Tom just as he pulled in.

"I know. It's a quarter past seven. Sorry. The pizza took a bit longer than I expected," he said as he opened the passenger door to Paige's car and handed her the pizza. "I picked up a couple of soft drinks too."

"Good, I thought I'd starve to death waiting for you," she laughed as she waited for him to get settled before she handed the pizza to him. "Veggie?"

"Oh hell no. All meat. Need protein on a stake out, right?"

Paige laughed, "Yeah, okay. I guess you're right." She put the car in gear and started out toward the street. "Hand me a slice, will ya? I'm starving."

Tom opened the box and took out a piece. As he handed it

to her, he asked "Have you ever talked to this Linda Coffey before?"

"No, it was a first. I thought it was a bit strange she reached out to me. It's not really been public I was investigating, has it?" Paige tried to catch a long piece of cheese strung out and down her chin.

Tom took a drink from his soda to keep from laughing. "Not really, no. But news gets around in the precinct, remember?"

"Yeah, yeah. News travels faster than Virginia Creeper. Anyway, why female this time? Have you had any thoughts?"

"I'm still at a blank," Tom said. "It all seems so random. Maybe this victim got in the way of the real target and McCain had to improvise?"

Paige made a quick right turn causing the pizza box to nearly slide off Tom's lap. "You may be right. I didn't think of that." She stopped slightly around the corner from an aging townhome complex and shut the car down. She licked her fingers and motioned for Tom to hand her another slice. With her clean hand, she grabbed the binoculars from the dash and focused in on the door.

After checking all around to make sure no one was watching, he relaxed in his seat, munching on his own slice of pie. "Were you able to glean anything? Did you see him again in the Collective?"

With a mouthful of pizza, Paige mumbled something which resembled no so Tom nodded like he understood.

————

After watching for two hours, and not seeing anyone except a scrawny teenage boy wearing shorts in the cold and a hoodie, Paige closed her eyes and tried to tap into Victor McCain.

Nothing. She shifted her thoughts toward her missing sister, Junna, hoping to find her thinking about anything. Paige, their brother Shepherd, Jay, anyone. Nothing.

She looked over at Tom, who was looking in the side-view mirror and lightly drumming his thumb on the edge of the pizza box. "I think we need to go knock on his door, and the doors of his neighbors if he's not home. See if anyone knows anything."

Tom turned toward her, "It's well after nine now. Do you think they'll be up?"

"Of course," Paige smiled as she started her car to pull closer to McCain's door. "If not, they couldn't have been asleep for long. It's not like it's two in the morning. Not everyone is an old fogie like you."

"Haha," Tom said. "I don't go to bed until nine-thirty."

Paige giggled as she parked and stepped out of the car. She enjoyed the banter she and Tom were developing together. It made her think of her partner and boyfriend, Jay. A feeling of loneliness swept through her. She missed Jay. More than she cared to admit.

As she met Tom on the sidewalk, they walked together toward McCain's door, then knocked. A middle-aged woman with a neat bun on the top of her head opened the door, barely peeking through the crack.

"Hello, my name is Detective Paige Aldridge, and this is my partner, Tom Miller. We're looking for Victor McCain. Is he home?"

"Victor? No. I'm sorry. He moved out many months ago. Nice guy. Big." The lady seemed to blush.

"Do you have any idea where he may have gone?" Paige asked.

"No, he didn't leave an address or anything. He just sort of disappeared. Vanished into thin air."

Paige shuffled her feet. "Okay, thank you. Here's my card. Please call me if you happen to remember or see anything."

The woman carefully took the card from her hand. "Is he in some sort of trouble?"

"No, no. We just need to talk to him about something. Not a big deal." Paige could sense the woman was a little nervous for him. "What's your name?"

"Jenna McDonald. I'll call you if he turns up. I haven't seen him in a long time."

"Thanks again, you have a good night," Paige said as she nodded and turned toward her car.

"Dead end? Or do you think she's hiding anything? Want to try the neighbors?" Tom asked.

"Dead end. If he's been gone that long, I doubt they'd know anything."

Chapter Six

Kurt shook his head. "Dude, you're lucky you're alive. Did your Spidey-senses go off?"

Victor knew Kurt was talking about the feelings he got in the presence of a fallen angel. Whenever one was around, he got the sense the world was not quite right, even if they were possessing someone instead of in their own bodies. Victor filled Kurt in about the accident, having to get his car towed to a guy he knew and catching a ride to his other car, a red 69 Chevelle.

"Nothing. This was something different. The guys told the cops I cut them off when I got on the interstate, then shot them the bird, neither of which happened. They swore up and down I did. It was weird.

"That's so bizarre. Do you need to call Winston back from vacation?"

Winston Reynolds had once been one of Victor's rivals. Now he was his right-hand man when it came to fighting the things that go bump in the night. "Nah. He's over in Europe with his aunt and uncle. Let him enjoy some time away. We've got this."

"You're the boss. Any-hoot, I've got the list of names you wanted, the other victims of the serial killer. The cops have a really cool name for him, The Devil's Mark Killer. Cool, huh?"

Victor laughed at his friend. "Kurt, cool is not the word I would use. What do you have?"

"Okay. Whatever. The first victim was Charlie Pratt, a fifty-five-year-old retired teacher. He was murdered almost exactly a year ago. The others were murdered in two-month increments. Victim number two was Leonard Ingram, thirty-two years old and an assistant manager at the Target over off Westport Road. Number three, Andy Bell, a thirty-seven-year-old author who writes kids' books. Number four was David Nichols, a sixty-six-year-old banker at PNC, and the last one Brian McIver, a forty-two-year-old nurse at Norton's downtown."

"What about the woman we found in the alley this morning?"

Kurt clicked a few times with his mouse and pointed to the screen. "Brenda Mazza. They updated the file on her about an hour ago. She worked at an art gallery."

"Yeah, Giancarlo Altezzoso Gallery. Ever heard of them?"

"Dude, my idea of art is a Marvel superhero poster. I have five of them. Want to see 'em?"

"Uh, no. Ruth Anne lets you hang this crap in the house?"

Ruth Anne was Kurt's fiancé and had seen her own fair share of grief at the hand of the Church of the Light Reclaimed. It was how the two of them met. "Oh, she doesn't care. As long as I keep them in the basement."

The man was a true geek. "Do the cops have any idea how the six of them are connected?"

"Man, they are dead in the water, pun intended."

Victor thought about it for a moment. "Whoever it is, they're picking up the pace. Two murders in the same day? Unless we have a cult-type thing and there's more than one killer, then the guy is picking up speed. I'll need to find him soon. A guy like this who gets to like what he's doing, won't stop."

"True that. What can I do to help?"

"I might as well start at the beginning. Print off the street addresses for me and any of the relevant data and I'll start my own investigation in the morning."

"You got it, Big Guy. If anyone can do it, you can."

———

Charlie Pratt lived in the Highlands, an area of town known for its dining and nightlife on Bardstown Road. Pratt's home was a well-maintained Craftsman-style house on Crowley. Victor parked out front and made his way onto the wide front porch and pressed the doorbell.

Morning drifted in on a crisp winter breeze and he zipped up his bomber jacket while he waited. There were lights on inside the house and right when he was about to push the doorbell again, he heard footsteps.

A middle-aged woman glanced through a pane of glass in the door and hesitated a moment before opening it. She was on the short side and skinny, with hair tinged with gray. Her eyes were brown and wary.

"Can I help you?"

Victor introduced himself. "Are you Mrs. Pratt?"

"Yes. What can I do for you, Mr. McCain?"

Victor noticed she did not invite him in. He knew her first name, Carol, and she worked as a secretary for the Jefferson

County Board of Education. "Mrs. Pratt, I'm investigating your husband's murder. There have been several more and I've been asked by interested parties to look into what's going on."

A hand went to her throat and her face paled. "More? When?"

"Today. May I come in?"

She swung the door open and stepped out of the way. He thanked her and walked inside, first stomping his boots on her welcome mat to knock off the snow. She showed Victor into a living area by a fireplace unlit and unused. He sat in a white wing chair, and she took the small sofa across from him.

"Who hired you, Mr. McCain?"

Direct. Victor liked that in people. "I can't tell you, but what I can do is promise to share anything I learn with you. I understand the police have, to this point, come up empty."

She let out a heavy sigh and dry washed one hand with the other. "Yes, though I do believe they've tried. They think, at this point, Charlie was the victim of a random killer. I've done a lot of research myself since Charlie was--since Charlie died."

"I'm sorry for your loss, Mrs. Pratt. What can you tell me about your husband? Had he any problems with anyone? I understand he was retired. Where did he teach?"

"Please, call me Carol. Yes. He taught for thirty years at a couple of different high schools, the last ten at Sacred Heart. He turned fifty-five, had his thirty in and wanted to try something else. He'd only been retired for a bit over a month when it happened. And Charlie got along with everyone. There was no reason for this to happen to him."

"Do the names Brenda Mazza or Brian McIver mean anything to you?"

She shook her head. "No. Are they new victims? Were they killed the same way?"

"Yes ma'am."

She closed her eyes for a moment and without opening them said, "I've been having nightmares. And in them, I'm in bed and Charlie is calling out to me. The room is pitch black and the light by my bed won't work. When I get out of bed to go find him, I can sense another presence in the room. I turn towards him, but it's not Charlie." She swallowed hard, her hands now still in her lap, clenched so tight the knuckles turned white.

She continued, "The thing is so large, it takes up the entire corner of the bedroom and I can smell it more than see it. It smells of decay, smoke, and something else: blood. I grew up on a farm and we cleaned and dressed the deer my dad and brothers shot. I'll never forget the coppery scent of blood. And in my dream, it's reaching out to me, and I begin to scream. And then I wake up."

As if putting action to words, she opened her eyes and stared at him. "I've had the same dream every night for the past year. I've been seeing a therapist about it, but it hasn't helped."

Victor felt the hairs on the back of his neck stand on end. A demon. "Losing your husband, the way you did would be hard for anyone to deal with."

"I don't think that's it. I don't know how I know, but it's real. At any rate, I've had enough. I called a realtor this morning and by tomorrow there will be a for sale sign in the yard. I gave my two-week notice. I have a sister who lives in Arizona. I'll be gone in two weeks regardless if the house has sold or not."

They talked for a few more minutes and then Victor left. When he got behind the wheel of the Chevelle, he stared at the house for a moment. Demons.

Why did it have to be demons?

Chapter Seven

Paige drew a hot bubble bath. It was nice to have a morning off, so she could ease her way into the day and bubble baths were her favorite way of doing it. *Well, a huge mug full of cream and sugar with a touch of coffee helped,* she thought as she placed the mug on the side of the bathtub. She couldn't remember the last time she had a day off, so even just a morning was a blessing.

The afternoon was going to be very busy with plans to interview the families of the victims again, starting with Charlie Pratt's wife. Paige now had a description of McCain, and maybe someone would remember something that could lead to his capture and conviction. Maybe they knew McCain somehow.

She closed her eyes and lowered herself into the warm water. She thought about the murders, wondering where in the world McCain could be. Slowly, an image started to form at the forefront of her thoughts. McCain slowly came into view. He was thinking about something.

As she waited for the thoughts to clear in the Collective

Conscious, she tried to focus on the area around him. What was he looking at?

Finally, the words came to her. "Charlie Pratt, a fifty-five-year-old retired teacher, Leonard Ingram, thirty-two years old and an assistant manager at Target, Andy Bell, a thirty-seven-year-old author, David Nichols, a sixty-six-year-old banker at PNC, Brian McIver, a forty-two-year old nurse."

Paige's mouth opened as if to say something. He was thinking about his victims. "Where are you?" she whispered. She could see his hands on a steering wheel. He was thumb-drumming as if he were listening to music, but nothing was on. Thanks to the way the Collective Conscious worked, she could see through his eyes. He was driving through... Finally, she saw something familiar as he glanced through the windshield. A Heine Brothers Coffee. The one in the Highlands. She knew where he was. Was he after another victim?

As she tried to focus on exactly where he was going, the vision faded.

"Damn it," she screamed as she jumped out of the tub, covered in soap. She half wrapped a towel around her and ran to find her cell phone on the nightstand in her bedroom. As she reached the bedroom, she yelled, "Hey Siri, call Tom Miller ... mobile."

Siri made the call as she grabbed the phone with wet hands. No answer. Impatiently, she waited for voicemail to kick in. "Hey, Tom. It's me. Victor is driving through the Highlands as we speak. I'm going over there right away and see what I can find. Call me as soon as you get this."

She threw the phone on the bed and grabbed some yoga pants and a sweatshirt. As she fought hard to pull on the yoga pants and fell over on her side against the bed, she really wished she had dried off first. It was like trying to pull a glove over a melon. After bouncing around the room, she finally had enough clothes on to feel comfortable leaving the house. Paige pulled her wet hair up in a ponytail, grabbed her keys and made her way as fast as possible to the Highlands.

———

As she drove up and down Bardstown Road, Paige didn't notice anyone who resembled Victor McCain. She decided to stop and go inside the Heine Brothers and grab a coffee, remembering her mug at home was full and very cold. As she took her first sip, she thought about Mrs. Pratt. She lived over on Crowly, not too far from here. Victor must live nearby, she surmised. She sat at a table near the window and watched the street. A few people were walking and window shopping, while others were going in and out of restaurants for lunch. Nothing looked amiss. Blissfully, no one was aware a serial killer could be among them.

Paige jumped out of her skin when her cell phone rang in the pocket of her sweatshirt, causing her to almost throw her coffee in the air. It was Tom. She'd better fill him in but not in the middle of the coffee shop. "Hey Tom, can I call you right back when I get in my car? Everything's fine. I'm just grabbing a cuppa Joe. Okay, talk soon." She slid the phone in the pocket of her sweatshirt, took one more look up and down the street and decided to leave.

A chill ran through her as she walked to her car and after getting in she started it up, turned the heat on high, and called Tom to fill him in. When she hung up, she decided to drive by Mrs. Pratt's home to case it out before she stopped by later in the afternoon. She had a hunch.

After a thirty-minute drive in traffic, she slowly drove past the house, noting there was a red Chevelle parked in front, right at the steps which led up to the door. She went around the block to pass again. As she approached the corner a block away, she heard tires squeal as a truck hit a car right in front of her, blocking the entire road. As Paige got out of the car to help, two men started to argue.

"Hey, I'm Detective Paige Aldridge with the Louisville Police Department. I witnessed what happened," she said as the men stopped to look at her and calmed a bit. "I'll call this in."

One of the men nodded slowly as he took a long drag from his cigarette. He then dropped it on the sidewalk and stepped on it to put it out. He seemed remarkably calm to have just been in an accident.

She reached for her cell phone and hit the number for the precinct and looked toward Mrs. Pratt's house. She dropped her phone and it smacked hard on the concrete. Victor McCain just stepped out onto the front porch and was heading for his car.

Chapter Eight

Victor opened a folder on the seat next to him and glanced at the pages Kurt printed out for him on the victims. Charles Pratt was murdered on the walking path at the new East End Bridge. They named it the Lewis and Clark Bridge after the two men President Thomas Jefferson sent out to explore the Oregon Purchase, from St. Louis to the Pacific Ocean. George Rogers Clark lived in Louisville and was now rewarded with a bridge named after him. Victor wondered what the two explorers would think about it.

He tossed the folder on the seat next to him, lost in thought. His incredibly wicked brother, Mikey, was buried in one of the bridge pillars, still alive as an Infernal Lord, one of Satan's twelve-foot soldiers, the Fallen Angel's answer to Jesus' twelve disciples. He knew his brother would never die, as he did not need to eat, drink or breath to survive. While he didn't think Pratt's murder and Mikey were connected, he decided to drive over and walk the path to see...what? If he felt anything? See if his Spidey senses tingled?

Victor was still getting used to being the Hand of God and all the perks and burdens which came with it. When a Fallen Angel was nearby, he could feel them like an incredible sense of wrongness. Same for demons. Yet it hadn't worked for Infernal Lords.

Still thinking, he put the car in drive and headed towards the interstate. When he got to the intersection to turn left, there was a fender-bender with a car and truck playing bumper cars. Their day sucked. Instead of turning left, he went the other direction. When he did, he saw a thin woman with long brown hair and wearing yoga pants stare at him, her mouth open. He nodded in appreciation, a fan of the yoga pants.

Then it appeared the woman recognized him, but Victor was sure they had never met. Victor shrugged it off and merged into traffic. In his rearview, he saw the woman run to her car. Cop car. It was unmarked but he knew a cop car when he saw one. He thought for a moment about slowing down and letting her catch up to see what might be going on. Then he thought, *to hell with that* and floored the Chevelle and took the next right, cutting through Cherokee Park.

He worked his way over to I-64 and accelerated up the ramp. Glancing in the rearview, he saw no sign of the police officer. He punched the quick dial for Linda Coffey. After several rings, it went into her voicemail. He tossed the phone onto the seat next to the folder and tried to put it out of his mind for the moment.

He cleared his mind and enjoyed the early morning drive. When he got to the bridge, he parked in a gravel lot underneath the overpass on River Road. He locked the Chevelle and hoofed it across to the path and walked up to the bridge, his hands thrust deep into his pockets. It took about fifteen minutes to get to the bridge itself and the point where Mikey would live out the next several hundred years, with any luck.

Nothing. He had hoped he would feel his brother buried deep in concrete and vice versa, but it wasn't going to happen.

Victor turned to look down the Ohio River to the city. The view was beautiful. He breathed deeply and tried to let the stress leave him. No luck. Pratt died on this very spot a year ago. According to the police report, he'd gone walking to get a few steps in on his Fitbit. Pratt was carrying a few extra pounds and was trying to lose weight. A female jogger found him bleeding out with the Devil's Mark symbol carved into his chest. What a way to start your day.

He glanced down the path as four guys on ten speeds were headed his way from the Indiana side of the river. The path allowed bikers and walkers to cross from one state to the other and enjoy the view while they did so. All four wore the spandex biker pants which showed off a bit too much for Victor's tastes. He pictured himself wearing a pair and busted out laughing.

His laughter stopped when the lead biker, instead of swerving to avoid him, peddled at full speed and crashed into him, taking both to the ground, the bike spinning away down the path. The other three braked to a hard stop and they were on him. The guy who hit him head-on was a middle-aged black man with a thin mustache and a bright green helmet. The man let out a growl and tried to bite his nose.

Victor responded by jamming a thumb into the man's left eye, pushing hard. The man screamed and tried to roll away. Victor let him and he heard one of the other guys, a wiry man wearing a blue helmet with red stripes, shout to the other two, "Grab his legs. We'll toss him over."

Victor looked through the railing of the bridge to the

water a good thirty feet below them and decided, "screw that." A young Hispanic man who looked like he worked out hard, reached to grab his foot and Victor pulled it back and then positioned it right into the young man's groin. The man spun away and vomited onto the bike path.

The third man, who he would bet worked in a library, managed to snag one leg while Skinny got another and they tried to lift him into the air. They learned trying to pick up two-hundred and seventy pounds of fighting deadweight was harder than it looked.

The logical part of Victor's brain noted he still did not detect the presence of a fallen angel. Either the demons learned how to mask their possession, or this was a new thing. He found it impossible to believe four random men would decide to attack him, right after two others did the same thing. The lizard part of his brain broke in and reminded him if he didn't figure out how to kick some major ass soon, the logical part of his brain might find out how gravity and water worked together when you add in thirty feet of drop.

Mustache, his left eye swollen shut, rejoined the fight, grab-bing Victor by the head and choking him while at the same time lifting him. Victor seized the man's helmet in both hands and ripped it off him, the man's chin strap nearly breaking the man's jaw in the process. Now armed he swung the helmet in a vicious arc, slamming it into the temple of the Librarian. The man hit the pavement like a robot with his power switch turned off.

With his leg free, he scissored sideways and planted a size twelve Timberland boot into Skinny's nose, breaking it, a spray of blood turning the railing red. The man dropped Victor's leg and stumbled backward, freeing him from all but Mustache.

With a near two to one weight advantage, Victor heaved himself upwards, snagged the smaller man's shirt, and tossed him over his head. Completely rid of his four would-be attackers, Victor got to his feet. When Mustache tried to get up, Victor picked up one of the bikes and pounded it across his shoulders. This time the man went still, out cold.

Victor surveyed the damage and yanked his phone from his pocket. At least three of the men would need an ambulance and he had a sneaky suspicion none of them were responsible for what happened. His first instinct was to say, "tough shit" and leave them there, but he couldn't do it. He tapped in 9-1-1 and put the phone to his ear.

As he made the call, he glanced over the rail and to the Indiana side of the river. A road ran parallel to the river, and he saw a woman with long sandy hair standing next to a dark-colored Porsche. She was watching through binoculars, and he wondered if she'd already called the police, but he didn't see a phone in her hand.

The 9-1-1 operator came on and asked him what his emergency was. He told her but didn't hear her response. The woman lowered the binoculars and stared at him, and while he couldn't be sure from this distance, she looked pissed. He felt cold fingers slide down his spine and the hair on his body stand on end. He began to jog down the path to the Indiana side of the bridge, his eyes never leaving the woman. He disconnected the phone and shoved it in his pocket as he broke into a full sprint.

The woman watched him for another moment, then opened the door to her Porsche, got behind the wheel, and took off with a roar. Victor came to a halt, panting from the run, knowing he would never get to her in time. The car disappeared out of sight under the bridge, and he was not about to cross four lanes of interstate traffic to try to see where she went.

Victor walked slowly back to the bicycle outlaw gang to

wait on the cops and the paramedics, thinking about the woman. And what he thought was, she wasn't a part of his fan club. He didn't think they'd ever met, but one thing was for certain, if she was involved, her Porsche would never go fast enough. The bitch was going to pay.

Chapter Nine

After Paige settled the argument between the bumper car drivers, she climbed into her car to call Tom again. Before she could push to dial his number, something felt off. She sat still in her seat and closed her eyes. Hoping the Collective Conscious would provide some insight.

"I need to find him," she whispered to herself. A vision began to appear as if a movie were playing on the back of her eyelids. Slowly the fog cleared, and she could see the images. She was seeing through someone's eyes. She watched as the person looked at the bridge, then at his car. Victor. She was seeing what he was seeing. After a moment, everything went crazy. Four men came screaming toward him on bicycles. Victor was being attacked. Several images of men on bicycles, helmets, blood, flashed before her eyes. Fighting the urge to open her eyes and take off towards the bridge, she kept watching. It was almost impossible to follow. Split seconds between fists and faces, trees and bicycles, the sky, the bridge, the pavement. Another face. Image upon image flashed and changed. Paige saw enough to know there was a huge fight going on.

Victor was a true beast, beating four men to a pulp like in a high action film. Things had finally calmed down enough to see Victor survey the scene. Unable to see if the four were dead or alive, she saw Victor pull his phone out of his pocket to dial 911. Her vision was interrupted by more fog, and she struggled to see what Victor was seeing. He was looking over the bridge at a woman. The woman had binoculars, watching the scuffle from below the bridge. Paige shifted directions and tried to look through the woman's eyes. Nothing. Absolutely nothing. Like trying to peer into the dark. A familiar feeling crept over Paige, but she couldn't put her finger on it. What was going on?

A call from Dispatch interrupted her thoughts. She fumbled to answer her phone, almost dropping it a second time.

"Detective Aldridge, we have a report of a beating, multiple injuries, on the East End Bridge. I know you're in the area, are you able to respond? Units are still a bit out," Meagan from Dispatch asked.

"Uh, yeah, sure," Paige jumbled through the words as if she were drunk. "Heading that way now. Everything is settled here and waiting on units."

Trying to bring herself out of her trance, Paige started her car and turned around in the street. *She had him*, she thought to herself as she wondered if she should let Tom know. There wasn't time. She had to get to the bridge, pronto.

She sped around the block and past pedestrians while flipping her lights on her dash. A few minutes later, as she approached the bridge, she saw Victor's Chevelle. Parking so she blocked him in, she grabbed her gun and ran toward the scene.

Victor was crouching over one of the beaten men, a man with a mustache, checking his pulse. Paige fought the urge to confront and outright arrest him but looking at what he had just done to these four men, she thought better of it for a moment. "What happened here?" she asked and flashed her badge, while keeping a gun in her other hand. Safety off.

"These four assholes jumped me," Victor said. He stood and looked at her quizzically. This made Paige very uncomfortable. She wished she had the luxury of jumping in his head at this very moment, but she couldn't risk giving him the advantage of her guard being down.

"Do you know them?" she asked, becoming more uneasy by the second.

"Nope, can't say that I do," he laughed without humor. "I was minding my own business, going for a walk to clear my sinuses, when these rejects from the Tour de Nerd came barreling across the bridge right at me. Before I knew it, they were on me. I had to defend myself."

Victor was rattling off the story as Paige was checking each one for signs of life yet keeping a side-eye on Victor. Everyone was breathing. Unconscious, but still alive.

"You're lucky they are alive, sir," she said as she looked up at him.

"Yeah, I get that a lot," he said as he leaned against the bridge railing, mindful of the blood spatter.

Confused, Paige looked up at him as he absolutely towered over her. He made her unsteady. "Sir, would you mind sitting down on the curb? Just over there?"

"What's the matter, Detective? I'm the victim here," he replied as he glanced across the bridge, perhaps hoping for the Porsche's return. He ignored her request to sit and remained standing. He rotated his left arm while massaging his shoulder.

"Are you hurt?" she asked him, noticing the wince and groan he made while stretching out his shoulder.

"Nah, just getting too old for this crap." He ran a hand

over his dark beard and took a deep breath, obviously getting lost in thought.

One of the men bled heavily from his lip. Paige took a handkerchief from her pocket. "Jay," she whispered to herself, remembering her partner always carried a handkerchief for just such occasions. Usually so Paige could cry into it. As she put pressure on the beaten man's lip, she tried to locate Victor's thoughts in the Collective Conscious. She felt she had a second after all.

She could hear his deep voice ringing in her ears like a freight train horn. "Gotta figure this out," he thought. "What do these guys have in common with the interstate dudes? Why the hell do all these people want to kill me? Is the blonde responsible?"

Sirens could be heard in the distance as help arrived. Victor started to move down the path to his car when she held up a hand.

"Hang on, there. I need to get some information from you." The way he looked at her made her feel like she was only inches high and as fragile as a lotus blossom.

Paramedics ran to the scene and Paige filled them in.

After Paige was settled, he said, "Whatever you want to know..." he smiled at her.

"First of all, I need some ID." She held out her hand toward him, stepping carefully away from the mounds of beat-up flesh at her feet. She watched closely as he pulled his wallet from his pocket and handed her the license she had seen in her visions.

"You live at 218 South Clay Street? Isn't that the Derby City Mission?" When he nodded it was, she continued, "If you live at the mission, are you homeless, Mr. McCain?"

"Nah. I decided chasing material wealth wasn't for me.

They give me a room and in return I handle security and background checks for the mission. Gives me peace of mind."

She heard footsteps running up behind her and turned to see Tom jogging towards them. "Why didn't you call me?" He moved to stand defensively between her and McCain.

"There wasn't time," Paige replied.

"Damn it, Detective Aldridge. Jay was right. You are like a five-year-old. Call me next time. Okay?"

"Yeah, okay."

A huge smile broke out over Victor's face as Tom stepped toward him to ask questions and she wondered why.

Paige broke in, "It seems, Mr. McCain was jumped on the bridge by these four men," she pointed at them as the EMT's began pulling stretchers from the ambulances. "He took care of them himself."

Tom frowned at her. "Let him tell it, please Paige?"

Paige nodded. She knew better. Victor needed to tell his side. Paige only chimed in because she had witnessed the whole thing in the vision. It seemed natural to tell it. She'd have to be more careful. She glanced around the area and realized this was almost the exact same spot where Charles Pratt was murdered.

First, he talks to Pratt's widow. Then to the scene of the murder. Was he getting off on reliving the moment, feeding off Mrs. Pratt's pain? She'd seen this kind of thing before, but it made her wonder where the attacks fit in. And who was this blonde he was thinking about? Was it the woman watching him from the road? She returned her attention to Tom and Victor.

"Did you know any of these guys? Or the men who attacked you at the off ramp? Did you do something to make these guys angry? The other two claimed you tried to cut them off, it was road rage. What about this time?" Paige fired off questions trying to get him off balance in his answers.

McCain was growing angrier by the moment, and she watched him try to keep it in check. "Listen, Detective, I don't know these guys from Adam. I never cut off the other two dudes either. You've got my statement and you've got that." He gestured with one thumb over his shoulder.

Both detectives looked where he was pointing. High up on the bridge arch they saw several cameras. McCain continued, "The Department of Transportation should be able to provide you a video of what went down here. I was minding my own business and they jumped me. End of story. I don't know why. When they wake up, why don't you ask them?"

"We'll do that, and you better be playing this straight with us." Paige demanded.

They talked for a few more minutes then Paige let him go. Both detectives walked him to his car and Paige moved hers up to let him drive away. McCain let loose with a bit of rubber when he sped away. Tom started to pepper her with questions of his own. She raised a hand and cut him off, thinking. Victor McCain was not what she expected, and it bothered her.

Chapter Ten

Victor drove to the Derby Mission deep in thought, most of it about Detective Paige Aldridge. She was smaller than he expected, and pretty too. Linda Coffey was the most beautiful detective he'd ever met, but Aldridge wasn't far behind her.

Why would the detective on the Devil's Mark Killer be responding to an aggravated assault call? She wouldn't unless there was a connection to the case. And there was her partner's admonition to call him the next time, like he expected trouble. Was this a general thing she did, investigating on her own? Or was it because he knew she was talking to him and was worried about her safety. This would suggest they knew about him in some way. Interesting.

This case was starting to make his head hurt. He starts working on finding the murderer, then all of a sudden people start attacking him unexpectedly. True, he'd pissed off enough people since becoming the Hand of God, but he doubted it was a coincidence. Were the bad guys also aware he was investigating and if so, how? He knew Coffee would never tell anyone. Something to consider. And how did the sandy-haired woman fit in? He needed answers and wasn't sure how to find them.

He shot into the lot, got out of the Chevelle, and went inside the mission. He made his way to the office of Brother Joshua, the man behind Derby City Mission and his boss, of sorts. Brother J, as Victor thought of him, told him who to go after and who to kill. Kind of like his own personal Nick Fury.

He found J as he always did, sitting behind a scarred metal desk, papers scattered across it in an order only he knew. A black man of average height and around fifty years of age, Brother Joshua wore reading glasses low on his nose. Victor couldn't remember ever coming to look for J and not finding him right here. There was another thing Victor knew about J: he was sometimes filled with the spirit of the archangel Uriel, one of the few angels allowed in the presence of God. In other words, not a man to be messed with.

Victor knocked on the door jam and Brother Joshua waved him to a chair. The preacher removed the glasses and tossed them on the desk, then steepled his fingers and rested them against his chin. "Tell me," he said without preamble. A man of brevity.

Victor took a few minutes and explained how he came to be involved in the Devil's Mark killings, the attacks by the brothers and the bikers and the interest of the detectives.

"I don't think the attackers were possessed though. I never felt a whiff of a fallen angel. You know how I get the heebie-jeebies around the divine. Have you ever heard of this kind of thing?"

He nodded and said, "There are many types of possession, not all of them by the divine. You say the men on the interstate claimed you cut them off and you're sure you did not?"

"J, there was no one anywhere near me when I took the

ramp. I'd remember it if I cut someone off and they were pissed."

"And the bikers, from your description, were not henchmen material, correct?"

"I'm quite sure the closest any of those dudes came to working out was taking their bikes in and out of their cars. Guys like them would never attack a guy of my size unless they were packing a gun. Even four of them weren't enough and they'd have known that."

Joshua closed his eyes for a moment, and I felt the air around us grow thick, the way it does when the static charge builds in the air during a thunderstorm, and right before the lightning bolt strikes. When he opened them again, I knew we were no longer alone. Uriel was in the house.

Brother Joshua opened his eyes and, to most observers, there was no difference in his appearance or demeanor, but Victor knew. Uriel possessed incredible power, and even though they were on the same team, Victor found himself in both awe and intimidated. Not a thing he often felt.

"Hand of God, you must be careful going forward. The forces you are now challenging are unlike anything you have encountered thus far. There are people among the tribes of man who have abilities as dangerous as they are subtle."

Victor shrugged. "If they're men, bring'em on. I will drag their subtle asses into the light and pound them into submission."

Joshua/Uriel smiled. Victor guessed not many talked to the angel the way he did. Then again, the good guys knew what they were getting when they asked him to become the Hand of God, so they'd have to live with it. Considering Uriel both guarded the gates of Hell and sent people to spend eternity there, they were likely not much different.

"What do you know about Readers?"

"I know they like books. I'm betting you aren't talking about those kinds of readers."

"I am not. A select few are given the ability to "read" thoughts. There are only so many allowed at a time, much like Lucifer's Infernal Lords. In addition to reading thoughts, they can also plant them."

Victor let out a low whistle. "Like suggesting I cut them off and they need to exact some payback?"

Joshua/Uriel nodded. "Exactly like that. The issue for you is you cannot detect them like you do fallen angels or demons. You will never know when one is around you and ready to strike."

"I think I saw one of these Readers while on the bridge." Victor filled in the archangel on the woman he saw watching the fight with the bikers and how she looked ticked off he won. "I'm guessing you aren't allowed to tell me who they are and where I can find them?"

"You know I cannot."

Victor swore under his breath. Uriel was under strict orders from God to only be *so* helpful and it ticked him off, but he'd long since learned to get over it. "Fine. I take it when I find this particular Reader, I'm allowed to terminate with extreme prejudice?"

"You may send them to their judgment day at your earliest convenience."

"Cool beans." Victor's phone rang and he held up a finger seeing it was Coffey. Joshua/Uriel nodded permission.

"Joe's Bar and Grill."

"Listen, we have to meet. Right now. Where are you?" Coffey sounded out of breath.

"Chillin' at the Derby Mission with Joshua and Uriel. What's going on?"

"Not on the phone. Meet me at Zachary Taylor Cemetery," she said.

Victor felt confused. "You want to meet at the monument of a dead president?"

"Now, Victor."

Coffey disconnected the call. Victor stared at the phone for a moment, his mind racing.

"Go."

Victor looked up and stared into the eyes of the archangel and thought he saw...what, anticipation? Excitement? Never a good sign from Uriel.

"Yeah. I'd better. Thanks."

Victor stood and fast timed it out of the mission and almost ran into Detective Aldridge and her partner.

Aldridge collected herself and said, "We have a few more questions for you."

Victor tried to brush past them. "Not now. I'll be happy to come downtown later."

Officer Miller grabbed him by the arm, hard, and said, "Yes, now."

Victor spun and used the palm of his hand to pop the officer back a step, regretting it the moment he did it. "Look, I'm sorry..."

Miller pulled out his gun and shouted, "Up against the wall, asshole. You just assaulted an officer."

Victor raised his hands and tried to apologize again. "Listen, I'm sorry. Natural reaction. I didn't mean it that way."

Aldridge reached behind her and brought out a pair of handcuffs. "You heard him, against the wall."

Victor groaned and did as they said. Aldridge brought first one arm, then the other, behind his back and cuffed his wrists hard.

Miller holstered his gun and began to read him his rights. "You have the right to remain silent -"

"I have the right, but usually can't," Victor cut in.

Miller finished his spiel as they walked him to the police car. They opened the rear door and started to force him into the car when they heard it. Men screaming. All their eyes turned up the street to see a dozen men, dressed in martial arts uniforms and swords racing towards them.

Victor sighed and said to Aldridge, "Houston, we have a problem."

Chapter Eleven

Caught off guard, Paige spun around on her heels and nearly fell to the ground. As she regained her step, she looked at Tom. In her mind, she mouthed the words get back. Stunned, Tom took a step behind Victor and planted himself against the side of the Mission. Not moving under Paige's control.

Victor stood tall, as if ready to pounce on them even with both hands cuffed behind him. Paige raised her hand toward him, yet he plunged forward, meeting the first attacker head-on. They hesitated and Victor then went at them one by one, shoulder first and legs flying, until one of them nicked him above the elbow, causing Victor to duck away. The man caught Victor on the backswing with the hilt of his sword, stunning him. Victor fell like the proverbial ton of bricks. He landed on another man, his shear mass taking his would-be attacker to the ground where the man banged his head on a nearby curb.

Paige managed to dodge swing after swing of the blades hurled toward her. She grabbed one man's arm and swung it around to slice another's leg.

At this point, Paige let Tom go as she tried to get into the minds of their attackers. No luck. She hit a wall in the Collective Conscious; time after time, with each one. She tried to send them thoughts to stop or drop their weapons, but she couldn't get through. A familiar feeling slapped her in the face. *They were already being controlled.* But by whom?

Not knowing what to do, Paige continued to try and fight her way through them. One of the attackers grabbed her and put his sword to her throat. She stood helpless. She watched as another attacker swept Tom's legs out from under him and took his gun as he fell to the ground. The attacker then kicked Tom in the face, rendering him unconscious.

Gun in hand, he pointed it at Tom's head. Paige's attacker managed to grab her gun and tossed it towards a third attacker who pointed the gun at Victor.

Paige took a deep breath. She still had a sword at her throat, and she could feel herself being pressed harder to the body behind her. She looked around desperately and saw a stray cat hiding behind a garbage can. Before she knew what she was doing, Paige focused on the cat. It crouched, then launched full force at her attacker's face. This caused him to step back and for a moment, loosen his grip. Paige snatched the sword from his hand and went to work. She spun around, handily slitting his throat. He fell to the ground.

Victor, starting to come around again, froze in stunned amazement as he watched a light engulf Paige. She almost grew a foot taller in it. He watched as she lifted her arms and yelled, "No more! Let them go!" The remaining attackers slowly stopped moving. Their swords fell from their hands making clunking sounds on the pavement. The guns were dropped. Confused, they all looked at each other.

One of them finally said, "Harry, what's going on? What happened?"

Harry stood with his mouth open, "I... I."

Exhausted, Paige fell to her knees. After a moment, she crawled over to Tom. He was still unconscious. She looked at Victor who had managed to get himself into a sitting position but was looking at the whole scene, trying to figure out what the hell just happened.

Paige knew whoever had control over the men was gone. She took a deep breath and, in her mind, told them to all go home, lay down, nap, and believe this was all a bad dream.

The remaining men picked up their swords, turned and walked away, their confusion obvious.

Wiping a bit of blood from her throat, she looked at Victor and imagined this might have been the first time this guy was rendered speechless. "Well, we have two dead warriors. No sense in dragging the others into it," she said to him. "I have to call this in."

Victor nodded.

Paige called dispatch and explained there was an officer down and she and Tom were attacked by two men with swords and was told police and an ambulance were on their way. Paige moved to Victor and removed the handcuffs. She pointed to the blood on his arm as he got to his feet. "Hurt much?"

He glanced at the arm and shrugged it off. "Not much. My head hurts more. Mind telling me what the hell just happened?".

"No time. Hurry, go back inside. Hide. We can talk when this gets cleaned up. I'll be able to talk in a few."

"Uh, well, thanks," Victor managed to say as he stood above the scene. "I've got somewhere to be. We can catch up later."

Tom started to wake, and Paige knelt and comforted him. "Tom, our story is we came here to talk with a suspect and were jumped by *two* men. It was only you and I. Tom, they were controlled by someone. I sent the rest away as soon as they broke free." Paige said as she looked up at Victor.

"I get it, but what about him?" Tom asked, tossing a thumb in the big man's direction.

"We will figure that out soon," Paige said.

The sound of sirens grew closer. Victor nodded at the two detectives, offered up a salute and jumped into his car and left.

They watched him go. In the door of the mission a middle-aged black man wearing horned rimmed glasses watched them. His gaze met hers and she felt...what? Immense power? Something ancient?

He offered a half nod then went inside and closed the door. Now she felt like Victor. What the hell was going on?

Chapter Twelve

The Zachary Taylor National Cemetery, burial site of the 12th President of the United States, was empty of live people save for Detective Coffey leaning against her unmarked Ford near Taylor's mausoleum. He pulled in behind her car, parked and got out. She glanced his way and returned to scanning the cemetery, her eyes never resting in one spot for long. Cop eyes.

"You're late," she said.

"Good to see you too."

She faced him and started to say something when she saw the bandage on his upper arm. He had managed to stop long enough to get his emergency kit from the rear of his car and quickly apply a pressure bandage to the sword cut. "What happened?" she asked, the concern clear in her voice.

Victor filled her in on the different attacks, the existence of Readers and the blonde with a hard-on to kill him. He didn't tell her about Detective Aldridge's glow, and he wasn't sure why not.

"You're sure there's a demon?"

Victor arched an eyebrow, and she raised her hands in

surrender. He said, "Mind telling me why we're meeting in a cemetery? You know in my line of work cemeteries are not all that much fun."

She nodded towards the monument. "Follow me."

The two of them walked towards the monument and then behind it. Off in the distance near the far tree line, Victor could see what looked to be an open gravesite, far away from any other tombstone.

"Did you know this cemetery is built on the land owned by Taylor's family?" she asked.

"History major, remember? The land was owned by Taylor's father, Richard. A gift for his service during the Revolutionary War." Victor nodded towards the open grave. "What's up with the grave?

"You'll see."

When they got to the opening Victor looked down and into a deep grave. At the bottom, rested a coffin which appeared to be made of iron. All of it. There was a hole large enough for someone to crawl out of near the top. Victor could see the edges had been pulled into the coffin.

"Bloody hell," he said.

"About a year ago, the groundskeeper noticed a dirt mound which had not been here before. When he walked over, he found a hole and was able to see part of the coffin, the part with the opening. He called in a ground crew, and they dug the rest of it out but haven't moved it yet because of the red tape with this being a national heritage site. He thinks someone dug it up and then punched a hole in it to rob the grave. There's rust around the edges. He thinks it made the coffin weaker and easier to get into."

"Or out of. I bet he found it empty. Am I right?"

"Yep," Coffey replied. "And this burial is not listed

anywhere in the cemetery records. It predates the cemetery itself, so they think."

Victor swore under his breath. "A coffin made of iron. The perfect thing to keep in an Infernal Lord."

Coffey nodded. "Or a demon. Look closer at the casket."

Victor got down on his belly and did as she asked. And then he saw it. Smack dab in the middle of the top, the same image which was being carved by the Devil's Mark Killer. Victor rolled over and stared up at the sky, and then the detective.

"How'd you find out about this?"

"The photographs of the coffin were logged in for the police report about the grave robbery. A cop on the night shift recognized the symbol from the reports being circulated about the serial killings and called me."

"And when was this casket discovered?"

"A few days before the killings began."

Coffey began to walk to her car and Victor hopped up and joined her. He said, "Well, if there was any doubt we were dealing with a powerful demon before this, there's not anymore. And it had to have been buried by Richard Taylor."

Coffey got to her car and turned to face him. "What are you going to do?"

"Hunt it down and send it right back to Hell. No passing go. No get out jail free card."

"I'm here for you if you need me."

Victor leaned in and kissed her. She asked, "What's next?"

Victor scratched his beard and thought for a moment. "I'm afraid I'm going to have to cheat on you with another detective."

Coffey raised an eyebrow and rested her hand on her gun. "Oh, do tell."

Victor laughed. "I'm going to go see Detective Aldridge. I

TONY ACREE & LYNN TINCHER

think she knows more about our side of the case than she's letting on."

"The demon side? What makes you think that?"

"I have no idea. It's a hunch. My hunches are usually right."

"You know she's gorgeous, right?"

"I never noticed. I only have eyes for you."

Coffey offered an unladylike snort, got into her car, and drove away. Victor glanced towards the unopened grave with a casket made of iron, then to the mausoleum holding the remains of Zachary Taylor.

"Well, Zach. If your daddy could kick its ass, then I figure I can too."

Of course, the demon spent over one-hundred and fifty years in the dark, getting angrier and angrier. Piece of cake, right?

Chapter Thirteen

After returning home with Tom in tow, Paige invited him in.

"Please, have a seat on the couch. We need to do something," she said, and, she had to admit, she enjoyed bossing Tom around.

"Yes, ma'am. Just what is it we need to do?"

Paige opened the top of a storage ottoman and pulled out a bag. "I need to make an Abet Stone for each of us."

"A what? Abet Stone?" Tom questioned.

Unpacking a small bag she brought with her, she spread out a wide cloth for them to sit on. A large circle was printed in the center of the cloth. "Yeah, it's for protection against demons."

Paige carefully placed candles around the circle and sprinkled salt around the perimeter. She added water from a container to a beautiful clear bowl that she placed in the center of a pedestal with a candle under it. Several candles were lined all around, six of them remaining unlit. All completed a circle. Bottles full of oils and smaller bowls were meticulously placed around the larger bowl like the ingredients of a recipe ready for a television show chef.

One at a time, Paige picked up four bottles. She added a few drops of essential oils from each into the water in the largest bowl and lit the candle under the bowl to heat the water. The scent of lime, basil, bergamot, and lavender filled the room.

As she added the second round of water, the steam began to swirl in front of the light of the candles.

Paige chanted, taking a flame from a single white candle to each of the remaining six candles for each location as she went. "I call upon the powers of the North and all the spiritual and elemental beings associated with the powers of the earth to protect the performance of this rite."

Slowly she turned toward the next candle and lit it. "I call upon the powers of the East and all the spiritual and elemental beings associated with the power of air to protect the performance of this rite. I call upon the powers of the South and all the spiritual and elemental beings associated with the power of fire to protect the performance of this rite. I call upon the powers of the West and all the spiritual and elemental beings associated with the powers of water to protect the performance of this rite."

Now she moved to the center of the room. "I call on the powers of the great space above and all the spiritual and elemental beings associated with the spirit to protect the performance of this rite ... I call upon the powers of the vast below and all the spiritual and elemental beings associated with the underworld to protect the performance of this rite. About us, below us, all around us, this sphere encloses about us while we perform this magick rite."

Tom squirmed, a bit uncomfortably, on his little piece of cloth.

After the candles were lit, Paige continued, "Divine Goddess and Gods, angels, elementals and spirit guides, I thank you for the beautiful energy of white love and healing you shine upon us. I ask for your help in releasing all that does not have our highest good in mind. I ask you help guide us with cleansing this space so only beings of light and love may enter here. I ask to receive a beautiful healing white light of protection and blessings as we look into the past. Protect me and mine from any harm. Allow not our thoughts to escape this circle nor allow anyone else's to enter. For this, I give my heartfelt thanks." Paige waved her hands through the mist that now seemed to explode from the bowl, causing it to swirl like a tornado in the air.

Still within the magical circle, Tom watched from behind Paige as her hair took on a light blue glow. As the steam from the bowl formed images, Paige drew in closer to see them.

"In this night … with all our might … give us vision … give us sight … In the light of the moon … within the circle of four … come to us power to open the door … between this realm and the one we cannot see … harm no one and mote it be." Paige repeated the chant three times before she closed her eyes and let the power grow within her. A powerful light emanated from her and filled the room.

Slowly, Paige added flower petals and other herbs to the water as Tom watched her. Tom had seen this before when he visited Visette, another Reader, and her mother in New Orleans. He realized what was about to happen. Visette had taught Paige well.

Paige took out three black obsidian talismans. She lay them in a line in front of the water bowl, waived her hands over them, and began a chant.

"I charge these talismans with the name of the Abet Stone.

Protect our homes from all that is dark. Protect all who dwell there too. Protect the places where we reside."

She lifted her arms in the air.

"Protect with light that is true. Protect with light that is pure. Protect through day and night. Protect from harm. Protect from negative energy. This spell cannot be broken. So mote it be."

Paige then positioned her hands so they slowly waved over the stones.

"Protect our cars. Protect our passengers. Protect our drivers. Let no harm come to anyone in them. Let our cars be protected from harm. As I speak these words, they are true forever and always from this moment forth."

The Abet Stones started to glow a shade of orange which seemed bright enough to blind.

"Send back the harm that is put upon us. Send it back to where it came. We do not accept harm to us. Protect us from all that is harmful. Protect us from negativity, and hatred. Protect us from injury and illness. We do not harm others, so others cannot harm us. As I speak it, so shall it be."

Paige seemed to pulse along with the light emanating from the candles and the stones. A breeze started to swirl in the room.

"The Abet Stones are our power to protect against evil. The Abet Stones keep out harm. The Abet Stones do not allow demons or negative entities to pass through it. These Abet Stones are our domain, and we alone determine what is allowed to pass. No dark entities shall pass through the Abet Stones. As I will it, so mote it be."

Paige continued, "We fear you no more, you cannot harm us. Your words and your soul no longer hold us. We are free from you now. Your power is gone. The power is ours now. It is ours alone. Our minds are our own, and forever shall be. Be gone with you now, so mote it be. We are unseen. We are protected. We do not show ourselves to thee. We hide ourselves in our own protective field. We are protected within our own invisibility. Nothing can harm us. We are unseen. As I speak these words, so mote it be."

"These Abet Stones are now shields. They are for full protection. These Abet Stones will protect against anyone or anything who tries to bring harm to us. No harm shall come as long as the Abet Stone remains."

"No one shall be able to remove the Abet Stone from its place. Let this Abet Stone remain and protect from this moment on. I place upon this Abet Stone a protective power. Its wearer is always protected. No harm shall pass this Abet Stone's protective shield. Protective energy has been summoned upon them. Heed my words of protection forever more."

Paige put one stone on a chain and passed it to Tom.

"I give to you, the Abet Stone, the power to protect. Protect us from harm. Protect us from illness. Protect us from injury. Protect us from pain and suffering. Protect us from anything or anyone who wishes ill will upon the wearer. As I command it, so shall it be.

"I call upon the power of the Full Moon's light. Heed my call. Charge the Abet Stones with your power so it may protect us. May the power of the moon forever charge them. Thank you oh moon, I am grateful for your energy. So mote it be."

Carefully lifting the rest of the Abet Stones from the line, she placed one on a chain around her neck alongside a green stone she had originally worn for protection. She put the next one on the last chain and put it in her pocket. "For Victor," she said as she held her own stone carefully in her other hand at her neck.

Chapter Fourteen

Victor pulled a card Detective Aldridge gave him out of his pocket and dialed her number.

"Victor McCain, where are you?" she answered.

"Hello to you too, Detective. I'm on my way to the Raven and so are you. We need to talk. You know the place?"

"Yes. I can be there in twenty minutes."

"Works for me. Leave Tom Thumb behind."

"He won't like it. We're a team."

"Then tell the team member to wait in the car. You can bring him takeout. I've got things to share and won't do it if he's around. I get the feeling he doesn't like me."

There was a pause. "Agreed. I'm on my way."

Twenty minutes later Victor was sitting in his favorite booth, the one with a view of all the entrances to the Raven. The place used to be Molly Malone's, but the owner decided he wanted to go independent and made the change. While Victor loved the new decor, what made him really happy was the food was still excellent. Detective Aldridge walked in, right on time.

Victor was nursing a Guinness. He pointed to the bottle, eyebrows raised.

"That's fine," she replied and slid into the booth across from him.

Victor caught the attention of the waitress and pointed to the bottle. She nodded and brought one over for the detective.

"Would you like to order something to eat?" the waitress asked.

"I'm not hungry," Aldridge replied.

Victor grunted. "Then you can watch me eat. I'll have the leg of lamb tonight." Looking at Aldridge, he asked, "Are you sure you won't join me?"

She offered a half-smile. "If you insist. I'll have the same."

The waitress walked away and Aldridge said, "You called the meeting. What did you want to tell me?"

Victor took a swallow of the Guinness then set the bottle to the side. "I think you and I are working for the same team, but at cross purposes." He slipped his phone out of his pocket and selected a photo Linda had sent him via text. "Recognize this?"

Aldridge stared at the photo for a moment, then said, "It's the symbol used by the Devil's Mark Killer. Where did you get this?"

"Off an iron coffin in the rear of Zachary Taylor Cemetery. Away from all the other fine folks buried there. It's been in the ground since before Zachary Taylor was president. Most likely put there by his father."

She sipped her beer. "And you think someone robbed the grave? To get what?"

Victor shook his head. "No. Not to rob it. Someone broke out of it. Well, not someone, something."

She froze with the bottle to her lips. "What are you saying?"

"I think Richard Taylor and some friends buried a demon in an iron coffin. I think somehow the coffin weakened, may have rusted, and the thing broke out. And I don't think the thought of demons is a surprise to you, is it now, Detective Aldridge?"

There was a pause in the conversation as the waitress returned with their meal.

Victor offered her a smile and said, "Claudia, there's a police officer sitting in an unmarked car outside, would you take him some Shepherd's Pie and something to drink?"

She said she would and left.

"Tom's going to love you," Aldridge said.

"I grow on people. Usually like a bad fungus. Back to the devil at hand. You're not surprised, are you?"

"Before I answer, why do you think I wouldn't be?"

"Because when we were attacked by the Jackie Chan Fan Club, you did something. I got popped pretty good on the head and it's a bit fuzzy, but you did something to make them all stop. That takes power. And they were being mind-controlled, just like the other idiots who attacked me."

Aldridge glanced around the room to make sure no one was paying them any attention. "One last question of my own before I answer. Why would you know about demons? You don't strike me as the religious type."

"Lady, until a few years ago, I didn't give a rat's ass about theology, religion, or heaven and hell. That all changed when I became the Hand of God. Now I track down and kill things that crawl out of iron boxes in hidden parts of old cemeteries. Part of my job description."

"A bounty hunter for who? God?"

"You've got it, sister. It's complicated but the orders come from the Big Guy himself. Now it's time for you to answer my question."

She paused another moment, sizing him up, and he saw her fight the desire to keep her secrets secret. And he saw her give in to the moment.

"You're right. Demons are not a surprise to me. Ever heard of Readers?"

"Recently. Wait. Are you telling me you're a Reader? I figured it had to be something. And the evil blonde who's been having all these people attack me, she's a Reader too? There are both good guy and bad guy Readers?"

"Of sorts," she said. "This lamb is really good, by the way."

"The Raven is da bomb. Don't change the subject. Why did you think I was the Devil's Mark Killer?"

"I searched for people thinking about the mark and I saw your thoughts. I could see what you were seeing, and you were standing over the dead body of the girl. I suggested you look at your license to find out who you were."

Victor laughed. "I wondered why I did that. I was over the dead body because Detective Linda Coffey called me. She knows what I do for a living and wanted me to see the mark and get my take on what was going on."

Aldridge looked surprised. "Coffey? The one who was suspended over--" There was a pause as she looked even more surprised. "You're the guy who got shot, right outside here."

Victor offered a small bow. "Yep. The one and only. The bullet barely missed my heart, thanks to Linda shoving me. She was suspended because she went after my brother while breaking a billion cop rules. What the fuzz brass didn't know was my brother was making his second trip in the land of the living. He was like the thing buried in the iron box. Satan calls them Infernal Lords."

"Is he still on the loose?"

"He's...where he can no longer hurt anyone. Let's leave it at that."

"Ok. How did Coffey know about the body?"

Aldridge didn't look happy.

"Anonymous tip. Before you go getting your cop panties in a wad, she did the proper follow-up. The call came from a burner phone. We think someone who knows our connection to each other made the call. The question is, how did little-miss-buzz-kill get on to me? The attacks started almost right away. She has to be connected. And that's why I think you and I need to work together before someone else dies."

Aldridge thought a bit and offered a small nod.

"I agree. In fact, we were thinking along the same lines, at least about the other Reader wanting you dead." She slipped the Abet Stone out of her pocket and slid it across the table. "Wear this. It will help keep you safe."

Victor picked up the string and twirled the stone. "Pretty." He slipped it over his neck and tucked the stone under his shirt. "A fancy rabbit's foot?"

She laughed and it sounded good to him. "Something like that. It will help keep you safe."

"From Linda's cooking?"

Paige laughed, "No, from demonic psychic attacks and mind control."

"Cool. What's next, Detective?"

She thought a bit and said, "We have to assume if this is a demon, it's not doing these murders at random. It has some sort of plan."

Victor nodded in agreement. "Well, if I'd been planted for over one-hundred and fifty years, I'd be looking for someone to punish for putting me there."

"You think the victims have something to do with the Taylor family?"

Victor shrugged. "It's an idea worth exploring. If you want to look on the cop side, I have a computer guy I can set to exploring their family histories."

"Then I think we have a plan, Mr. McCain."

She offered her hand and Victor took it.

"Call me Vic. It's what all my detective friends call me."

"Oh, you have a lot of detective friends, Vic?"

"Nope. Just you and Coffey. And some days I wonder about her."

She drained the last of her beer and started to get out her wallet.

"Your money's no good here. I've got it. You'd best get out to Tom before he comes in and tries to shoot me."

"Thank you. I'll call as soon as I have anything. I'll contact Detective Coffey and see what we can do to coordinate things."

She got up and left the Raven and Victor watched her go. He fingered the stone now hanging around his neck. He had often felt that being with some women was like having an anchor tied around his neck. This one managed to slip one on him without even trying.

Chapter Fifteen

Tom watched Paige as she walked slowly to the car. He took a napkin and wiped the residue of the Shepherd's Pie from his lips. He all but swallowed it whole.

As Paige opened the car door he spoke. "Hey, thanks for this. It was delicious."

"Don't thank me. Thank the Hand of God." She couldn't help but giggle at the thought.

"Huh?" Tom asked. "The What of Who?"

"The Hand of God. You know, God gives him instructions, he does what he's told. Hunting down demons and the like."

"No, no I don't know," Tom placed the food container in the back seat. "Why don't you enlighten me?"

Paige filled him in on the discussion with Victor as Tom pulled out onto Shelbyville Road.

"Do you actually believe him?" he asked her.

"I...I don't want to. Everything in my logical mind says not to. But...I can't help it. With all the strange things going on in the world, in my life, over the last few months, I can't discount anything."

Tom nodded. "And he took the stone from you, no questions asked?"

"Yeah, it was almost like he already knew. Or at least trusted me. I dunno. Anyway, we're going to start looking into possible relations to Taylor. It may even be a few generations back."

"At least it's a start. A small something to latch on to."

"Vic thinks you don't like him," Paige nudged Tom's arm.

"Well, the jury is still out. Someone has it out for him, that's for sure. Which means someone somewhere doesn't like him." Tom couldn't help but laugh.

"Silly…" Paige's voice drifted away as she pulled her cell phone from her pocket. "I need to brush up on my history."

She opened an internet browser and googled "Zachary Taylor". She then read aloud to Tom.

"Zachary Taylor, 1784 to 1850, served in the army for forty years, commanding troops in the War of 1812, the Black Hawk War in 1832, and the second of the Seminole Wars from 1835 to 1842. He was a war hero through his service in the Mexican War, which broke out in 1846 after the U.S. annexation of Texas. After being elected President in 1848, Zachary Taylor entered the White House. At the time, the issue of slavery and its extension into the new western territories had caused extreme tension between the North and South. Taylor sought to hold the nation together, even as a slaveholder. He was ready to accomplish this by force if necessary. He fought with Congress over wanting to admit California to the Union as a free state. In early July 1850, Taylor suddenly fell ill and died.

"Zachary Taylor was born on November 24, 1784, in Orange County, Virginia. He was a descendant of Elder William Brewster, a Pilgrim leader of the Plymouth Colony, a Mayflower immigrant, and a signer of the Mayflower

Compact; and Isaac Allerton, Jr., a colonial merchant, colonel, and son of Pilgrim Isaac Allerton and Fear Brewster. The descendant of a long line of prominent Virginia planters, he was raised on a tobacco plantation outside Louisville, Kentucky. His parents moved there and settled along the Ohio River around the time of his birth.

"He did not receive much of an education as his mother taught him to read and write, but was well-schooled in farming, horsemanship, and using a musket. In 1808, Taylor left home after obtaining a commission as a first lieutenant in the army. In 1810, he married Margaret Mackall Smith, and they went on to have six children. Ann Mackall Taylor, Sarah Knox Taylor, Octavia Pannell Taylor, Margaret Smith Taylor, Mary Elizabeth Taylor, and Richard Scott Taylor. Their second daughter, Sarah Knox Taylor, would marry Jefferson Davis, the future president of the Confederacy, in 1835. She died three months later. Taylor made his home near Baton Rouge, Louisiana, on a 2,000-acre plantation with some 80 slaves. He owned a second plantation in Mississippi."

She looked at Tom, who was pulling into the police station. "Not much to go on so far, but I do have some names to look up."

After entering the police station, Paige started to do some research. Before she could even look at her first search results, Chief Waters burst into her office.

"Detective Aldridge, I need you and Officer Miller to head over to the boat ramp in Cardinal Harbor in Prospect. I know, it's Oldham County, but it looks like they may have another Devil's Mark Victim.

"Any details," she asked as she gathered her phone and put on her leather jacket.

"Only that the vic is female, mid 20's, no ID, and has the mark carved on her forehead."

"On our way." Paige raised her phone and said, "Hey Siri, call Tom Miller."

Chapter Sixteen

"Alright, Kurt, what do you have for me?"

Kurt sat in front of three huge monitors. Victor saw one screen filled up with Ancestry.com, the other with a spreadsheet, and the third full of a list of names. He pointed at the genealogy website.

"Well, I've found an anomaly. You were right, all the dudes, Pratt, Ingram, Bell, Nichols, and McIver, were all descended from friends of Richard Taylor. They formed part of a Freemason Lodge when it moved from Lexington to Louisville. I found a letter signed by all of their ancestors authorizing the move.

"Cool enough. What's the anomaly?"

"None of Brenda Mazza's family, directly or indirectly, were associated with the Taylors or any of his friends. In fact, her family didn't migrate to the US until the early 1900s. She doesn't fit the pattern."

"Huh. How many other guys were in Taylor's mighty band of Freemasons?"

"Two more, both of whom have direct descendants still

living in the area. One, Mike Hawkins, lives off Zorn Avenue, over on top of the hill. The other is Kevin Muldoon. He lives out in Lively Shively."

"No Taylors in town?"

"That would be Hawkins. The direct line ran out of boys and Hawkins's grandmother is the oldest of his direct line. Maybe he'll be left alone?"

"Maybe. Any chance you missed a connection with Mazza?"

Kurt turned and stared at Victor, his eyebrow raised. A move Mr. Spock would be proud of. "Okay, okay. Text me the addresses of Hawkins and Muldoon, assuming they're both still alive?"

"Living and breathing as far as the Internet is concerned."

"Groovy. Dig into Mazza, see what else you can find out about her."

"Will do, Big Guy."

Victor went out to the Chevelle and took a call from the body shop fixing his Ford. The damage was around fifteen grand and would take a couple of weeks. Son of a bitch. Luckily, he got the guns out of the secret weapons safe in the rear of the car before the guys hauled it away, but it left him exposed. Now the weapons were under a tarp in the trunk. He'd need to make sure he didn't get pulled over by the cops.

He glanced at his text from Kurt and read the address into his phone GPS and was off. Hawkins lived just off Zorn Avenue up on the Heights. Once in the neighborhood, Victor tracked mailboxes and found a gravel drive heading off into a grove of trees with the right number on the box. When he turned into the drive, with his window down, he smelled smoke.

Victor rounded a corner and could see the house was on fire. *Bloody hell.* He slammed the car into park and got out and ran to the front door. He yanked his phone out of his pocket and started to dial 9-1-1 when he saw a figure through the front window. It was huge, wide-shouldered, around seven feet tall with the head of a raven. A raven with wolf's teeth, walking casually through the fire. *Double bloody hell. A demon. The demon.*

There was no time to run back to the car and get his katana. Victor took the sword off a crazed Asian vampire Infernal Lord and kept it around for emergency demon fights. One way to kill a demon is to go all Highlander and cut its head off.

No time. He sighed, shoved the phone into his pocket, yanked the gun out of its holster, and kicked the door in. He knew the gun would likely only make big, bad, and evil laugh, but it made him feel better to have it in his hand. The door smashed into the living room making the demon stop and turn towards him as Victor walked into the front room, the fire raging mere feet away. The feeling of wrongness hit him like a sledgehammer, and he realized later he was growling. Hands of God have been fighting demons and their ilk since the days of Cane and Abel. Let's just say they don't like each other.

The demon smiled and said in a voice like gravel being poured down a metal shoot, "The Hand of God. I see you have come to die."

"Actually, I'm here selling Girl Scout cookies. I figured I might get a sale before the house burned down. I have Samoas." He glanced into the house and shouted, "Hawkins."

A man a few inches shorter than Victor appeared in the hallway on the other side of the fire. He had short blond hair and a mustache. He wore Army fatigues sporting captain's patches and carried a Mossberg 920 shotgun in his hands. If the fact his house was burning down around his head with a demon in the living room bothered him, you wouldn't know it. He stood there casually with the gun pointed at the demon.

"Mr., I don't know who you are but you'd best be leaving."

The whole thing actually made Victor laugh and it pissed the demon off.

"You find this funny, Hand of God? I will yank out your heart and feed off it while you die."

"Dear Lord, you are a walking talking cliche," Victor said as he nodded his chin towards Hawkins. "Captain, you'd best be heading out the back while you can."

His response was to raise the shotgun to his shoulder and pump a couple of shells into the demon. It spun the Hellspawn around a bit, but the damage caused healed almost as quickly as it happened. For good measure, Victor did the same, putting a small grouping right in the thing's head. Same result as Hawkins, though the creature now seemed undecided on which of them to kill first.

"Dammit," Hawkins snarled.

The heat of the fire was intense, and Victor knew there was only seconds left before it collapsed the entire house. He reached into a pocket inside his bomber jacket and pulled out a small flask filled with water.

"Captain, I'm going to do something. When I do, head out and meet me at my car. Got it?"

The man nodded as Victor whistled at the demon like you would a dog.

"Here boy, here boy."

The demon turned and started his way. Good.

"Hey, you look a bit thirsty. Here you go."

Victor threw the flask as hard as he could right into the demon's chest. The thing was so massive it was impossible to miss. The glass hit home and broke and water splashed all over the creature. The demon let out a scream loud enough to make Victor cover his ears, then the thing began to claw at his skin, his long nails stripping off huge strips at a time.

Holy water, blessed by Urial himself. Bet that stung like a son of a bitch. It wouldn't be enough to kill him, but it would keep his attention for a bit. Victor glanced up and Hawkins was running out towards the rear of the house. He made a retreat out the front.

Victor got no more than a few feet from the house when it gave up the ghost and caved in, completely engulfed in flames. The demon was still howling. Hawkins jogged into view carrying a duffel in one hand and the shotgun in the other. Victor hopped in behind the wheel and Hawkins jumped in the other side and tossed the duffel into the back seat. He held onto the shotgun.

Victor turned the car around and floored it. The demon strode out of the fire and yelled what he assumed were insults in a language Victor didn't understand as they left him in the dust. He held a hand out the window and gave the demon the finger, a language he was sure even ancient demons understood. Hawkins watched the side mirror until they turned onto the main road and the demon was no longer visible.

He stared at Victor a moment and then said, "The Hand of God. Nice to meet you."

Victor had to admit, he was used to the few people who found out who he was reacting a bit differently. His reaction suggested a familiarity. "Well, I usually go by Victor, but, yeah, that's me. You don't seem surprised at hearing the name."

He watched out the window with a faraway look, not seeing the scenery, but something else. "I'm not. It's the name my great-great-great-grandfather, Richard Taylor, went by. The Hand of God."

Victor almost drove off the road.

"You're telling me your many great grandfather was a Hand of God?"

"Yes sir." He hitched a thumb to the duffel behind us. "Get us somewhere and I can prove it."

"He hunted demons?"

"Yes sir. Demons, fallen angels, hellhounds, among other things."

Victor recalled what he knew of Richard Taylor and then it hit him like a thunderbolt.

"Wait. Didn't he die in his early eighties of natural causes?"

"He did. Died in his sleep."

"He didn't die in the line of duty, so to speak?"

"No, he didn't. He retired from being the Hand of God when he was in his sixties."

It was all Victor could do to keep breathing. He believed the only way to stop being the Hand of God was to die on the job. Now this guy was telling him it wasn't true. Bloody hell. There was a way to get out alive.

They were going to see Brother Joshua and it was time for the two of them to have a come to Jesus moment.

Chapter Seventeen

Paige stood over the victim at Cardinal Harbor boat dock. Yes, everything looked the same. The crucifix in the mouth. Everything. She sighed as she carefully sat on the ground next to the girl. She looked to be about fifteen. The youngest victim so far. She swallowed hard to hold back tears that pooled behind her eyes and nausea that began to consume her. Unconsciously, she touched the stone on the necklace she wore around her neck.

Looking up at Tom, "Just a child? What's the connection?"

"No idea. I didn't expect this for sure." He kneeled beside Paige and brushed aside the girl's light blonde bangs from her forehead revealing the Devil's Mark more clearly. The blood had dried in a short dripping pattern which ran along the creases in her forehead. "Look, she was strangled. See the lines on her neck?"

Paige nodded. This young girl reminded her of Hannah. She was the adopted daughter of fellow Reader and FBI Agent, Randy Peterson and she was possessed by a demon.

—————

The memory came flooding back to her. The exorcist, Evan, was lighting candles around the bedroom as Isaac stood by Hannah. She was stretched across on the bed with her wrists and ankles bound to the bedposts. She was panting like a dog on a hot summer day while she stared at the ceiling. As Paige entered the room, Hannah's eyes shot to her. Paige accidentally let their eyes lock for a moment. As she did, nausea again swept through her, causing her to run to the bathroom to vomit. Evan paused for a moment to watch them and then continued to light the candles.

"We are in for a rough night. I want everyone to be prepared." He did not look up from his task of lighting candles. "My partner, Peter, cannot be here to help so I will need you all to focus on me," Evan said as he finally looked at each of them.

Paige entered the room again. "Paige, I do not want you to look at her. Whatever it takes, don't let your eyes meet again." At that precise moment, a loud low growl escaped from Hannah. She pulled and fought hard against the restraints that held her bound to the bedposts.

Junna thought she was in a nightmare or a movie. This can't be happening, she thought to herself. *Wake up Junna, wake up,* she pleaded as she pinched the underside of her own arm. Of course, it didn't work. Nothing worked. A chill ran through her as she realized she was going to have to deal with this one way or another. There was no longer a choice, no longer a way out.

"I need everyone to stand over there," Evan said as he pointed to the far side of the room. "Stay together and don't say a word. Isaac, you and Agent Riggs stay here near me." He paused and turned toward the group. "You will likely see things you never thought possible, and I need you to remain as quiet as you can. Repeat in your mind everything I say, but don't say them out loud. Do you understand?"

Everyone nodded. Agent Riggs stared at Paige making her feel small and inadequate. She couldn't figure out just why he was so angry with them.

"Okay then, Isaac? Are you ready?"

Isaac slowly nodded as he swallowed the lump in his throat.

Paige was dizzy. Jay reached out and took her hand helping steady her nerves just a little, and then took Junna's hand. Hoping for extra strength for them both, Jay held on tight.

"In the Name of the Father and of the Son and of the Holy Ghost, Amen," Evan said loudly as he approached Hannah. She froze and listened carefully. "Most magnificent Prince of the Heavenly Soldiers, Saint Michael the Archangel, look after us in our war in opposition to principalities and powers against the leaders of this world of shadows, this realm of darkness, in opposition to the forces of evilness in the high places."

Paige tried to think the words in her head, but she couldn't keep up. She looked at Junna's puzzled face and realized she was struggling as well. "I can't understand what he was saying, much less repeat anything," she whispered.

Junna nodded, licked her lips, and bowed her head.

"Come to the sustenance of men whom God has fashioned to His likeness and whom He has redeemed at an immense price from the oppression of the evil spirit."

A dark, evil laugh escaped Hannah's lips, but her lips did not move. Her expression was only blank and staring at the ceiling.

"The consecrated Church holds You in the uppermost regards as her keeper and guardian. The Lord has entrusted the souls of the redeemed to be led into heaven. Pray accordingly to the God of Peace to overpower Satan, that he may no longer enslave the men, women, and children and do damage to the Church and the children of the earth. Earthbound sinners and offenders are we all."

"Ha! You think this can stop me?" A voice even darker than the laughter emanated from Hannah's lifeless little body. "This is almost comical. I'm going to enjoy this immensely."

Terror overtook Paige. She gasped for breath and tried to turn around to face the corner. Jay took her in his arms and hugged her tightly. She fought off the urge to slug him to get him to let her go. Wanting desperately to run from the room and out into the dark cool air, she tried to push Jay aside. Agent Riggs put his cold hand on her shoulder. This made Paige stop in her tracks. He pointed her to the corner of the room. Like a scolded child, she returned to stand by Jay.

"Who is that? What's happening?" Paige asked Jay.

"Shh, Paige. Be quiet. I don't know what's going on either."

Evan continued after the commotion settled on the other side of the room. "Offer our desires to the Most High, that without impediment they may draw His absolutions down upon us; take hold of the dragon, the old serpent, which is the demon, tie him up and throw him into the bottomless pit so he may no longer hold this child prisoner."

"You are an idiot," the voice from Hannah interrupted. "You have no idea what you are dealing with." The voice then laughed slowly, calmly. Hannah's head slowly moved to one side. Her eyes were a solid jet black like polished coal. Junna caught a quick glimpse of them before she turned away. Hannah's skin was as white as baby powder; even in the glowing candlelight casting a soft yellow glow around the room. Junna noticed the candles did not flicker, but seemed perfectly still. She drew in a deep breath and exhaled it slowly, leaving a fine mist in front of her. The temperature in the room had dropped considerably, but Junna had not noticed it until that very moment. She wrapped her arms around herself to keep warm.

Ignoring Hannah's taunts, Evan looked at Isaac. He was pale but vigilant. Evan continued, "In the Name of Jesus Christ, our God and Lord, strengthened by the Virgin Mary, Mother of God, of Blessed Michael the Archangel, of the Blessed Apostles Peter and Paul and all the Saints and dominant in the holy power of our faith, we humbly take on to defend against the attacks and deceits of the evil force in this room; in containment of this child."

"Let me show you. I want to show you what I am," the voice continued as both Hannah's head and body turned slowly toward Isaac. Her lips were still not moving. The candles flickered quickly before going dark. Completely dark. Silence filled the room. It was the only thing that could. The feeling of emptiness consumed them, but no one made a sound. No one made a move.

The only sound Paige could hear was her heart pounding. She feared everyone else could hear it or at least hear her heavy breathing. It felt like her heart would explode through her chest at any moment. She wanted to scream. To fight the feeling, she bit down hard on her bottom lip.

Finally, Evan's calm voice broke the silence.

"God comes; his enemies are spread and those who detest Him escape before Him. As smoke is driven away, so are they driven; so the immoral depart this life at the company of God."

There was laughter. Laughter so dark and sinister even Evan wanted to run. He reached for the flashlight in his pocket, but as he found it, the candles suddenly came back to life, filling the room with the soft, warm glow. As his eyes adjusted to the room again, he noticed Isaac. He stood as if frozen in his tracks, his eyes were unblinking, and both of his hands were around his own throat. His face was turning blue. "Riggs," Evan shouted, as Agent Riggs seemed to lunge through mid-air across the room to Isaac's side.

As Agent Riggs fought with Isaac to remove his hands from self-strangulation, Evan reached for the cross he had around his neck and pressed it to Hannah's chest.

"Behold the Cross of the Lord, escape the company of the enemies. The Lord of the family of Juda, the children of David, has won over the enemy control. Most sly serpent, you shall not provoke this child any longer. You will leave her be. Flee from our sight. Give us back this child of God." Evan then pressed the cross to Hannah's forehead. Braced for a great fight, he expected something to happen. However, Hannah didn't flinch.

Without her lips moving, the voice sneered at Evan. "You will see my power is great. You are unprepared for what you are trying to accomplish here. You do not even know what you are dealing with. A demon? I fight with God? Ha ha ha."

Isaac fell to the floor. Agent Riggs fell across him trying to do CPR. Jay tried to run to his aid, but Riggs held up his hand to stop him. Jay returned to his place with Randy, Paige and Junna. All the four of them could do was watch silently. None of them knew what to do. After a few minutes of struggle, Agent Riggs stood and slowly shook his head. Isaac was dead.

"God wants all men to be saved and to come to the truth and the light. He wants all to be saved through the grace of Jesus Christ." Evan said over Hannah's body.

"Ha ha ha," the voice laughed. "Please, by all means, continue." Whoever this was seemed to be enjoying this; enjoyed taunting everyone.

Evan was now even more unsure of himself. He did not know what he was dealing with, but he continued. "God the Father orders you. God the Son orders you. God the Holy Ghost orders you. Christ, God in the flesh, orders you. He who has built His Church on the solid rock and acknowledged that the gates of hell shall not triumph against His people, because He will live with them forever until the end of time." Panting, Evan fell across the bed. The candles flickered again but did not give up their light.

Breathlessly, Evan whispered, "Be gone, Satan, architect, and master of all deceitfulness, adversary of man's deliverance, liar, evil one. Holy, Holy, Holy is the Lord, God Almighty. Lord, hear my request. May the Lord be with You and with Your strength of mind. May the Lord be with us all."

"Let us pray," he bowed his head that was already almost on the bedside. Everyone bowed along with him.

Junna wiped her nose. Tears had been streaming down her face, but she was unaware until she bowed her head, and her nose ran.

"God of heaven, God who has authority to give existence after death and respite after exhaustion, we respectfully bow down ourselves ahead of Your Wondrous Majesty and we beg of You to set us free by Your power from all the oppression of the infernal forces, from their traps, their fabrications, and their enraged impiety. Please Lord, lower Yourself, save us. Keep us with You, keep us out of harm's way. Please save this child. Please force the evil from her. Expel the evil into the dark once more. We humbly ask You through Jesus Christ Our Lord. Amen." Evan sank to the floor, exhausted.

"Are you quite finished now?" the voice asked him. "I have some things to take care of."

Paige felt like passing out. She swayed against the wall, holding herself up with both hands. She could hear a voice deep in her head repeating itself. She couldn't quite make out the words because they sounded like they were underwater. She struggled to hear them, but the words eluded her. Jay took her by the arm and helped her to the floor. Randy sat beside her as she looked at him, her eyes pleading for help. She looked toward the bed, searching for Evan, but she caught Hannah's eyes. They immediately fixed on her; piercing her very soul as she felt them suck her in, drag her down to the depths of hell. As they did, Paige passed out.

———

Jolting back to reality, Paige touched the wrist of the victim and turned over her hand. "Wait, look," Paige said. With her gloved hand, she pried open the victim's fingers. "What's this?" She pulled out a crumpled piece of paper and very carefully unfolded it.

"Detective Aldridge, Meet me at 11:00 PM at the Falls of the Ohio. Bring the Hand of God with you."

Chapter Eighteen

Victor stood in front of the desk of Brother Joshua and barely contained his fury. Mike Hawkins sat in a chair off to one side, his duffle bag resting on the floor at his feet. Victor paced back and forth in front of Joshua's desk then stopped, pointed a finger at the man and said, "You lied to me."

Brother Joshua, his calm never slipping, gently shook his head. "I did not."

"You told me I would not survive being the Hand of God."

"Actually, what I told you was, this is the kind of job you die from. A true statement with the rarest of exceptions. In fact, you have nearly died on several occasions despite being at the top of your game."

This time Victor pointed a finger at Hawkins. "Yet G.I. Joe over there says Robert Taylor retired from being the Hand of God. Care to explain how he did that, Oh Wise One?"

Brother Joshua glanced at Hawkins before replying. "Robert Taylor is one of those rare cases of transition."

Victor sat down heavily in the other chair in the room. "Do tell. I'm all ears."

Hawkins spoke up before Brother Joshua could reply. "He suffered a stroke. He wasn't physically able to continue."

"I'm sorry," Victor said, "a stroke? I've never read anything about Zachary Taylor's dad having a stroke"

Joshua said, "It was not an obvious thing. It manifested most in his cognitive abilities. It made his work as the Hand of God nearly impossible."

Hawkins nodded. "One night my great-grandmother, Sarah, prayed to God from sundown to sunup, to spare him. She stayed on her knees the entire night next to the bed where my great-grandfather slept. The next morning, a man knocked on their door."

Hawkins unzipped the duffle and removed a worn leather-bound book and showed it to Victor. "This is her diary. It's how I know about the Hand of God. She wrote about the things my great-grandfather did while he was the Hand of God."

He turned to a spot near the end of the diary and stared at the yellowed pages. "Following Robert's stroke, she wrote how a black man named Joshua, wearing the mantle of God, appeared upon her doorstep and told her God heard her prayers and her husband would no longer be required to be the Hand of God."

Victor sat stunned and stared at the man behind the desk. "Wait, a black man named Joshua...was that you? Or is this just a coincidence his name was also Joshua?"

Brother Joshua simply returned the stare, not speaking.

"No coincidence. This man is the one who talked to my great-grandmother. I don't know how I know, but I do," said Hawkins.

Victor said to Joshua, "That would make you, what, over two-hundred years old?"

Brother Joshua said nothing.

"Dammit J, I need answers."

Brother Joshua said, "All you need to know is you can count on one hand in the entirety of human existence, how many times someone survived serving as the Hand of God."

Hawkins stood up and faced Joshua while throwing a thumb in Victor's direction. "Then lets up those totals. If he's tired of being the Hand of God and wants to retire, then let him and I'll take his place."

Victor laughed. "Slow your roll there Captain America. You don't know what you're asking."

Hawkins practically bristled. "I assure you, sir, I do."

"No, you don't. You heard J. What your great grandpa did is the rare exception, not the rule. You're asking to commit suicide."

Hawkins turned to Victor. "What I'm offering to do is something you seem not to have the stomach to keep doing. I'm offering to serve, to fight. I was willing to die for my country and I'm more than willing to die for my God."

Victor shot out of his chair. "Watch your tongue, kid, or you will find out just how much stomach I have for a fight."

"Kid?" Hawkins' fists balled in rage. "You think I won't kick your ass from here to Hell and back?"

"Enough."

Brother Joshua never raised his voice, but it struck the two men like a thunderbolt. They turned to him and once again, the presence of Uriel was unmistakable. Hawkins took a step back and quickly crossed himself. Victor simply stood still, not moving.

To Hawkins, Joshua/Uriel said, "Serving as the Hand of God is invitation only. You don't ask to serve, you are chosen.

And you," he said, turning to Victor, "will be released from service when and only when God decides you are no longer needed. Do you understand me, Hand of God?"

Victor faced the archangel, one of the most powerful angels in existence with jaw clenched, refusing to back down. "You mean when he kills me."

Brother Joshua/Uriel's smile was completely without warmth and terrible to behold. "Be. That. As. It. May."

All the anger, all the fear, all the hope of finding a way out of being the Hand of God, drained from Victor, and a deep sense of fate settled upon him, followed by a weariness of body which felt endless. He offered the archangel a short nod.

Victor turned to Hawkins and offered his hand. "I'm sorry. I shouldn't have jumped down your throat. Things are a bit tense around here. Especially when all you want to do is to open a can of whup-ass on Satan and his gang."

Hawkins grasped the offered hand. "I'm sorry if I suggested you weren't willing to do the job. I get it. I really do. If I can't be the Hand of God, I'd like to at least help."

"Even if it gets you killed?"

"I seem to have no choice, considering a demon is hunting me and just tried to kill me. Speaking of which, how did you know to come to my house?"

The two men returned to their seats and Victor filled in the Army captain on what he knew. "It seems the demon is on a revenge tour, trying to wipe out any direct descendants of the men who put him in the ground. There are only two of you left. You and a guy named Kevin Muldoon. Do you know him?"

"Never heard of him. I guess we should go warn him?"

Victor stood and Hawkins did the same. "Sounds like as good a plan as any other."

Hawkins dropped the diary into the duffle, zipped it, and

swung it over his shoulder and the two men headed to the door when Victor pulled up short. "Wait. Your great grandma wrote about Robert's time as a Hand of God?'

"Yeah, it was handed down over the years, kept secret. My mother gave it to me before she died."

"Any chance she wrote about burying a demon on the family farm?"

This time, it was Hawkins' turn to smile, and Victor thought, "damn if it didn't look a lot like Uriel's smile."

"Every chance."

"Well, hot damn. Let's go find Muldoon and then figure out how to bury the son of a bitch. Again."

The two men left and going out the door, Victor glanced over at Joshua and saw the angel's smile was back.

Hell yeah.

Chapter Nineteen

After returning home, Paige paced around her kitchen, waiting for a pot of coffee to brew. "Who is the person and how do they know about Victor?" she said out loud as she put cream and sugar in her cup. Absent-mindedly, she rubbed her dog Harry's ears. He happily danced around her, wanting to go outside. Paige opened the kitchen door leading out to her back yard and Harry bounded outside. She went to the counter and poured her coffee. "And this poor girl, what does she have to do with any of this?"

Paige sighed heavily and took a quick drink of her coffee. She burnt her tongue but didn't even really notice. She'd have to get in touch with Victor and convince him to go with her to meet the killer. Or should she just go by herself with Tom waiting in the wings? Why put Victor in more trouble? He's in trouble too, after all.

If only Evan was still alive. He excelled at working with Demons. Until he met his match in the Demon Lora. A few months ago, Lora managed to take on a physical body strong enough to kill Evan. Paige's sister, Junna, was now off running around with this Demon and Paige didn't know how to deal with that. A battle was raging inside Paige. Were the two of these events related somehow?

Paige went to the door and stepped out on her porch to watch Harry. He was barking furiously at a squirrel teasing him from a branch of a tree next to the fence. Harry suddenly turned and ran to another corner, still furiously barking. Paige could see a woman standing on the sidewalk across the street. Her view was blocked by some hedges in her neighbor's yard. Something seemed familiar. She felt as if the woman was trying to read her. But how was that possible? Paige knew the feeling from when her brother Shepherd was alive. Shepherd read her all the time. The feeling made her ill. Paige fought back and tried to read the stranger. She could see her head duck down behind the shrubs. Gone. She was gone. Gone from view. Gone from the feeling.

"Oh, no you don't," Paige screamed as she dropped her coffee and ran to catch up to this woman. Harry ran behind her. When she reached the hedges, nothing. No one. No sign of the woman. Paige kept running down the street, looking left and right between the houses and around trees, Harry barking behind her. But Harry lost the scent and so did Paige. Deflated, Paige headed to the house. "Come on Harry, it's time I go and find Victor. I need to ask him for help.

Chapter Twenty

On the way over, Hawkins brought up a Google Street View of the man's house. Muldoon lived in a brick ranch-style house with blue shutters and front door at the end of a cul de sac near the rear of the subdivision. A front porch ran the length of the front of the house with two green rocking chairs on either side of the door. A two-car garage was attached to the side of the house.

Victor stopped his car near the entrance to the dead-end street and looked around. It was now fully dark. Muldoon's front porch light was on and it was easy to see the two rocking chairs. There were lights on inside the house as well.

Victor turned into the cul-de-sac and hit the brakes when all the lights in Muldoon's house went out at once like someone flipped a master switch.

Hawkins turned to Victor and asked, "What are the chances this is a coincidence?"

"My statistics professor in college would say about a billion percent against."

Victor turned off the Chevelle's lights and tapped the gas

and let the car coast down the slight downhill street until he reached the man's driveway. Victor reached up and turned off his dome light. The two men got out with Hawkins carrying his shotgun. Victor went to the car's trunk and retrieved the katana and a small backpack he slung over one shoulder. He closed the trunk quietly. With his Glock in the other hand, they approached the house cautiously.

"First cut the power, then attack," Hawkins said.

"Agreed," Victor said. "Which means we aren't dealing with the Demon. They prefer the blunt smash and kill kind of assault. This suggests military trained thugs. The Church of the Light Reclaimed."

"Church?"

"Yep. Of Satanists."

"Lovely."

Victor went to one side of the door, Hawkins the other. When both men were ready, Victor nodded to Hawkins, and he tried the doorknob. He shook his head. It was locked. Hawkins whispered, "How do you want to play this?"

Before Victor could answer, they heard glass being broken somewhere in the house, then a door being slammed open.

Victor stepped in front of the door and said, "I vote for the direct method."

He raised a booted foot and, using all his weight, crashed it into the door right next to the knob. The front door exploded inward with splinters flying in all directions. Victor dove through the opening, going left, Hawkins right. Through the ambient light streaming through the shattered front door, Victor saw he was in a great room, with a fireplace and door to his left, another door down a short hallway to his right and a series of French doors on the far wall flanked by another opening to what he guessed was a dining room. An L shaped sectional faced the fireplace with a couple of armchairs on either side.

He took one step into the room when gunfire erupted from the dining room, and he dove down low next to the fireplace as the drywall next to where he was standing erupted from the impacts. Hawkins jumped behind the closest end of the sectional and let loose with the shotgun, the sound filling the room. Victor dropped the katana and reached into his backpack.

Victor shouted, "Hawkins."

The former soldier turned to look at him and Victor raised the concussion grenade in his hand. Hawkins curled up and covered his ears and closed his eyes. Victor yanked out the arming pin, counted to two and tossed the grenade into the dining room. A moment later it detonated with a huge roar and flash of bright light. Considering they cut the power, Victor counted on the intruders to be wearing night vision goggles.

He ran to the dining room and saw ceiling plaster falling onto a huge cherry table surrounded by ten chairs. Four men were lying on the ground moaning. They wore the dark blue coveralls favored by the members of the Church of the Light Reclaimed. And all four wore night vision goggles.

One of the men rolled over onto all fours and Victor kicked him hard in the head, sending him down for the count. When another tried to get up, Hawkins slammed the butt of the shotgun into his face, knocking the man unconscious. The other two weren't moving at all. Victor took zip ties out of the backpack and tossed two to Hawkins and they quickly tied the men's hands behind their backs.

Victor ran and picked up his katana and said to Hawkins, "We've got to find Muldoon and fast. Neighbors will be calling it in for sure with the flash bang."

The two men cleared the first floor, yelling for Muldoon and not finding him. Hawkins nodded to the basement stairs. Victor returned the nod and the two men started down, their guns raised. The stairs ended in a finished basement. Victor fished out a flashlight and shone it around the room. A huge pool table took up most of the space, with a large flat screen on one wall and a beautiful mahogany bar on another.

"Muldoon, are you here?"

A man of middle years stood up from behind the bar clasping a bottle of bourbon to his chest. He was around six feet tall with dark black hair and John Lennon glasses. He was dressed in a UK sweatshirt and jeans.

"Please, don't kill me. Take anything you want. I mean it. Anything."

"We're not here to kill you. We're here to get you out alive. Come on, we don't have much time. We have to leave and now," Victor said.

Muldoon shook his head. "I'm not going anywhere. I don't know you and I'm not going."

Hawkins offered a short bark of a laugh. "Can you believe this guy? Maybe we should leave him to the guys upstairs. We can cut them loose and when they come to…"

Muldoon clutched the bourbon even closer, if that was possible. "Who are you?"

Victor strode across the room, shoved the Glock into a pocket and leaned over the bar. Muldoon moved until his back was against the wall. Victor snatched the bourbon out of Muldoon's grasp and shined the light on the label. Willet's Family Reserve. "Nice bourbon," he said and turned and headed for the steps. He motioned Hawkins to go ahead of him and the younger man disappeared up the steps. He glanced over his shoulder at Muldoon. "Four men came here to kill you tonight. We stopped them. They will send more. If you truly want to survive the night, you need to go where the bourbon's going."

He was halfway up the steps when he heard Muldoon yell, "Wait. I'm coming."

Muldoon caught up to him and they made it upstairs to find Hawkins keeping watch. Muldoon started towards his dining room and mumbled, "What the hell?"

Victor grabbed him by the arm and spun him around.

"We need to leave, and I mean right now."

He half drug and half shoved Muldoon out the door and to his car. The three men jumped in with Muldoon sitting in the back. Victor held the bourbon out to him, and the man once again cradled it like it was a talisman which would keep him safe. Victor fired up the Chevelle and raced up the street. They heard the cop cars before they saw them, and Victor turned down a side street and waited for them to pass. Once they were out of sight, he left the subdivision and headed towards the Derby Mission.

He watched Muldoon in the rearview mirror. The man was near being in shock.

He asked, "Do you live alone?"

"Yes. I'm divorced. My wife and kids live in Maryland." He swallowed hard a couple of times. "Why would anyone want to kill me? I'm just a CPA."

"It's not what you do," Victor said, "but who you're related to."

"What's my brother done now?"

Victor shook his head. Another guy with brother issues.

Hawkins said, "Nothing, as far as we know. You have to go back a few generations to get the right guy."

Muldoon blinked several times then said, "I don't understand."

Victor said, "Don't worry. We're headed to the Derby

Mission. Once we get there, we'll explain everything and figure out what you should do next."

Hawkins looked over his shoulder at Muldoon and asked, "What's with the bourbon?"

"It's my favorite. Once I heard the shooting, I was trying to figure out what to do and I picked it up out of reflex."

Victor shrugged. "There are worse ideas. But we may ask you to open it once we get where we're going."

Muldoon said, "I'm saving it for a special occasion."

Hawkins laughed. "You survived an attack by four assassins. Doesn't that qualify as a special occasion?"

It was Muldoon's turn to shrug. "Let me think about it."

Chapter Twenty-One

After settling in the kitchen with a fresh cup of coffee, Paige dialed Victor's number. No answer. She waited a few minutes and tried again. Still no answer.

With a foot up in her chair so she could hug her knee, Paige drummed her thumb on the top of her coffee mug, she remembered a conversation she had with Tom.

"Tom, what do you know about what is to come?" she asked, not wanting to hear the answer.

"I know there are two sides to this. It's the balance. It's not so much good versus evil as it is right versus left. At least that was how it used to be. This demon, Lora, she's the one who changed things. Agent Riggs isn't evil; he's just misguided, as are the other Readers. A Reader can't read a Keeper so no one can know for sure what we think so we are in the dark as to Agent Riggs. I guess it's by design," Tom said as he looked around the room to make sure no one was close enough to eavesdrop even though he knew they were alone.

"I guess it makes sense. But how does Lora play into this? What does she want?" Paige asked.

"Well, since the beginning, there has always been good versus evil, right? God created the world, and Satan introduced Sin, and so on. Lora has been around since before time. She has always been one to cause trouble and wanted to control others. She revels in it. When she found out about the Readers, she saw their power of manipulation and wanted to use that power. If she could control the Readers … well … you get it, I'm sure."

"But how does this involve me?"

"As you know, the gift gets passed down. And like with you, it has to be learned again every time it does. So, when Lora manages to control a Reader something always happens and the Reader dies doing her bidding. She then has to start over. She somehow needs the Readers. Killing them just doesn't seem to fit. That is where Evan came in. He was extremely talented at getting rid of those who were under her influence. But he was only driving out her influence, not killing them. He had always succeeded until recently," Tom looked at the ground. "She's managed to get strong enough now she was able to kill Evan. Death seems to fuel her power. That's where you come in," Tom took another drink and scanned the room again.

"Your mother's power was the strongest of all the Readers. She was extremely talented at only using it when necessary and humble enough to control it. She was Lora's biggest target. Lora couldn't control her, so she possessed someone else and caused the accident that killed your family. Of course, your mother's gift passed to you. Lora then controlled Shepherd, both while alive and his spirit for a while when he died. That is until you. Even with all that was blocking you, you were strong enough to kill your own brother, strong enough to defeat him while *in* the Collective Conscious. Paige, we are hoping you can defeat her now and end this. Unfortunately, you will have to destroy the other Readers as well to get to Lora. Even your sister. The line of Readers has to reset. They've become weak. Visette thinks death is the only way."

Paige shook her head, "I'm not sure I can."

Paige shook off the memory, took a deep breath and stood up from the table. The woman that was reading her, who was she? It was familiar, but it wasn't her sister, Junna. Was she really one of the other Readers or a figment of her imagination? Is she connected to the Devil's Mark? She wondered about Linda Coffey and her connection. And the Hand of God...

She picked up her phone again and sent a text to Victor. "I'm on my way to see you. Be at your place in twenty."

Chapter Twenty-Two

Victor swung the Chevelle into the Derby Mission parking lot to find Detective Paige Aldridge leaning against the trunk of her car. He was once again struck by how beautiful she was and how he knew her beauty made forging a career in law enforcement harder in a boys will be boys organization like the LMPD.

Hawkins asked, "Who's that?"

Victor put the car in park next to the detective's unmarked car and replied, "The cops. Why don't you get Muldoon inside and explain what's going on while I have a chat with Detective Aldridge?"

Muldoon leaned forward to look between them. "I'll gladly share my bourbon with her if she wants some."

Victor mentally noted, *point made* but said, "I think the less you have to do with cops now, the better. Remember you have four would-be assassins in your house the Boys in Blue will surely have found by now."

Muldoon nodded reluctantly. "Good point."

The three men got out and Hawkins and Muldoon went

inside, offering up brief hellos to Aldridge. She turned and watched them go without comment. The moment they were inside she asked, "Who are the newbies?

Victor took a moment to explain what happened, starting with his fight with the demon at Hawkins' house and the rescue of Muldoon. "What really sucks is," Victor continued, "the demon has now managed to hook up with the Church of the Light Reclaimed. The guys who invaded Muldoon's home were card carrying Church members. We need to find out if the lady Reader from your side of the tracks is involved with them as well. It's bad enough if they are coordinating and worse if we are fighting a war on two fronts."

"Funny you should mention it. I got an invitation today. Well, we got an invitation today."

Aldridge handed Victor the note from the latest murder victim.

He read the note and asked her, "How'd you get this?"

She told him and Victor closed his eyes while crushing the note and taking several long deep breaths. When he reopened his eyes, she saw pain, determination, and a primal force kind of anger, all mixed together. This was one dangerous man.

"It's obviously a trap," she said.

Victor smiled but the smile only made him look more primal. "Yes. Yes, it is. And I love traps."

Despite the seriousness of the situation, she laughed. And once again Victor thought how nice it sounded. There was a little voice in the back of his head reminding him he had a girlfriend, and the girlfriend owned a gun. He gave the little voice a mental shrug.

"The Falls of the Ohio State Park is a strange place to want to ambush us."

Victor had to agree. The Falls of the Ohio was the reason the city of Louisville came into being in the first place. Before the river locks were built, boats sailing up and down the Ohio River would have to stop and portage around the falls, a large rock outcropping featuring the exposed limestone fossil beds from the Devonian period more than three hundred million years before.

Victor said, "It's different, that's for sure. There's a long stretch of Riverside Drive and they can block it from either end once we get in there."

"How do you want to do this?" Aldridge asked.

Victor scratched his beard a moment before replying. "They say for only you and I to come. I think if we brought a crew with us, they wouldn't show, and I dearly want them to show. It's time you and I started to start dishing out some payback for the people they've killed."

"I am curious about something, though," she said.

"Go on."

"If the demon is the one killing all these people and then leaving his mark on them, does it seem likely to you he'd leave a message for us to meet on a post-it note? You've established the men were direct descendants of Taylor but can't find the connection to the women. I am beginning to think we have a copycat."

Victor grunted. "The Reader lady?"

She nodded. "Which also makes me wonder how she knew about Detective Coffey and her connection to you."

"Once I wring her neck, I'll ask her. So, will it be you and I riding into battle and kicking some evil bad guy ass?"

"I'm ready."

"Are you OK with leaving Tom out of this?"

"Yes. He won't like it. He believes he has to protect my every move. But I agree with you. If we show up with the cavalry in tow, they may not show themselves."

Hawkins opened the door and stepped out to join them.

Victor made the introductions and explained what he and Paige planned to do.

Hawkins said, "You should really let me come along. You know I can help you."

Victor raised his hands and said, "Captain, this is not a reflection on your abilities. We simply don't want to chase them off. Between the good Detective here and I, we can rain down plenty of Hell if it comes to it. And look on the bright side."

"What bright side?"

"If they kill me, you just might get my job. While we're gone, go through your great grandma's diary and figure out how we get the demon in his iron box."

He shook his head and went inside the mission.

Aldridge asked, "Your car or mine?"

"We better take mine. I don't think having an unmarked police car at a place where death and destruction might rain down is a good idea." The two of them walked to the Chevelle and Aldridge opened the passenger door. Before she got in Victor said, "One more question. Speaking of being a cop, whether this is the Church or your Reader lady, I will be shooting first and asking questions later. The Church of the Light Reclaimed won't give a rat's ass you're a cop. They will strip your skin from you alive if given the chance. Are you going to have any problems with me shooting people?"

The detective paused for only the briefest of moments before responding. "No. No I won't."

She got into the car and Victor thought, *My kind of woman.*

Chapter Twenty-Three

Victor started the Chevelle and cranked up the heat and turned to face Detective Aldridge. "Before we go, I need to make a phone call, if that's alright with you."

She nodded and Victor dug his phone out of his pocket and called Kurt, putting it on speaker phone so the detective could hear as well.

"What's up, Big Guy?" Kurt asked.

"Kurt, Betty Lou needs to get out tonight."

There was a hoot from the computer guru. "About damn time. Where?"

"Detective Aldridge and I are going to walk right into the middle of a trap at the Falls of the Ohio State Park across the river and I'm going to need her help. How long to get her there loaded with the fireworks package?"

Kurt snicked, "You want video of you and the hot detective, is that it? Linda will not be happy, dude."

Detective Aldridge gave Victor the kind of look you get when someone is totally busted.

"Er, Kurt?"

"Yeah, Vic?"

"We're on speaker phone and she's sitting right here."

There was a moment of silence then Kurt spoke up, his voice squeaking more than a little bit. "Uh, Detective? I meant that as a... well...er...hmm..gosh, you know."

Aldridge laughed and let the poor guy off the hook. "It's all good, Kurt. No harm no foul."

Vic joined the laughter and added, "I won't let you off that easy. Wait till I tell Ruth Ann you think Detective Aldridge is hot."

"Come on, man. That's not funny. I better go and get Betty Lou ready."

Kurt hung up the phone and Vic put the phone in his pocket.

Aldridge asked, "Betty Lou?"

Victor threw the car in reverse and then headed out of the parking lot before he answered.

"A couple of years ago I used a drone to drop hand grenades on a family of Hellhounds. And it got me thinking about more uses for drones. I went out and bought a heavy lift drone and we set about modifying it. In addition to the four clamps we can use to drop an M67 fragment grenade, I had it outfitted with both a thermal camera and LIDAR to complement the standard camera it comes with. Kurt calls her Betty Lou, and he loves it when we deploy at night because of the old Bob Seger song, *Betty Lou's Getting Out Tonight.*

"Wait, you have access to M67 grenades? That's military grade hardware."

Victor turned onto the ramp to I-65 North and hit the gas, the Chevelle jumping forward. "Yeah, ain't it great?" Aldridge started to say something, and he held up a hand. "Look, I have a source who supplies me with anything I need this side of a rocket launcher. I just pay to replace whatever I use."

"What's the fireworks package?"

"In addition to an M67, we added a few other surprises for the bad guys. You'll see. I don't want to spoil all the fun."

She thought for a moment. "This all sounds really expensive. How does a guy living at the Derby Mission afford all this stuff? Does God provide you with a bank account?"

"Sort of. A friend of mine and I ripped off the Church of the Light Reclaimed for a cool thirty-million dollars. We use their own money to put them in the ground. Pretty cool, huh?"

She turned almost completely sideways in her seat to stare at him. "Thirty-million?"

Victor nodded. "Yep. Scouts honor."

Aldridge turned around and shook her head. "Victor, I think you are a long way from being a boy scout."

"True, but the Girl Scouts wouldn't let me join. I kept eating all the cookies."

"And with all that money you live at a mission?"

"One of the few perks of being the Hand of God is when I'm on church grounds the bad guys can't touch me. There's a church at the mission and therefore I can sleep knowing they won't murder me in my sleep."

She removed her gun from her holster, checked the magazine and to make sure a round was locked and loaded in the chamber before returning the gun to the holster. The gun was blue in color and Vic asked, "Is that a Walther? I've never seen a blue one."

"It is. A PPS M2 LE. I had the gun store cerakote the entire gun robin's egg blue. I like it. It's pretty."

"Don't blame you. The Walther is a good gun. What type of ammo are you carrying?"

"9mm 124 grain Blazer Brass. Nothing fancy. Besides, I don't really need it."

"Well, rock on with your bad self."

They stayed quiet as Victor exited I-65 at exit 0 in Jeffersonville and looped around to Riverside Drive and the entrance to the park. He pulled into a parking lot before they reached the street and shifted the car into park.

"I've got some things in the trunk you're going to want."

He got out and she did the same and they met at the trunk. Victor used his key to open it and tossed aside the blanket covering his weapons stash. Aldridge let out a low whistle.

"Jesus, Vic. You've got enough here to start a small war."

"Sure enough, Detective. That's what I'm fighting. A war. You help keep the public safe from bad guys you can lock up and put away. I keep them safe from the things the bad guys are scared of." He reached into a bag and came out with two com links, handing one to her.

"Well, I am fighting a war with something that goes bump in the night, myself," she sighed as Victor cast her a sideways glance.

"They are Bluetooth connected. And how about one or two of these?"

He lifted out a pair of goggles and slipped them around his neck. Next came a bag full of M67 grenades, the group of them looking like a bag of small green melons. "I think I'll pass. You start tossing those things around and we're going to draw a lot of attention," Paige said as she waved her hand.

"If I have to start tossing these around," Victor said, "I won't care if they draw attention or not. If I'm dead, I won't care."

Paige saw the katana and picked it up and slid the blade out of its sheath.

"Really? A sword?""

Victor held out his hand and she returned the blade to the sheath and handed it to him.

"Ever see Highlander? There's more truth to the movie than you think."

Victor grabbed an MP5 out of the trunk and quickly swapped out the gun's standard site for a LIDAR scope, then attached a silencer to the barrel. He put several more magazines into the pockets of his bomber jacket and motioned for them to get into the car. He hopped into the driver's seat and slid the MP5 and katana next to him by the door. Aldridge got in and belted up and they made their way onto Riverside Drive and into the park.

Paige thought for a moment. She was so far outside of the norm for her job. She paused for a second wondering if she really wanted to be a part of this. Kicking some snow off her shoe, she realized that, yes, yes, she did. Maybe this would help her with her own battle. Shake the dust off.

The Louisville city skyline shown bright in the chilly night air, all the leaves off the trees providing a great view of the Derby City and of the Ohio River reflecting the lights of the city. Snow covered the ground, and the park was deserted as they arrived at a quarter to eleven. Vic drove slowly watching for signs of the trap. He knew the Visitor's Center was at the far end of the road.

Victor glanced in his rearview mirror, and saw an SUV stop at the entrance to the park and turn sideways, blocking the road. Victor nudged Aldridge and pointed over his shoulder at the car.

"I saw them. I'll bet you dollars to donuts they did the same thing at the other end near the Visitor's Center."

Victor grunted in response knowing she was likely right. Riverside Drive paralleled the river before taking a hard right and over a hill into Jeffersonville. With both ends blocked the only way to exit the park would be to make them move the cars or head out on foot. Victor stopped about halfway into the park and reversed into a parking spot just as his phone rang. It was Kurt.

"Dude, Betty Lou gave me a great shot of you arriving. You guys saw them block the entrance?"

Victor once again placed the phone on speaker. "We did. And they did the same at the other end?"

"Yep. You're effectively trapped."

"What else do you have for me, Kurt?"

"You're not going to like it if you didn't bring more people with you."

"Spill it, dude."

"The moment you entered the park and they blocked off both ends three boats hit the shore about a hundred yards from where you are. I count twelve guys in total. And man, they seem to be armed to the teeth. All are carrying long weapons. Dude, I'm not sure this is a good idea. You want me to have Betty Lou drop her presents?"

"Not yet. Hold tight. I'll link you into our com system and let you know when to let them loose."

"Roger that."

Victor rang off and pulled up an app on his phone, tapped a few settings and he asked, "Can you hear me, Kurt?"

"Loud and clear."

"Paige?"

She nodded. "I hear him."

"Good."

He offered Paige a fist and she bumped it, then she pulled out her pretty Walther.

"Happy hunting, Vic," she said and got out of the car.

"Damn straight, Detective."

Victor joined her in front of the car and slid the strap of the katana's sheath over his shoulder, positioning the sword on his back in easy reach of his right hand.

Victor knew there was a good chance he would die tonight, and he could not have cared less. He was about to do exactly what he was built for: death and destruction. The Hand of God was going to deliver the ultimate justice and it felt damn good.

Chapter Twenty-Four

"How do you want to play this?" Paige asked.

Victor looked around and said, "You head up the river a bit to that dumpster and take cover there."

She looked to where he pointed and saw a large dumpster, the kind used to haul away large amounts of trash and waste. The Ohio River saw a minor flood a few weeks ago and when the water receded there was all manner of garbage and drift-wood needing picked up.

"How about you," she asked.

"I'll start down towards the Visitor's Center and see what I see. Kurt, site rep."

"The twelve are having a brief powwow, still about a hundred yards away. One of the guys is pointing towards where you are. Easy enough as you're the only car in the park. The people blocking the exits are holding their positions."

"Detective, let's move out. And remember, shoot then talk."

"I think it's time you start calling me Paige, don't you?"

He smiled and said, "Sure, Detective. When this is over,

we'll head to the Raven and drink the enemy's blood from a boot."

She gave a disgusted look and asked, "You don't really do that, do you?"

"Nah. We'll drink bourbon. But blood sounds cooler."

She shook her head and moved towards the dumpster while Victor moved the other direction. He took a moment to enjoy the view of the city shining across the water from him. He loved his town, and he would be damned, so to speak, if he was going to let a bunch of Satanist-loving douchebags win.

"Kurt," he asked. "Anyone else in the park besides us and the bad guys?"

"Negative. The only other things in the park seem to be a pack of dogs down near where Detective Aldridge is taking her position."

"You can call me Paige, Kurt."

"Sweet. Thanks, Paige. You're really cool. I think you're the kind of person to help keep Victor in line. I mean, after all, he's always in trouble, it's kind of his-"

Victor cut in and said, "Kurt, focus."

"Sorry." There was a pause and Kurt said, "Uh oh. Vic, bogie on the hill behind you. He's moving down the ridge towards your position."

Victor raised the MP5 to his shoulder and sighted down the LIDAR scope. Things took on a multicolored 3D look like the laser sight rendered the world around him visible in the darkness. He found the man bent low and running while holding what looked like a sniper rifle. Great. Victor tracked him and took careful aim when the man stopped to check his bearings, like a rat stopping to sniff the breeze. He squeezed the trigger, and a short three shot burst struck the man center mass, and he went flying down the other side of the hill out of sight, the suppressor lowering the sound of the shot to a hard cough sound.

Kurt said, "Rumble rumble, scratch one weasel. The dude ain't moving. Nice shooting, Tex." He paused briefly, then continued. "Paige, four are coming down the river towards where you are, can you see them?"

"Yes, they are back lit by the city. I can see their silhouettes."

Victor stopped behind the trunk of a towering oak, limbs stretching leafless fingers to the sky, and glanced through the night scope. He saw the other eight break into two groups of four, with one heading more or less in his direction, the other working to flank them on the side of the Visitor's Center. He saw each man wore night vision goggles and relayed the information to Paige and Kurt.

Kurt said, "Figured as much. Which do you want first?"

Victor thought for a moment, then said, "There's almost no wind. Drop the Enola Gay on the group of four men closest to me."

Paige asked, "Enola Gay?"

"You're going to like this. The color matches your gun. Let it fly, Kurt."

Kurt let out an evil snicker. "Just like Thunder Over Louisville," referencing the large fireworks show held during Derby Festival Week.

"Boys and their toys," Paige said, and he could hear the sigh in her voice.

Victor pulled on his own goggles and pressed a button on the side and, like his gun scope, the world around him lit up in a LIDAR view. There was a time when he wore night vision goggles much like the Church goons. He liked these a lot better.

A moment later there was a thud in the middle of the four

men and a dark blue smoke began pouring out the end of the EG-18 military smoke grenade. With no wind the area quickly filled up with the smoke and the men disappeared from view. He knew the kind of night vision goggles used by the Church could not see through smoke. But he could.

Drawing the katana, Victor charged silently into the smoke, the men as clear to him as if on a sunny day while they were like the three blind mice plus one.

One man ran straight towards him to get out of the smoke, unaware of Victor's presence, and with one smooth stroke Victor removed the man's head from his shoulders as he ran by, the sharpness of the katana slicing through bone and cartilage like a sharp pair of scissors cuts through paper. The head and body hitting the ground was the only sound made.

He pivoted to his left and another man turned in his direction, evidently hearing the noise of the body falling. Victor drove the blade straight into the man's chest, piercing straight through his heart and out the other side. The man's finger squeezed the trigger of his assault rifle as he died, swinging the weapon in a small half circle as he fell, hitting one of the two men left standing in the head. The shot man dropped like a puppet with his strings cut. Victor withdrew the sword and concentrated on the only man left.

The final Church goon raised his gun to his shoulder and tried to look everywhere at once and shouted, "Blane, Carlos, Gus, what's happening?"

Victor moved behind him quietly and as he drove his katana through the man's back, he said, his voice low, "Judgement day's happening, asshole."

He yanked the katana from the man and watched him fall to the ground. It took less than thirty seconds to kill all four men. Victor felt the adrenaline rushing through him and the cold, hard concentration which came with it.

In his ear Paige asked, "Victor, are you OK?"

"Peachy. Four less rats to worry about."

The smoke began to clear, and Victor ran towards the cover of an oak tree, a brief memory of a raid on a Taliban stronghold when he killed nearly a dozen men the same way, using smoke for cover and a big ass knife, came and went. His reverie was interrupted when the other four men to his right let loose and tore huge chunks out of the oak tree as he reached cover.

Victor offered up a quiet apology to the ancient oak and promised he would get revenge on the tree's behalf. Victor also knew the tree, if it were possible, wouldn't care, knowing it would likely outlive him many times over. Victor glanced up towards where Paige waited for the men to reach her. He knew she was as tough as they came, with abilities he didn't begin to understand. He hoped it would be enough.

———

The four men hunting Paige approached the dumpster, the leader on the other side opposite Paige. She took a deep breath, held her gun out and peeked around the edge when her foot slipped in the snow and mud, and she went down on one knee. Her necklace holding the Abet Stone caught on the dumpster and was ripped off its chain. She reached for it just as a severe dizziness hit her hard. She fell face down in the mud on the bank of the river. She slowly opened her eyes, turned her head and looked toward the water.

Paige could hear a voice in her head as pain started to take over.

"Fragrant air may you define to purify this space of mine. Clean and pure be this lovely place I have chosen as this sacred space."

Paige noticed the surface of the water began to sparkle.

She blinked hard and watched the small, dancing lights. She crawled through the snow to the edge of the water and could see her reflection as the lights brightened a little. She stared at it for a while as if she were looking at a stranger.

The voice continued. *"May the goddess enter the water now to prime dear Paige for our vow. May Apollo's light release the shower. May Apollo's magic transform your power."*

Her reflection stirred and began to swirl. Then it stopped as quickly as it appeared. Paige's face slowly became blurred into a reflection of her mother. She remembered her mother's face peering into her crib at night. She remembered the last time she saw the same sweet face was in the swamp when Visette performed the spell to increase Paige's power.

"May the goddess enter the water now to prime dear Paige for our vow. May Apollo's light release the shower. May Apollo's magic transform her power. May the goddess enter the water now to prime dear Paige for our vow. May Apollo's light release the shower. May Apollo's magic transform her power."

Paige could no longer hear the voices of the Collective Conscious. Everything was quiet.

A vision started to form. She watched as it took on the form of her mother. She was just an image, the same image that appeared to her in the swamp months ago, but it didn't matter. Her mother moved her hand so it passed in front of Paige's forehead, and it felt like a veil was removed and her senses returned to her.

Paige felt the presence of something vile. Something evil. Nausea swept over her, and she remembered what it felt like to be controlled by another Reader. The other Reader was here and trying to control her.

That was her mistake. Paige was no longer confused or afraid. Everything was clear. She knew what to do. She rose slowly from the snow and the mud. Her breath was slow and steady. Her hair, damp and mud-caked, managed to glow a brilliant white light at the end of each strand. She slowly opened her eyes and a bright blue light shot from them, subtle yet strong. Then her eyes rolled back into her head, and she smiled. She was powerful, in control, and unafraid.

Everything fell into place. As she got to her feet, she could feel her mother's presence. She stood and found herself face to face with the closest of her assailants.

At the same moment, a pack of wild coyotes, the ones Kurt thought were a pack of dogs, drew closer. A new feeling came over her. She instantly knew there were six of the coyotes. She knew there was an alpha male, almost the size of a wolf, three other males and two females. And most surprising of all, she knew what they were thinking. Though that wasn't quite right. They didn't think like humans did. They thought in images. They were both curious and on edge with these new people in their territory.

And then she felt the final surprise as the alpha male let out a low growl. They felt what she felt, the anger and fear she felt for the men hunting her. She was a member of the pack and the desire of the men to hurt her meant they wanted to hurt the entire pack and the alpha male sent the image equivalent of a question mark: what do you want us to do?

She responded with an image of the pack running to her aid, and they did.

The man with the gun, his night vision goggles making him look like an alien bug, raised the gun and pointed it right at her forehead. Things began to move in fractions of a second. She made a quick read, searching for thoughts of someone wanting to shoot her, and the man's thoughts were there, instantly, and she had him. She sent the thought for him to turn his head and look over his shoulder. And he did.

The pack arrived at the same instant and she sent the alpha

male an image of what she wanted, and she felt his eagerness for the hunt. The alpha streaked past her and launched himself into the air, slammed into her would-be murderer and took him to the ground while he clamped his powerful jaws onto the man's neck. They hit the ground and the alpha started to shake his head from side to side and ripped out the man's throat.

The other three men began screaming as they pointed their guns at the alpha but were afraid to shoot out of fear of hitting their comrade. Paige felt the triumph of the alpha and sent to the remaining five coyotes what she wanted of them.

They spread out behind the three men and then attacked. The pack charged forward and hit the men hard enough in the back to take them all to the ground, the screams of the men mixed with the growls of the coyotes. She watched the fury unfold and she felt the copper taste of the blood in her mouth as if she were one of them.

Paige took the opportunity to look at their surroundings with the heightened sense of the pack. Someone else was there. The other Reader. She could feel it. Controlling. Angry. She couldn't make the thoughts out, but she could *feel* them. Unlike anything she was ever able to do before.

Paige took a deep breath and turned toward Victor who stood by the oak, as the lights dimmed around her. With her heightened senses, she saw the utter shock and awe on his face, despite the total darkness.

It wasn't long before all four of the assassins lay dead on the riverbank and she felt her connection to the coyotes end as the pack raced off down the river and out of sight.

"Uh, Paige?" Victor started when Kurt broke in.

"Did all those dogs just attack the bad guys?" Kurt murmured in her ear.

"Yes. Yes, they did," Paige said.

"Bloody hell," said Victor.

Paige turned around to try and find the other Reader, but knew it was pointless. They were gone. Paige picked up her Abet stone and made a promise to herself to find them and when she did, she would end things once and for all.

———

Victor found it hard to believe what he saw happen to Paige. One moment she was down on the ground, the next she's up, her hair glowing with a man pointing a gun right at her. Before he could even get the MP5 up to shoot the guy a pack of coyotes raced in and killed all four men. She turned to look at him and he knew she was seeing him as clear as day with glowing eyes. Then between one blink and the next, the light was gone, her eyes returned to normal.

His stunned inaction was broken when Kurt said, "What the hell?"

"What's going on, Kurt? Talk to me," Vic said, obviously shaken by what he just witnessed.

Kurt replied, "The two men standing by the SUV at the entrance to the park are down, as in face down on the pavement and not moving. Thermal says they're cooling off. Dude, they're dead. I was so busy watching the dog fight I didn't see anything. Did you bring back up?"

"No, I didn't. Paige, did you take them out with the whole glowing hair and eyes thing?"

"I didn't and I don't hear anything either."

Victor checked on the four remaining ambushers through the night scope and found them crouched low and moving towards their fallen partners in crime. Two of them took potshots at Victor but they missed by a wide mark. No doubt seeing eight guys go down in a matter of minutes, half of them by crazed coyotes, would make any aim shaky.

He started to target in on the closest one when he saw movement in the scope attacking the four from behind at the same time Kurt yelled in his ear, "Who is that?"

Whoever or whatever it was moved at a speed no human could match. He saw an arm rise, weapon up, as they shot one man after the other in quick succession. They died before they knew they were even under attack. As the last body fell, the person turned to face where Victor was hiding, and the gun disappeared into a pocket. The assassin started walking slowly towards him and Victor instinctively knew by the way the person walked it was a woman, and somehow familiar. She pulled off what looked like a knit cap and shook out long hair. Woman for sure.

He lowered the scope but held the rifle pointed in her direction as she got closer. She stopped about ten feet away and said, "Victor, if you shoot me, I'll be very put out."

Bloody holy hell. For one of the few times in his life, Victor found himself speechless. The woman had long raven black hair and appeared to be in her mid-twenties. Though she was older. Much, much older.

"What? No, how are you, Elizabeth? No, you look great, Elizabeth? This breaks my heart, Hand of God."

Kurt asked, "Vic, who are you talking to? Who is it?"

"Elizabeth Bathory," Victor managed to squeak out.

"I know that name," Paige said.

Victor was nodding his head and wondered if Paige could still see him. Kurt let out a sound somewhere between a moan and a choking sound.

"You may know her better by the name people called her back in the day. The Countess of Blood."

There was bewilderment in her voice. "Victor, Bathory

died in the 17th century. Surely, she's not *that* Elizabeth Bathory. Unless..." Her voice trailed off.

Detective Aldridge was a sharp study. "Unless she's an Infernal Lord?"

Elizabeth stepped up in front of Victor and began to pout, as with her enhanced hearing she heard the conversation. Both ends. "Who is this woman you are talking to? Is this the Samantha who was my rival for your affections?"

And evidently close enough for Paige to hear her as well. "Wait. You dated an Infernal Lord? And who is Samantha?"

Kurt whispered over the com, "Dude, you are so busted."

To Elizabeth he said, "Elizabeth, it's not Samantha. It's a cop." To Paige he said, "And Paige, as for who Samantha is, that's a longer conversation and my relationship with Elizabeth is complicated."

"I bet," she snorted.

Elizabeth offered a wicked grin and said, "Wild? Yes. Carnal? Yes. Complicated? No."

Before anyone else could say something, Victor jumped in. "Look, we need to get the hell out of here and go somewhere to talk. The Jeffersonville cops will be here soon. Someone had to have heard the Church guy's guns."

"Agreed," Paige said. "I'll move the SUV out of the way. What about the bodies?"

"Nothing to be done about them. I'll get Brother Joshua to use his contacts to spin it and keep us out of it. Let's move."

Victor jogged towards his car and Elizabeth kept pace. He glanced at her and asked, "Did you kill the men by the SUV?

"Yes. They were easy to kill. No fun at all."

"How did you get here?"

"Uber. He was cute, too."

"You didn't, uh, well..."

"He still lives, Hand of God. I have told you. I am a new person. I am a good girl now."

"Uh, huh."

They reached the Chevelle, and climbed in. As Victor fired up the car he thought about the Infernal Lord. The previous year she saved his life and helped to stop a bombing that would have changed the world and plunged it into chaos. She'd told him at the time she wanted to find a way to earn God's forgiveness, despite being damned for all time. Victor wondered more than once after she disappeared if there was an evil too evil to be redeemed. He still didn't have a clue what the answer was. He didn't even know if he would earn his own trip to the Pearly Gates.

And because of her attempted conversion Satan wanted her dead as much as he wanted Victor dead. Heaven help her if her bid for salvation was all for naught and she ended up once again in Hell. It made him shudder at the thought.

They stopped long enough to pick up Paige who got into the backseat without complaint. Victor knew it was not out of deference to Elizabeth, but to keep an eye on the Infernal Lord. He could tell Paige had her gun in her coat pocket, her hand on the gun. She had no way of knowing bullets would only piss Elizabeth off, but if it made her feel better, so be it.

Paige asked, "Where to?"

Victor thought for a moment then said, "I think we need a tank."

Elizabeth raised an eyebrow and said, "You have me. You do not need a tank."

"Believe me, you're going to love this one."

He knew Elizabeth would love where they were going. Detective Aldridge? Not likely. But hell, when your friends are all in low places, you go to low places.

Chapter Twenty-Five

Over the years the Riverside Inn has been many things. Several different bars, a couple of different restaurants, to name a few. Now the Riverside Inn was a biker bar headquarters for the Tyranny Rides motorcycle gang.

When Victor pulled into the parking lot it was after midnight and there were several bikes there, despite it being the middle of winter. One does not get to be a member of Tyranny Rides by being a wussy. He selected an open spot next to one where Detective Coffey sat waiting, having gotten there first after Victor called her.

They all got out of their cars and introductions were made. When Victor introduced Elizabeth to Linda, the detective found her hand going to her gun, then she grimaced and dropped the hand to her side. Elizabeth laughed, making Linda even angrier.

"And just how does she figure into this?" Linda asked through gritted teeth.

Victor shrugged and said, "Yet to be determined. Let's go inside and we can all lay our cards on the table."

Victor led the motley crew to the front door which sported a closed sign despite every light being on inside the building. The inn, a one-story wooden structure, sat right on the river with a dock to allow boats to tie off and gas up while getting lunch or dinner during the summertime. When the Ohio River flooded earlier in the month, the inn found about a foot of water inside despite a healthy sandbagging effort by the gang.

Victor rapped his knuckles against the door, and it was opened by the man he would always think of as Evil Santa. Cleatus "Tank" Bone was only an inch or two shorter and about seventy pounds heavier than the bounty hunter. He sported a long red beard which reached down about his belly button, with long red hair pulled into a ponytail. He was the leader of the biker gang and wore a T-shirt with a leather vest despite the cold.

Victor knew a quick way to get a pool stick upside your head was to call Tank by his given name, Cleatus. He hated his first name with a passion and Victor used to call him by it until they'd reached a deal for his help with a raid on a bad guy hangout. The bikers, while not quite the upstanding citizens he would prefer to deal with, were good when it came to getting down and dirty.

Tank stepped to the side and waved for them to come inside. He made a point of offering Paige and Elizabeth a smile he felt was inviting but came across more like a grizzly bear with attitude issues. He snagged Victor's arm and motioned for him to stop and wait for a private chat.

The inn's bar took up the center of the room, with an open door behind the bar leading to the kitchen. Tables filled up the left side of the bar with pool tables on the right. The bar was empty except for Tank, four other bikers sitting at a table in the corner watching basketball on a large flat screen

TV and the bartender, a lady named Saray, an attractive woman of about thirty with long black hair pulled into a ponytail. She was wiping down the bar despite the fact it already shined.

The rest of Victor's gang took the table furthest away from the bikers and sat. Saray came over to take their dinner orders and Victor's mouth began to water. Not only was she a great bartender, but she was one hell of a cook to boot.

Tank said, "Why didn't you tell me you were bringing another cop into my place. I get Coffey coming, she's your girl. I get it. But this one here, she screams cop,' he said as he pointed to Paige. "As for the dark-haired chick, she…"

Tank trailed off as he stared at Elizabeth, and she stared right back with a hint of a smile on her face. She oozed sensuality and knew the effect she had on men. Hell, it had worked on him.

"I don't have a choice and, for what it's worth, she's not like other cops. She deals in my kind of problems. Her name is Detective Aldridge. As for the other woman, her name is Elizabeth and is one of the deadliest women on the planet. I'd tell you to stay clear, but I can see by the look on your face you will have to touch the flame to learn your lesson. Just remember I warned you."

"What are you dealing with this time, is it like the hunt for Mikey?"

Tank and his gang helped Victor, Linda and his one-time girlfriend, Samantha Tyler, take on an Infernal Lord, a demon and a hoard of zombies. A lot of his guys didn't return.

"It's exactly like that. We are trying to get a handle on how bad and needed a place to work things out. Thanks for letting us hole up for a while."

"I like you McCain, but you only get the place because you agreed to pony up renting the place for things like this." He rubbed a hand across his expansive belly and continued, "You going to need me and the boys again?"

"Maybe. Are you sure you guys are willing to dip a toe in the demon stream again?"

"Hell fire, Vic. That's the most fun I've ever had. I'd do it again in a heartbeat."

Victor clapped Tank on the shoulder, and it was like slapping a boulder. He joined the others at the table and sat down next to Linda. She was finishing up telling Paige about Samantha. Victor and Samantha met when Satan hired him to track her down for stealing the thirty-million from the church. Victor agreed to do it to save his brother's soul. In the end, he found Samantha, but still lost his brother to the dark side. The two remained close until she was possessed by a demon and things got complicated. She was better, but their relationship had ended.

He pushed the thoughts of her out of his mind with a major effort and got down to business.

"First things first," he said. "Elizabeth, how did you find me? Only three people knew where I was going. One is sitting here and the other two wouldn't have told you."

Elizabeth crossed one long leg over the other and started to bounce her foot. "You are so full of yourself, Victor. I was not tracking you. I was tracking the men tracking you. The Fallen Angel himself set these men to finding and killing me. I found out they were supposed to do so after they made a trip here to Louisville. I thought to myself, why would Satan send this many men to Louisville if not to kill Victor McCain. And I planned to launch my own ambush to kill them first. I watched you and the dog woman kill many of them and decided why should you two have all the fun."

If Paige took issue with being called a dog woman, she hid it well. She glanced at Elizabeth, then to Victor and asked,

"Are we sure we want the help of an Infernal Lord? Doesn't her very existence suggest she's not to be trusted?"

Linda said, "I'm with Detective Aldridge on this one. We don't need her help."

Victor glanced at both women, then at Elizabeth, who said nothing in her defense before answering. He drew a deep breath and let it out slowly. "Actually, we don't know yet if we need her help or not. Linda, you know I trust my instincts. My instincts have told me from the first time I met her, she's telling the truth. She wants to earn salvation. I, of all people, cannot throw stones. If she wants to help, I'm willing to take what she can offer."

The two cops stared at Elizabeth a few beats more before both grudgingly nodded their acceptance. There was a brief pause while Saray sat plates around for the women and one for Victor. Without asking his preference she'd brought him the Tank Burger, fries and a Guinness.

Paige said, "If Victor says you're in, you're in."

"What I want to know is," Linda said, "Victor says he gets spidey sense like feelings anytime he's around a demon or a fallen angel, but not you or other Infernal Lords. Why not? I don't want to come across any other surprises."

Victor had often wondered the same thing and wanted to hear the answer as much as Linda. When he'd first met Elizabeth, he had no clue she was an Infernal Lord. It's something which might have led him to the great hereafter, but she'd saved him instead of killing him. It was one of the reasons he trusted her. She could have killed him dozens of times but had not.

"It is because I am not one of the Divine. Every Infernal Lord was once human. While we are given certain gifts by the Fallen One, we are considered lower beings. Victor, by being the Hand of God, is in tune with the divine and feels their presence. By our own nature, we Infernal Lords radiate a kind of evil which helps us overwhelm mere mortals, but it is not something Victor can sense. Though my former master has cut off many of my gifts."

Paige said, "I saw how fast you moved in the park. That was supernatural speed, not mortal speed. You still have some abilities."

"This is true. My physical traits remain the same. And some other things, as well. For instance," she pointed to Tank, who leaned his chair against the wall and stared at her with open lust on his features, "I know the fat man will be headed to Hades when he dies."

Linda let out a short bark of a laugh. "Listen Sister, it doesn't take an oracle to know Tank is headed straight to Hell when he catches the death train."

Elizabeth waved her off. "It is not a guess. Infernal Lords can read auras. It's a way for us to know when we have found someone we can use. Or someone on the edge we can push to the side of evil. You, for instance, are on the edge. If we were not allies and I was still working for the Dark Angel, you would be someone I'd push until you crossed the line."

Linda gripped her fork hard enough to turn her knuckles white. "You don't know a thing about me, you Hellspawn bitch."

"Truth hurts, Detective?" Elizabeth pointed to Paige, "This one, on the other hand, is out of the reach of any of my former master's minions. As for Victor…"

She looked at Victor and opened her mouth a couple of times as if to say something, then closed it, with a puzzled look on her face.

"As for Victor, what?" the Hand of God asked.

"I am afraid I cannot say," Elizabeth responded.

Victor felt a cold fear deep inside. "Why can't you?"

She again opened her mouth to say something but stopped. After another moment she managed to say, "It is not allowed."

Victor felt the fear turn to anger, his rage trying to bubble to the surface. "Not allowed by who?"

"You know the answer as well as I, Victor McCain, Hand of *God*."

Which made him even angrier. He would never know if what he did in God's name would allow him to make the trip to Heaven until the moment he died, because God would not allow it. And it sucked.

He mentally gave himself a slap to get over it. It was what it was, and it wasn't going to change. "Linda, you were going to try and track down who bought the burner phone. Any luck?"

She shook her head. "It's a dead end. It was bought at a Walmart, but there's no video showing who bought it and they paid cash."

Paige said, "We know at least one Reader is now working with the Church of the Light Reclaimed and the demon which is loose. The combination makes things tough for us."

Elizabeth took the last bite of a steak and dabbed at her lips with a napkin. Victor knew Infernal Lords don't have to eat to stay alive, but Elizabeth was a true foody. She asked, "What is this Reader? Explain, please."

Paige gave both Linda and Elizabeth a quick rundown on what they were and how they operated. When she finished Victor said, "We need to find a way to get ahead of the game. Up to this point, we've been dancing to their tune. That must change. We now have two of the demon's intended targets at the Derby Mission. We need to find a way to leverage that."

Victor gave them an update on Hawkins and Muldoon. "Hawkins is going through his great grandmother's diary now to see if she documented how Taylor and his merry band of demon hunters got the demon in the ground to start with. If a bunch of 18th century men found a way to plant a demon in a graveyard, then we should be able to as well. Elizabeth, do you have any suggestions which might help?"

"If you want power over a demon, you must know his name. That is where you should start."

"Okay," Victor said. "I'll see if Hawkins can find the name in the family history."

Elizabeth stared at the ceiling then said, "They may also have used a talisman. They are extremely rare, but they are known to exist."

Paige said, "I have dealt with a demon. I know someone I can talk to who may be able to help."

Victor said, "Good. Any luck on determining what the women may have in common? We've found the link to the men, but Kurt's coming up with nothing connecting the women."

"Not yet. I've got Tom and the task force checking into a few things. We will keep at it."

"Sounds good. Then I think what we need to do is have Linda keep working the cop angle, Paige you see what your contact might know about burying a demon while Tom and Kurt keep trying to find a link between the women. I will get with Hawkins and see what he's come up with."

"And what do you want me to do, Victor McCain?" asked the Infernal Lord.

"Try not to kill anyone unless they are trying to kill you. How will I contact you?"

She gave him an eye roll, then changed her gaze to Tank and raised a chin in his direction. "I will be with that one. I think he needs to be broken."

Victor looked at the huge biker and shook his head. The

image of Elizabeth and Tank in bed nearly gave him the willies.

"Uh, then we all have a plan. Let's get moving and we can all get together for dinner tomorrow."

Everyone but Elizabeth got up and headed to the door. Victor was the last one out and he turned and offered Tank a weak smile. Tank gave him two thumbs up as Elizabeth started to saunter in his direction. Victor closed the door and crossed himself, offering up a short prayer for Tank.

He was going to need it.

Chapter Twenty-Six

Exhausted, Paige slowly made her way to her car. What happened at the Falls of the Ohio had taken a lot of her energy. She couldn't stop now. Not in a million years, would she be able to forgive herself if she stopped now.

As she started her car, she asked Siri to call Visette.

"Hey, you!" Visette's sweet voice answered. "I was just getting ready to call you."

"Great minds…ha ha," Paige responded. "I have so much to tell you and so much to ask of you."

"I know. I saw it in the mist. And I'm here to help. My plane just landed."

"How's that for timing?" Paige laughed.

"Pretty damn good if you ask me. Pick me up, will ya?"

"On my way." Paige hung up the phone. She wasn't sure Visette knowing when to show up to help her was a surprise to her. It shouldn't have been. Visette could see the truth in the mist with her spell. Always. She was a Reader as well as a powerful witch from a long line of powerful witches. And she was the one who trained her in the use of her gifts.

Traffic was nonexistent on the way to the airport after being a nightmare earlier in the evening. Paige figured it was the line of cars waiting to get into Lights Under Louisville. Every year the Louisville MEGA Cavern was converted into an underground holiday light spectacular for the Christmas season. People lined up all around to drive through and enjoy the lights. Paige wished she had the time to do something like that; just for herself. She often resisted the urge to control everyone and make them pull off to the side of the road when she was in a hurry. She refused to abuse her power; besides, she wanted to avoid the questions everyone would ask after it happened.

Finally, as she pulled through the pick-up line at the Louisville Muhammad Ali International Airport, she could see Visette standing at the curb, leaning on the handle of her carry on pull behind bag. Visette spotted her in the car and waved. Paige pulled to the curve and hit the button to pop the trunk.

After depositing the bag, Visette hurriedly hopped into the front passenger seat. "Great to see you," she said. "I wish it were under better circumstances."

"Me too. Do you think we will ever get to the point of better circumstances?"

"Most likely not," Visette sighed as she toyed with the corner of the flap on her light blue handbag.

"Do you have a place to stay?"

Visette shook her head. "I don't. Is your guest bedroom available?"

"It is. Hey, I have something to tell you. Unless you saw this in that mist of yours. Did you have any idea I could suggest actions to a pack of coyotes?"

"You're right. I did see it in the mist. Did I know? No. Hell

135

no. I had no idea that was even possible. Animals aren't in the Collective Conscious, right? I've never noticed."

"Well, there was one time when I was watching a squirrel in the courtyard of the hospital when I went to see Jay. I would think of something, and it would just do what I thought. I blew it off as coincidence. Then yesterday I jumped into the mind of a cat and had him attack a bad guy. And now coyotes at the Falls of the Ohio, that was no coincidence."

"I agree. I can't imagine. I tried it myself on a cat I saw on Beech Street before I left New Orleans. Nothing. It just did its own thing. I swear I felt it snub me."

"As cats normally do," Paige laughed. It felt good to have some small talk, although Paige could feel the discussion was about to change. Change to something dark. Before Paige could even start, Visette was ready to explain why she had come.

"A demon. I know we have to trap one. I had to do a bit of research, but I know it was common to use spirit traps known as "witch bottles" to capture spirits. My Grandma told me of burying one once. Under a tree, near the swamp. Far away from our house. Anyway, these bottles would be filled with hair, fingernail trims, or other physical traces such as blood or urine of a target. This was used to trick the evil spirit into thinking it had found whoever it was after. When the demon entered the bottle to look for them, the bottle would be sealed shut, then wrapped with little glass squares tied together, along with mirrors to keep the spirit inside its prison. Then the bottle would be buried, often at a point of running water. There are different accounts of this, with some spells requiring a binding ritual to be performed before the spirit can be sufficiently confined inside the bottle. Unfortunately, this spell is said to be able to capture human souls as well."

Visette cleared her throat as Paige drove, looking like she was far, far away, and continued. "These demon traps were very widespread in Medieval Europe in places where fear and insecurity made evil spirits and demons a very real thing for much of the population."

"But," Paige interrupted, "a bottle? Catch a freaking demon in something as simple as a bottle?"

"It's what you do with, and to, the bottle that counts. There are accounts written in the Old Testament of the Bible, where the legend of King Solomon states a ring was given to him by the majestic Archangel Michael, inscribed with a magical seal. It was named the Seal of Solomon. The ring gave him the power to control demons. It was mentioned in the Christian, Islamic, and Jewish religions. The belief is roving demons could be trapped and bound within different objects. They believed these things were quite stupid and would follow bright and shiny things or symbols or artifacts and then became completely mesmerized to their doom for all infinity."

Paige nodded in agreement, thinking she could use this information in her battle with the demon Lora. Which seemed like a lifetime ago.

"Get white chalk and draw these circles and symbols," Visette told her while handing her a drawing from a yellow legal pad. "Sorry, I drew this on the plane here."

Paige took the drawing in her hand and glanced at it as she drove. The drawing was of three circles, nestled one inside the other. Along the entire outside circle were what looked to be runes while the middle circle seemed to loop through a large triangle. The inner circle had symbols. Some swirled, some were dots, and there were two more triangles, one inside the other.

"When the time comes, as you draw the circle, I will be preparing the witch bottle. We can do this. And with the help of your new friend, Victor."

"How so?"

Visette took a deep breath. "We need his blood."

Chapter Twenty-Seven

Victor parked at the Derby Mission and turned off the Chevelle but didn't immediately go inside. He sat there and thought about what Elizabeth returning meant. It wasn't so much he didn't believe her story as it was she was a wildcard with unknown motives and consequences. Their brief love affair was more like a bonfire than a flame but burned out just as quick. Add in having her there with Linda and discussions of Samantha and he felt like his personal life was spiraling out of control. At least he could say the women he fell for were not ordinary in any way.

And then there was Detective Aldridge. In a way she was like him: fighting supernatural threats to the mortal world, putting her own life on the line. There was a lot about her he didn't understand, how her powers worked, how they affected her. She proved to him several times she was tough enough to handle the job. He found his thoughts drifting her way more and more.

And he had to admit to himself, Elizabeth not telling him

what she saw in his aura pissed him off. It was as if God wanted him to sacrifice everything while at the same time, not giving him any rewards on this side of the Great Beyond. He knew life wasn't fair. He also knew he was in this position due to his own actions. It didn't mean he had to like it.

He said a few more profanities under his breath and went inside. Down the hall he saw Brother J's light was on in his office despite the hour and he ambled in that direction. He knocked and entered to find Brother J behind his desk, Hawkins in a chair flipping through his great-grandmother's diary and Muldoon stretched out on a couch in the back of the room. His shoes were off and a blue Solo cup in one hand dangled just above the floor, while the other arm covered his eyes. The bottle of Willet's was on the floor next to the couch and about a third gone. He also noticed Solo cups by both J and Hawkins, surprised J even drank bourbon.

Victor saw a stack of cups on the lone filing cabinet in the room, went and grabbed one, then walked over to Muldoon, cleared his throat and held out the cup. Muldoon raised his arm and looked at Victor with his cup held out. He sat his own cup on the ground, picked up the bottle and poured Victor a double, then returned the bottle to the floor and re-covered his eyes. Good man.

Victor plopped down in the other armchair opposite Hawkins and sipped the bourbon. Damn if it wasn't one of the best things he'd ever tasted, the whiskey exploding across his taste buds and the burn down his throat. A welcomed feeling.

Victor glanced at Brother J. and said, "I didn't know you drank bourbon."

Brother Joshua replied, "There's a lot you don't know about me, Hand of God."

Victor tipped his cup in J's direction acknowledging the

truth of the statement. He then turned his attention to Hawkins. "Any luck on figuring out how they got the demon buried?"

Hawkins sat the book to the side, his frustration obvious. "Not really. She writes about how it was a struggle and that several other men died helping Robert Taylor in the plan to capture and bury the thing, but no details on how they did it. I went back and reread the entire thing seeing if it was mentioned elsewhere and I simply forgot, but no luck there either. I'm sorry. It seems I'm not much help."

Victor hid the frustration he felt, as it was not the younger man's fault. "Any chance she at least wrote down the demon's name? If we know the thing's name it may help us with all the spooky stuff."

Hawkins furrowed his eyebrows and picked up the diary. "You know, that rings a bell. Give me a sec."

Hawkins searched through the diary while Victor filled in Brother Joshua about the attempted ambush, that the Church of the Light and one of the Readers were now a tag team, and the reemergence of the Countess of Blood.

Brother Joshua steepled his hands on his desk and rested his chin on his fingers. "Bathory showing up is quite unexpected. What was your sense of her?"

Victor shrugged his rather large shoulders. "She seemed sincere, and she did help take out the Church goons. Yet, if she has an agenda here, I'm not sure I would know. She's had a lifetime of lying and getting what she wants. If you want to go by my gut, I'd say she's on the up and up. Her offer of help seems to be without strings attached."

Brother Joshua merely offered a short nod of his head and picked up his cup of bourbon, took a sip, and said nothing more. The man would have made a hell of a poker player. His features gave away nothing.

Hawkins spoke up, breaking his reverie. "Well, it looks like another dead end. She talks about one of the other men who kept track of the names of all the demons and things they tracked and either trapped or killed. He evidently wrote them down in a book called *Daemonii et Diaboli: Liber Nomini*. I have no clue what the title means."

Brother Joshua said, "It's Latin for Demons and Devils: The Book of Names."

Victor said, "Great. Sounds like just what we need. Where do we find it?"

Hawkins set the diary down with a sigh. "I have no clue. I've never seen it. I've been through everything of Robert and Sarah's I could find and I would have remembered something like that."

Muldoon, without moving a muscle on the couch, said, "I know where it is."

Victor almost dropped his cup in surprise. "You do? Do you have it?"

Muldoon sat up and poured himself some more bourbon and took a swig. "Kind of. I don't have it at my place. It's at my grandpa's place, a cabin out in Shelby County. Well, it used to be his. It was left to me in his will. He had a small library of books in a back room. I went through them and the book you're talking about is there. I knew it was Latin but the closest I got to learning Latin is E Pluribus Unum, so I ignored it."

"About damn time we got a break going our way," Victor said. "I know it's the middle of the night, but I'm going to get the book. I won't be able to sleep. You game Hawkins?"

Hawkins stood up and stretched. "Damn straight."

Victor said, "Excellent. Kevin, how do we find this cabin?"

Muldoon drained the last of the bourbon in his cup, picked up the bottle and walked over and sat it on Brother

Joshua's desk. "Watch this for me, please." He turned to Victor. "You'd never find it. I'll have to show you."

"I'd really rather you not leave the mission. As long as you're here, the bad guys can't touch you. You go out with Hawkins and me, all bets are off."

Muldoon gave Victor a shrug of his own. "Does it really matter? I can't stay here at the mission for the rest of my life. No offense," he offered to Brother Joshua.

"None taken," replied Brother Joshua.

Hawkins stood up and shouldered his duffle bag. "Then let's go get us a book."

Victor's phone rang as he stood up and Muldoon went to put on his shoes. It was Linda. He answered, "Look. I can't talk for long. We have an actual lead on getting the demon's name."

He filled her in on Kevin Muldoon's cabin in Shelby County and the importance of the book.

"Want me to come along?" Linda asked.

"No. I need you to get some sleep and then keep digging on your end doing cop stuff. You're our main access to all the official stuff while Paige is doing Reader stuff. I'll take Hawkins with me. We'll be okay."

"You'd better. Trouble seems to follow you around. I don't want any more holes in you."

She'd been standing right next to him when an assassin's bullet nearly ended his life. "That makes two of us. I'll check in when we get back to town. What did you need?"

"It's not important. I just wanted to talk about Bathory being involved. It can wait."

Victor was happy about putting off talking to Linda when it concerned Elizabeth. The longer the better.

The two said their goodbyes and Victor turned to Hawkins and Muldoon. "Let's go check out a book."

The three men left the Derby Mission and for the first time since the Devil's Mark Killer intersected his life, he felt like he was seizing control of the situation. Victor knew a good defense was a good offense that destroyed the opposition. He planned to take the ball and ram it down their throats and make them choke on it.

Chapter Twenty-Eight

Muldoon directed them out onto I-64 East and the three men rode in silence, each with his own thoughts. Victor spent the drive doing his best to keep Elizabeth and Tank out of his mind. It was hard to do. About a half hour later, they got off on Highway 53 and headed north through Shelbyville and several miles out the other side. Muldoon told Victor to slow down and eventually pointed to a beaten down dirt track heading out into a thick grove of trees.

The Chevelle was not the best vehicle to take down a snow packed dirt road, but beggars couldn't be choosers. Tall oaks and pines crowded close on both sides of the road and Victor more than once worried he would hit a tree when the rear end of the Chevelle fish-tailed in the snow. He felt better when the car's headlights showed the outline of a cabin, sitting straight ahead and at the bottom of a hill in a natural bowl depression in the land.

Muldoon said, "I'd park the car up here. If you go down the hill, it's not likely you're going to make it to the top and I really don't want to walk all the way to Shelbyville in the snow in the middle of the night."

"Roger that," Victor said.

He stopped the car and turned off the engine. They got out and Victor went to the trunk, got a Maglite, and turned it on. When he pointed the strong light towards the cabin, he noticed a steady breeze was forcing a heavy mist to drift down into the area around the cabin. He knew it was supposed to be warmer in the morning and mist often formed when warmer weather passed over a colder patch. But it was the middle of the night. Right now, the air was every bit as cold as it was earlier in the day, if not colder. The hair on the back of his neck stood straight up and motioned for the other two men to stop.

"What's wrong?" Hawkins asked.

Victor didn't answer right away, stood still and watched as the cabin started to disappear from sight. He moved the light around them in a slow circle. The mist was only down next to the cabin, nowhere else. "This isn't right," he finally managed to say.

"We get fog here quite a bit, since it sits down low like that. It's no big deal."

Victor wasn't convinced. "Hawkins, are you armed?"

"No, but I can be. You think it's needed?"

"I do. Get your shotgun, just in case."

Victor returned to the trunk, opened it, slung the MP5 over his shoulder and retrieved his katana. He lifted out a Glock 19 and asked Muldoon, "Do you know how to use this?"

Muldoon took the offered weapon, checked the chamber and tucked the gun into the back of his jeans. "Yep."

"Good enough. Let's go," Victor said.

His Maglite was able to show glimpses of the cabin as they

walked closer. It was a true single story log cabin and appeared to be about the size of a smallish ranch house. A large chimney rose up on the left side and Victor saw there was a porch running the length of the front of the cabin.

"Jesus Christ, what's that?" Muldoon gasped when the Maglite flicked across a window and there appeared to be something staring at them from inside the cabin. Between blinks it was gone. Victor glanced at Muldoon who now had the Glock in his hand.

Hawkins said, "Maybe a trick of the light? Only one way to find out, right Vic?"

After another moment of silence, he agreed. "We need that book. Perhaps our imaginations are getting the best of us. Stay sharp. And Kevin?"

"Yeah?"

"Don't shoot one of us in this mist. Alright?"

"Yeah. Sure. I won't."

Victor led them towards the front of the cabin and the mist became so thick it was harder to see the two men, one on either side of him. It seemed to cling to his skin, the air damp and cold. He moved another couple of steps closer to the cabin and then yelled for them to stop. He sensed more than saw Hawkins and Muldoon pull up short.

"What is it?" Hawkins asked.

Victor pointed the Maglite straight down at the ground and saw footprints. Much larger than his size fifteen and with a stride length even longer than his six-foot six frame. They started on the ground in front of the first step and up to the porch. They didn't seem to come from anywhere, with the snow unbroken from where Victor stood to the steps and on either side. It was like a very large creature had been dropped from the sky. There were no claw marks or boot treads. Victor's mind flashed on fake Bigfoot footprints.

Hawkins, on Victor's left, turned on a flashlight of his own and shined it off to the side. He said, "Did you guys hear that?"

"I haven't heard a damned thing. What did you hear?" Muldoon asked, his voice going a bit higher than usual.

Hawkins said, "I...well...I thought I heard…"

"What?" Victor asked.

"Chains."

Victor tried to watch the area where Hawkins aimed his light and strained to hear the chains but didn't. "I didn't hear anything. Muldoon, are you sure you didn't hear anything?"

Victor glanced to his right and then searched the area with his Maglite. "Muldoon?"

Muldoon was nowhere in sight and gave no response to his shout. Victor pointed the light at the ground where the man's footprints stopped next to Victor's and then nothing. Bloody hell. It was like the man teleported away.

"Hawkins, Muldoon is gone."

"What do you mean gone? Where'd he go?"

"Gone as in I've got no fucking clue, man."

"There's that sound again," Hawkins said. "Wait. I think I see someone."

Hawkins moved quickly away and was lost from sight as he was swallowed by the mist.

"Mike, hold up. Wait," Victor said, but the man was gone from sight. After a moment, he shouted Hawkins' name, but got no reply. Hadn't he seen any horror movies? Splitting up at the cabin in the woods always brought on disaster. Victor knew legends like the cabin and the woods often were based on long ago stories that were true.

Victor spun around when he thought he heard someone behind him, the MP5 up and ready. Nothing. He felt the primordial fear rise inside him and the fight or flight response demanded he pick one. The lizard part of his brain screamed at him to run to his car and leave the other two to their fates. Survive. Live. Run.

Victor let out a low growl and turned towards the cabin's door. Being afraid pissed him off. And when he got angry, he got violent. He raised the gun and let a burst hit the wooden front door, splinters flying off in all directions. Victor charged up the steps and followed the large footprints up to the door and slammed a boot right next to the doorknob, not even stopping to see if the door was unlocked. The door practically flew off the hinges and slammed hard against the jam.

He dove into the cabin and rolled to his right and came up hard against a leather couch. He scanned the room with the LIDAR scope he had left on the automatic rifle and fought to control his breathing. He knew he was being hunted. By what, he had no clue. He needed to be calm and think clearly. He needed to find the threat.

It turns out, the threat found him. Victor heard the sound of chains mere moments before a length of chain came flying and wrapped around his neck. Victor dropped the Maglite and let the MP5 hang loose by its strap, as his hands grappled with the chain.

There was a hard pull and Victor went flying through the air, the fact both his hands held tight to the chain was the only thing keeping it from breaking his neck. He slammed hard into the far wall and knocked several framed paintings to the ground. The breath was nearly knocked out of him, too. When he landed on the ground, the chain dragged across the ground, hauling Victor with it. Victor struggled to his feet, planted them and yanked hard with all his strength on the chains. He felt something heavy on the other end slide in his direction but then it stopped.

Victor realized he now could make out a large figure in the

room with him. One moment it was completely dark, the next there was a soft glow. And the glow was coming from his katana. The sword was made by the greatest sword maker of all time, Muramasa, a samurai who lived in the 1500s. It was said he went insane and, it turns out, it was worse than that. He became an Infernal Lord and it was claimed a bit of Muramasa himself was imbued in every sword he made after joining Satan's ranks. Victor took the sword as the spoils of war after killing the Infernal Lord,

Now his frickin' sword was glowing, something it never did before, and the light revealed what appeared to be a huge gray man, his facial features almost non-existent. Where his eyes, nose and mouth were supposed to be, there were only depressions like a nylon stocking being pulled across someone's face. Its hands were huge and its right hand was wrapped around the length of the chain now around Victor's neck. Part of his brain wondered what the creature was and then the answer came: it was an Am Fear Liath Mor, a Greyman, a monster from the mountains of Scotland. Victor swallowed hard, not because of the creature, which was scary enough, but because the answer came from the katana.

Bloody hell. His sword was talking to him.

Victor stopped resisting and instead charged the Greyman and yanked the katana out of the scabbard. The Greyman started to yank the chain again and as he did, Victor swung the katana in a huge arc. There was no finesse, no tactics. He simply channeled his anger and used brute strength. The sword cut off the creature's arm at the elbow and it howled in rage, the sound muffled coming from the nonexistent mouth.

Victor began to reverse the swing to deliver a devastating blow and cut the creature in half when it backhanded him with his left hand. The blow caught Victor square in the chest and sent him flying across the couch and he landed by the door. The Greyman came at him again as it crossed the room, shoved the couch out of the way and aimed a blow which would crush Victor's head like a grape.

Instinct took over and Victor dove under the blow, twisted in the air and slashed at the creature's hamstrings with the katana. The blade sliced through sinew and bone as one would slice through water. The creature let out another muffled howl and tumbled backwards onto the cabin floor.

Victor rolled onto his side, gripped the trigger of his MP5 and emptied the entire clip into the creature's head. He realized he was screaming the whole time he did so, but he didn't care. This was something out of a nightmare and he wanted it dead.

When the clip emptied, he dropped it again and he saw the creature twitch and spasm a few times then went still. Not wanting to take any chances, he raised the katana high and brought it down in a vicious stroke, severing the head from the rest of the body.

Victor got to his feet as pain exploded with every movement he made. He kicked the head hard and it flew through the broken door and into the snow, the pain the effort caused worth it.

He retrieved the Maglite from where it had rolled under the couch and pointed it out the door. The mist was almost completely gone and Victor figured it must be connected to the monster lying at his feet. Dead monster, no mist. Also, there was no longer a light emanating from the katana. "What the hell? Do you also make breakfast?" The sword remained silent.

He went outside and searched for Hawkins and Muldoon. He found both men at the side of the cabin by the chimney. Both were unconscious but breathing. He carried them inside, one at a time and laid them gently on the couch. In the flashlight's glow, he saw Hawkins must have taken a blow to the head, as his right eye had begun to swell shut. Muldoon had a huge knot on the side of his head.

With the two men inside, Victor, bruised and bone weary, found the door to the bedroom and opened it. On the far wall was a bookshelf. He showed the light across the spines and found the book he was looking for: *Daemonii et Diaboli: Liber Nomini*. He offered up a silent prayer to God for allowing him to keep breathing for a bit longer. He knew this time he almost didn't make it.

When he returned to the main room, he found Hawkins awake and trying to bring Muldoon around. He looked at Victor and said, "It feels like Mike Tyson sucker punched me."

"Not too far off," Victor said as he panned the light across the body of the Greyman.

Hawkins let out a low whistle and saw the arm as it lay on the floor with the length of a heavy chain in the monster's hand. "I guess he tagged me with that?"

"Yep. And the same for Muldoon."

Victor told him about the fight and how the creature used the chain to toss him around the room. When he was finished, Muldoon sat up and groaned, and then he threw up.

Hawkins said, "I bet he has a concussion."

"Agreed," said Victor. "Let's get him on his feet and get out of here. I've got the book. We need to get to the mission because we have a huge problem."

Hawkins lifted Muldoon and each of them put an arm under him and walked the woozy man to the Chevelle. "What problem? We've got the book."

"Big grey and ugly back there. He was waiting on us. How'd he know we were coming here? Only five people knew where we were going. Three of them are here and Brother J. is above reproach. That leaves Detective Coffey, and it would seem she's been compromised somehow.

They got Muldoon in the Chevelle, and they began to make the treacherous drive back the way they had come. The whole time, Victor worried about Linda. He didn't want to call and warn her in case they'd bugged her phone. Perhaps they might find a way to use it to their advantage. Yet he worried. Somehow, they'd gotten to her. And he needed to find out how. And then there was his katana glowing and talking in his head. He worried Muldoon would get sick in the rear seat of his Chevelle.

Bloody hell.

Chapter Twenty-Nine

Victor, with Hawkins' help, got Muldoon inside the Derby Mission and to one of the rooms used for homeless men. Victor's room was down the hallway. He'd once lived in a very nice townhome but moved to the mission when he became the Hand of God so he could sleep without worrying about a denizen from Hell trying to kill him while he did.

Once they got him settled, Hawkins asked, "What's next?"

"We need to talk to J. Come on."

Hawkins followed him and said, "Man it's almost five in the morning. Won't he be asleep?"

Victor said nothing as he walked down to Brother Joshua's office and of course the light was on. Hawkins let out a laugh. Victor knocked and the two men entered. The man they were looking for was right where he always was when Victor needed him: sitting behind his desk. Victor laid the book in front of him and then he and Hawkins took the two armchairs, both men nearly dead on their feet.

"We don't read Latin. Care to help out?" Victor asked.

Brother Joshua pulled the book closer and then began to

thumb through the pages. After a few moments he said, "The demon's name is Aamon. He is one of the Princes of Hell and commands forty legions of devils in Hell. You will find him a formidable opponent."

"Is it ever easy? How did they capture and bury him?" Victor asked.

Joshua closed the book. "It doesn't say. It only mentions his name and where they buried him. It would seem there are quite a few Hellspawn buried around Louisville. They found burying them would be better than sending them to Hell and risk them returning to persecute mortals."

"Seriously? Not even a small clue? What is it with you guys? Is there something wrong with lending a brother a hand?"

Brother Joshua said, "You now know his name. That brings power. I have faith you will figure it out."

Victor shook his head in disgust. "Whatever." He glanced at Hawkins and then continued, "The good Captain here needs a place to sleep tonight as well."

Brother Joshua nodded and said, "His room is next to yours. He will be afforded all protections, of course."

The two men got up and walked down to the other end of the hallway and Victor showed Hawkins where he could bunk for the night. When Victor turned and walked towards his door Hawkins stopped him. "Now what?"

"We both get a good night's sleep and then tomorrow morning there are a couple of people I need to talk to."

"Then I'll tag along."

Victor shook his head and said, "'Afraid not." He saw Hawkins was about to protest and he raised his hands, "Look, they won't talk to me if you're there. It's not personal. Rest up. We're going to war with one of the princes of Hell and you will be there when it goes down. I promise."

The younger man seemed only slightly mollified, but Victor really didn't give a rat's ass. It was what it was. He left the Army Captain to his room and went to his own. Despite all that happened, he was asleep the moment his head hit the pillow.

———

Victor was up and out the door by ten a.m., stopping only long enough to eat a fast breakfast in the mission cafeteria. He drove straight to the Riverside Inn knocked hard on the front door of the inn and after a moment it was answered by one of the bikers, a guy named Rupert. When the Tyranny Rides gang went to war alongside the Hand of God against his brother, Mikey, Rupert was one of the few who survived.

Victor said, "I need to speak to Elizabeth."

"Jesus, McCain, we ain't open yet and I don't know anyone named Elizabeth."

"She's the one playing rodeo with Tank."

"Oh. Her. Yeah. One sec."

The biker closed the door and a few minutes later Elizabeth opened it wearing one of Tank's T-shirts and bare legs. It made her look like she was wearing a tent. Her hair was messed up and she seemed tired. That was a new one as Infernal Lords possess superhuman endurance to go along with speed and strength.

She opened the door wider and motioned for him to join her. The lights in the bar were dim and Rupert was no longer to be seen. Elizabeth walked over to a pool table, hopped up onto the table, laid on her back and stretched her arms above her head. Victor leaned a hip against the table and stared down at her and felt the attraction. He did his best to ignore it.

Victor asked, "Did you break him?"

She waved a hand one way then the other. "He sleeps now. Like a baby who snores. What do you need, Victor?"

"I know the demon's name. It's Aamon."

She swung her legs over the edge of the pool table, bumped him out of the way and sat up. "Him? So that is why he disappeared. He was buried surrounded by iron. And now he is free? This is very, very bad."

"Brother Joshua says he is one of the princes of Hell. That sounds bad alright."

She offered a humorless laugh. "Not just one of the princes of Hell, *the* prince of Hell. He is one of Satan's truly bad boys. The Fallen One searched the world over for him, but he was hidden from sight. The iron coffin hid him from us."

Victor knew iron was like kryptonite to Hellspawn. "Then how do we use his name to beat him?"

She crooked a finger to draw him closer and he did as she asked. She wrapped her legs around him and pulled him close, her hands on his chest. "Well, not like I just did you," she purred. "Did you miss me, Victor?"

He leaned in even closer, close enough to kiss her and said, "Yes, but I have a girlfriend now and I'm a one-woman man. How do I trap a demon?"

She dropped her legs and pushed him away, the pout in place. "You are no fun, Victor."

"I get that a lot. The demon?"

She let out an exasperated breath. "I suppose you can use it to summon him. Then we destroy him. You and I. We can do this."

"There will be others helping. Detective Aldridge, for one."

"The policewoman? We don't need her. You and I, Victor. We do this."

Victor shook his head. "She's in. So is Linda. And a guy named Mike Hawkins. They will be there, Elizabeth. Alright?"

"They will die. You know this, do you not? They will all die. Aamon will kill them."

"I think they will surprise you."

Before he could say anything else, there was a loud groan from the back room and Elizabeth giggled and hopped off the pool table. "Tomorrow, Victor, we will talk more. Since you won't be with me, I will once again drive the Tank."

She sauntered off and Victor spent time watching the sway of her hips as she disappeared and shut the door. Victor shook his head again to clear the image of Elizabeth and Tank from his mind. He wasn't successful. When he got outside, he called Paige. When she picked up, he asked, "Can you meet me at the Raven in a half hour for lunch? I have news."

"Yes. I'll be there and I have news, too."

He hung up and glanced once more at the door of the inn before getting into his car. He felt a strong urge to go inside, get Elizabeth and bring her with him. Then he closed his eyes, told himself to get it together, got in the car and headed to the Raven. Demons, Infernal Lords, Readers, mythical monsters and cops. If he wrote a book about his life, no one would believe it. Half the time he didn't believe it.

Victor McCain. Hand of God. Dead man walking.

Chapter Thirty

When Victor walked into the Raven it was the lunch hour, and the place was packed. He found Paige sitting in his favorite booth and he appreciated her remembering, even if she did take the side that would force Victor to sit with his back to the crowd. She was sipping a brown liquid from a bourbon glass, her eyes constantly surveying the room. Cop eyes.

He slid in across from her, glanced around the room and motioned for one of the waitresses to bring him what Paige was drinking. She looked tired but excited. She started to speak, but he held up a finger for her to wait. Shortly, the waitress brought over his own glass of bourbon, and he took a sip. He guessed Angel's Envy. Not as good as the Willet Muldoon poured, but a good choice. Especially the angel part, all things considered. His normal was Fireball Whiskey. What did that say about him?

He motioned to her to proceed with the glass, and she said, "Several things. First, Tom just called, and he has not found a connection between all the female victims.

"Go figure. I'll call Kurt, my computer guy, and have him

lend a hand tracking down possible connections. What about burying the demon? Any luck?"

"We can take turns. You called the meeting and you said you had news. Did Hawkins learn anything from his great grandmother's diary?"

Victor filled her in on learning about the book with the demon names and the trip to Muldoon's cabin in the woods to find it, the fight with the Greyman and the retrieval of the book and Brother Joshua's ability to read Latin and give them the demon's name, Aamon. He also told her about Elizabeth suggesting they summon the demon and then beat the ever-loving shit out of him.

She spun the glass in small circles on the table between them. "Having the name and doing a summoning would be a first step. She stopped twirling the glass and gave him a sharp glance. "Is there any particular reason a Greyman would be waiting for you there?"

He shook his head. "There was not. And you know what that means."

"Yes. Someone told them. Who knew you were going to the cabin?"

"Only five. Me, Hawkins, Muldoon, Brother Joshua and Linda. Hawkins and Muldoon were with me, and J. is beyond reproach."

Her eyebrows drew down in puzzlement. "Why would Detective Coffey tip them off? It makes no sense."

"I agree. There would only be two reasons: one, she's had her phone, car or home bugged, or all of them for all we know. Or she's been compromised."

Paige drained her bourbon. She waved to the waitress and motioned for another. "Do you think she's being controlled by the other Reader?"

Victor said, "I have no clue. Let's see if we can rule either or both out. Can you have Tom check her phone? Tell her it's a security check or something?"

"As the lead on the task force, yes. I can. And how do you suggest we check to see if she's being controlled?"

"Can't you just wiggle your fingers and tell?"

She laughed. "No, I can't. Just like you can't tell when someone is an Infernal Lord. Thoughts are thoughts and if I can't find the thoughts of someone doing the controlling, there is no way for me to know the controlled." Paige thought about when her brother, Shepherd, controlled both she and her sister, Junna. She then wondered, how did Junna know?

"Fair enough. Then we feed her some misinformation and see if they act on it."

"You don't think she deserves to know it might be a possibility? She is your girlfriend, after all."

"She is and it pains me to even think about it. But you just said, even if we ask, she won't know, and we won't know. If Tom finds an electronic way they are getting information, then we won't make her feel guilty."

"And if she's being controlled?"

"Then we feed them some misinformation and see what happens. If they act on it, then we know for sure she's been mind hacked and then we fix it. That way--"

Victor stopped in mid-sentence as the feeling of wrongness hit him like a ton of bricks. He slammed down his glass hard enough some of the bourbon sloshed out and onto the table, as he spun in the booth and scanned the crowd.

Paige quietly drew her Walther out its holster and held it down in the seat next to her. "What is it? What's happening?"

"The demon. It's here."

He stood and the people who were sitting close by looked at him and leaned away from him, the intensity rolling off him in waves. Finally, the crowd around the bar parted long enough and he saw him. A tall man who could pass for a Goth Magazine poster boy. His skin was pale, but his hair was long and raven black. As were his fingernails, which were each nearly an inch long. His T-shirt, jeans and boots were also black, and he wore a long duster. Also black. The demon had assumed human form to mingle among the mortals.

He smiled at Victor and the bounty hunter saw all the man's teeth filed down to sharp points, though he knew they were the teeth of a wolf. Bloody hell. People who walked near his table seemed to avoid it without looking at him, their natural warning system steering them clear.

Victor knew his options were limited. He had left the katana out in the car and the gun he carried under his bomber jacket would be of no use. Nor would Paige's gun. He said to her, "Put the gun away. It won't help. You see him?"

She did as he asked and said, "Yes. I don't need your special Spidey senses to figure out who you're talking about."

Victor cut a path through the crowd and stopped in front of the demon; Paige right next to him. Even sitting, Victor could tell the demon was nearly as tall as he was and ripped like a professional athlete. He sat drinking a glass of red wine, his boots crossed at the ankles, not a care in the world.

Victor said, in a low growl, "You got a lot of nerve coming here, asshole."

The demon took a sip of wine, then smiled and said, "I go wherever I want, Spear of Uriel."

The Spear of Uriel was what the fallen angels and demons called him, as he ultimately got his orders from the archangel. He started to call the demon by *his* name, but stopped himself, not wanting to tip off what he knew to the Hellspawn.

"I consider this place like home, asshole, and I will snatch you out of that seat, drag your sorry ass outside, tear off both your arms and then beat you to death with them."

The smile vanished from the demon's face and for a brief instant, a look of pure hatred flashed across the demon's features. But he got control of himself and hissed, "You try it and I will change form and kill not only you and the bitch with you, but everyone else here."

Victor knew it was a bluff. While he could change forms as he threatened, Satan would punish him severely. Demons worked in the shadows to bring about the fall of Man. Any overt actions in public revealing demons were real would push people to God by the millions and weaken Satan's power over them.

"What do you want?" Victor asked.

"I am giving you a warning, Spear of Uriel. Continue to interfere in my affairs, and I will kill everyone around you. Starting with the bitch you have with you."

Paige said, "You and what army, asshole?"

The demon continued as if she had not spoken. "Then your girlfriend, the rest of your team, the fool of a man who leads you, and then your mother."

Victor felt his blood run cold. "Is that all?"

The demon stood and met Victor eye for eye. "You will turn over the other two descendants of the men who trapped me by this time tomorrow night, or I will start coming for you and yours."

Victor took a half step forward, invading the demon's personal space, his nose less than an inch from the demons. "By this time tomorrow, I will be spreading your body parts across the state of Kentucky. Your time as a prince will be coming to an end."

The demon's eyes, two black holes that appeared to have stars falling through them, half closed as he said, "I will make you suffer like no one has ever suffered before since the misguided creation of your kind. You have my word, Spear of

Uriel."

The demon took a step to the side, then turned and left the Raven. Victor glanced around and noticed the entire restaurant had stopped what they were doing and had been watching him and the demon. He said to the crowd, "Uh, he owed money on some overdue library books, and I let him know he needed to pay up."

Some in the crowd offered halfhearted laughs, others simply looked away. Victor let out a long breath and motioned for Paige to follow him back to their table. Once they did, the waitress came over with fresh drinks. She said, "The owner says the drinks are on the house. That guy gave us all the creeps. Thanks for running him out."

Victor, "You're welcome." When she was out of ear range, Victor said to Paige, "What did you learn about burying the son of a bitch?

Paige gave him a rundown of her conversation with Visette and needing his blood to lure the demon to where they wanted. Paige said, "The key would be the demon being mad enough at you to want to kill you straight out."

"Well, do you think what just happened will do the trick?"

"Yeah, I think when he said he would make you suffer like no one has ever suffered before, I think he meant it. And good job, by the way. I half expected each of you to whip 'em out to see whose was bigger. We're good."

"And you really think you can trap big, bad, and nasty in a bottle?"

"Yes. We use a summoning spell to get him close to where Visette and I will be waiting, and your blood will lure him into the bottle like a hound to a rabbit."

"If you say it can be done, then I trust you, though it sounds complicated and a bit silly."

"Visette knows what she's doing."

"No doubt. And if any part of the plan goes sideways?"

Paige made a bomb going off sound and Victor laughed.

They both sipped their bourbon and then Victor asked, "Hey, do you know anything about talking swords?"

Paige nearly choked on her bourbon and said, "Seriously?"

Victor nodded and she said, "Seriously."

"Seriously?"

She propped an elbow on the table and a chin in her hand and contemplated him. She said, "I believed I lived the weirdest kind of life. Now I'm wondering if yours is not weirder."

"That makes two of us, sister."

Chapter Thirty-One

Paige drove home after her meeting with Victor and the confrontation with Aamon. She thought about the demon's warning to both stay away from what he was doing and to turn over the two men. She knew Victor would never give the men up and neither of them would stop trying to capture and destroy the demon. If they did not trap him by the high noon deadline, even more people were going to die.

She texted Tom to drop by her place and he was waiting for her when she got home. He started asking questions and she put him off until they were inside and the door was closed. She waved him to the couch and they both sat. Visette walked out of the bedroom and joined them.

Paige spent several minutes updating them about her meeting with McCain and the confrontation with Aamon. "Tom, we need to start off by checking all Detective Coffey's electronics. We don't want her to be suspicious, so you will need to call in the whole task force. Have both the cyber and counterintelligence groups there. Tell everyone there was a suspected hack of our systems and we are checking things out in an abundance of caution. Check their cars too. When they are finished, have them go check her home."

"Alright, I can do all that," Tom said.

Visette pulled her feet up and under as she sat and said, "But you don't think that's the answer, do you?"

"I don't," Paige replied. "I think Victor is right and there's a chance the other Reader is in her head."

Tom grimaced. "If that's true, we can't trust anything she's told us, can we?"

Paige said, "No, we can't. While they're checking all their phones, I want you to get her call log and track down the call that tipped her to the first female victim. Double check her work."

"Will do," Tom said.

Visette pursed her lips, then asked, "Do you plan to do as Victor suggested and provide her with misinformation?"

"Yes. I think we have to, don't you?"

Visette stared at her friend for a moment. "I suppose, but is this not, in a way, using her as bait?"

"If she's under the control of the Reader we need to know and by doing it this way, we can possibly set the Reader up as well."

Tom finished tapping out a text and put away his phone. "I've started the ball rolling on the electronics check. Everyone will be at the precinct by three. I'll get the numbers from her phone and let you know if I find anything."

Paige thanked him and Tom left for the station. When he was gone, Visette said, "Okay. Tell me more about Victor McCain."

"Well," Paige took a deep breath, "I'm not entirely sure what to tell you. He's some kind of Hand of God? He, well, as best as I can gather, he hunts people down for God."

Visette nodded slowly. "God, huh? And you believe him?"

"I think so. I've seen him do some interesting things. And for some reason, people seem to want to kill him."

"Well, that sounds familiar, doesn't it?"

Paige shifted her feet. "Yeah, kinda does. And I find him oddly attractive."

"How so?"

"I mean, he's rough around the edges but somehow he kinda interests me."

Visette almost choked from laughter. "And what would Jay think of this thought?"

Paige shrugged. "I'm not sure. I mean, Jay did try and kill me."

"You know as well as I do, he is being controlled by a Reader. He didn't do it."

"If he doesn't wake up from his coma, though, we'll never know for sure, will we?"

Visette walked toward Paige and put a hand on her shoulder. She didn't know what to say.

Chapter Thirty-Two

"He wants you to give us up? You won't, will you? Please say you won't," Muldoon begged.

Victor sat with Muldoon and Hawkins in the mission's conference room, and he filled in the two men about his meeting with Paige, some about who she was and the demon's demands.

"Lucky for you," Victor said, "you shared the Willet's bourbon so you're good. But it was close."

Muldoon swallowed hard and said, "I have more."

Victor laughed and waved him off. "I'm just yanking your chain, Muldoon. I don't take orders from demons. It's bad for business."

Hawkins sipped a Mountain Dew, then asked, "What about Coffey? Did Detective Aldridge think she's being mind controlled?"

"She has no way of knowing," Victor said. "About the only way we can know for sure is to set her up and see if the bad guys show up."

"Why can't Brother Joshua help?" Muldoon asked.

"Because evidently there are rules to this whole divine intervention stuff. They can offer me limited support, but it mainly comes down to what I can do on my own. It has something to do with free will and good and evil."

"That sucks," Muldoon said.

Victor nodded his head in agreement. "Yes it does. So, the question is how do we do it?"

Hawkins leaned back his chair until it rested against the wall and he stared at the ceiling. "Well, we obviously want to bring them to a place we can control and then lower the boom with little to no collateral damage."

"And I know just the place," Victor said. "Muldoon's not the only one who owns a cabin. My dad had one out in Harlan County. My brother bought it and now that he's out of the picture, it's mine."

"Sounds like a winner to me," Hawkins said

Muldoon said, "I hope you guys don't mind, but I think I'll sit this one out."

"Smart move, keeper of the bourbon," Victor said.

"Who else are we going to bring in on this? If they send more Greymen, it would be nice to have more firepower."

"I think I know just who to invite."

———

Hawkins, Elizabeth and Tank sat in the van Victor borrowed from the Derby Mission to pick up the other two at the Riverside Inn for the drive to Harlan County. Elizabeth practically glowed while Tank looked more tired than he'd ever seen the man. When Victor asked him if he was up to the task, Tank offered a "Fuck you" then climbed onto the bench seat in the back, leaned his head against the window and closed his eyes.

Elizabeth offered Victor a wink then told Hawkins to get

out of the shotgun seat so she could ride up front. The soldier did as she asked without any complaint, but when she offered him a smile to melt the heart of most men, he returned a dead eye stare and got in the back with Tank. The Captain was made of sterner stuff than most men.

Victor leaned against the driver's side door and called Paige.

When she answered he said, "We're going to put the misinformation plan into action. I have a place out in Harlan County. I'm driving out there now with Hawkins, Elizabeth and Tank. Once we get there, I'll call her and tell her I'm going out there for solitude to figure out how to use the book to bury the demon and see if the bad guys bite."

"Sounds like a good plan. Do you want me to come along?"

"No. I think you need to keep things moving on this end. Any news on the check of her phone?"

"Tom has the entire team in the station now and they're looking at her phone and car, then her house. I'll let you know what I find out." Paige said as she kicked at a fold in the rug.

"Don't be surprised if you can't reach me. Cell service out in that part of the country is not always reliable."

"Please be careful," she said.

"Why Detective Aldridge, I may start to think you really care."

She laughed and hung up the phone.

Victor got into the van and started the engine. "Please return your tray tables to their upright positions. We are on our way," he said.

Elizabeth snickered. "You are a strange man, Victor McCain. But I still like you."

"I think it's the aftershave," he replied.

She frowned. "But you have a beard. You don't use aftershave."

He started to explain it was a joke, but simply shook his head and drove to I-64 and headed east towards the Appalachian Mountains and Kentucky coal country. While he drove, he thought about the good times when his dad would take him and his brother, Mikey, out to the cabin for the weekend to hunt. They were happy memories and he cherished them, even with how his brother turned out. His father had died many years ago of a heart attack and Victor missed him every day.

Elizabeth seemed to sense his mood and left him to his thoughts while she softly sang something in Hungarian, the country of her birth. He wondered what she was singing but decided not to ask, especially if it was something from her youth, a time when she murdered literally hundreds of women and girls believing it would keep her young. I guess, in the end, it did, when Satan offered her near immortality in exchange for her faithful service.

He glanced in the rearview mirror at Hawkins. The man stared out the window and watched rolling bluegrass hills pass by. The man sat relaxed and peaceful, not like a man headed to a possible battle with any number of the denizens of Hell. The skin around his eye where the Greyman slapped him with his chain was starting to turn several different colors, but he seemed otherwise unaffected.

Tank on the other hand, snored loudly, his head against the window and Victor worried the snores were so loud they might break the window into a thousand pieces. Poor guy. Victor knew when it was go time, he would hold his own. The man truly did not know fear.

Several hours later, Victor turned off on the Corbin exit and the group stopped for a bite to eat at a Wendy's. Tank wolfed down three double cheeseburgers, two orders of large fries and multiple Frosties. The man put the food away as if it would be his last meal. Hell, for all Victor knew, it might be the last one for all four of them. The table talk was minimal and after less than an hour and a brief stop at a gas station, they were on the road again.

When they reached Cumberland, Kentucky, Tank let out a low whistle. In the heyday of the coal mines, Cumberland was a bustling town with nearly ten thousand people living in and around the city. When the coal began to run out and people left for other jobs, the town slowly began a death spiral. Now many stores on the main drag were either closed or bordered up. No bomb or attack hit the city. It was simply a matter of a slow death.

Victor pulled into another gas station and called Linda, after reminding the other three to keep quiet.

"Where are you?" she asked.

"I need to decipher this book and decided to do it where I know I'll have peace and quiet with no one to bother me."

There was a brief pause and she asked, "You headed to your cabin?"

"Yeah. I figure it's the only place to guarantee I won't be bothered. Once I figure out how to bury the demon again, I'll be back. Shouldn't take me more than a day or two. What's going on with you?"

She let out a long sigh. "They called in the entire task force to check our phones and cars. Someone was found to have some type of malware on their phone and now they're going over everyone's to make sure the task force isn't compromised."

"That has to suck," Victor said.

"We're sitting here wasting time when we should be out

trying to track down the--" She paused for a moment as Victor knew she was going to say demon. "The killer."

"Now you know why I'm not a cop. Too many rules. I'll call you when I'm headed home. You know I don't get any service at the cabin, so leave me a message. I'll drive to Cumberland late tonight and call you from there."

"Make sure you do. I love you."

Victor was momentarily taken aback as Linda rarely showed emotion where others could hear her. "I love you, too."

He hung up and found Elizabeth staring at him with an eyebrow raised, an amused look on her face.

"What?" he asked.

"You had better hope she is not dirty, Victor, as you are quite smitten with your detective toy."

"She's not a toy," he snarled.

He threw the van into drive as she laughed at him, and Victor drove through Cumberland and then started the climb up Black Mountain. About halfway to the top, he turned onto a bumpy gravel road heading up and into a notch in the mountain with more potholes than flat stretches. Victor, Elizabeth and Hawkins grumbled about the rough going. Tank never woke up, his snoring constant.

After about fifteen minutes, they came to a flat spot and a well-built hunting cabin came into view. It was a single-story wood building with a covered front porch running the full length of the front of the structure. A creek rock fireplace rose from the rear of the cabin. A light blanket of snow covered the ground, and the air was crisp and clear.

Hawkins said, "Looks in great shape."

Victor nodded his agreement. "I pay a guy to keep it up. I called him to let him know I would be here this weekend and told him to stay clear."

Finally awake, Tank asked, "So, what's the plan, McCain?"

"You and Elizabeth will take a position inside the front of the cabin for the duration. Hawkins and I will take station in the rear. Whoever sees something first will yell out. If you guys see someone coming up the driveway, then Hawkins and I will head out the back door and hit them from the sides."

Elizabeth offered Tank a sly grin. "Cleatus and I are good at many positions, aren't we, Cleatus?"

Tank's face seemed a bit queasy, but said, "I'm game."

The four of them went inside, with Victor and Hawkins carrying large bags filled with the weapons of war. Once inside, Victor made fires in both the fireplace and the Ben Franklin stove to knock off the chill, as the cabin was too far away from any other power source. He had installed a propane generator with a 500-gallon tank in the rear of the cabin for when he needed full power, but it wasn't the quietest and he wanted to hear the bad guys when they were coming.

Elizabeth and Tank each pulled a comfortable armchair to the front two windows, the blinds opened wide enough for them to easily see the road. Tank cradled a Mossberg shotgun. Elizabeth needed no such weapons but kept a Glock 20 in easy reach in case she changed her mind.

Hawkins set up a watch in the master bedroom by dragging an ancient wooden rocker to the bedroom window, his weapons bag dropped next to him. It made Victor smile thinking about all the McCain butts the chair rocked to sleep since his great-grandfather made the chair in the mid-1800's. He gave up rocking in it a hundred or so pounds ago.

Victor wandered into the spare bedroom and sat on the edge of a large cedar chest his own father made. The chest was still as sturdy as the day he brought it to the cabin. He glanced around the room at the pictures hanging on the walls, nearly all of them pictures of himself with his brother and father and a melancholy feeling settled inside him. His father was now dead, and his brother buried in the bottom of a bridge pylon. He always thought he'd be the one to die first, considering what he did for Uncle Sam overseas. Now he and his mother were the only ones left.

He could hear Elizabeth and Tank talking in the front room for a bit, then they went quiet. With the bedroom doors open, he had a clear shot to watch Hawkins. The man gazed out the window while he put together a sniper rifle, his eyes barely looking down while he worked, his movements practiced and sure. His face was serene, his breathing even. Hawkins told him his job in the Army was as a sniper and he was one of the best. There was no doubt the Captain must have seen his fair share of action while serving. If he ever needed a replacement, God could do worse.

The four of them sat and waited. There was no telling how long it would take for bad guys to show up if Linda really was under the control of the Reader trying to take him down. Victor prayed she wasn't and they would all pass a quiet late afternoon and evening and then they could head home in the morning, with Linda free and clear from mental domination. Despite his normal desire for death, action and mayhem, this time he wanted a peaceful evening in his ancestral cabin. That's all he wanted.

It only took three hours for all his hopes to go up in smoke.

The sun was beginning to sink behind the top of the mountain, the cabin bathed in the golden light of the setting sun when Tank appeared in the doorway.

"We've got company."

Chapter Thirty-Three

Paige parked in the detective's lot at the station and went inside, thinking about Victor and his rag tag band holed up at his cabin in Harlan and wondered what was happening. She'd sent him a test text and found out he was right, receiving a "this cell phone cannot be found" error message.

The Devil's Mark task force was working out of a large conference room off to one side. The room featured a huge mahogany table large enough for ten people to sit around it comfortably, along with several computer work stations on the far wall. What she loved almost as much as anything was a full-sized Keurig Coffee maker with several different types of coffee from which to choose. Thankfully, the days of over-heated bad police station coffee were becoming a thing of the past.

When she got there, Tom was sitting at the head of the table with Jerry Bender, the head of the LMPD Cyber Squad, going over the results of the bug sweep. Bender was not your stereotypical computer geek. He was well over six feet tall with a brush cut any Marine would be proud to wear. Tom looked up when she came into the room, but she waved for him to keep doing what he was doing while she fixed a large cup of Dunkin Donuts coffee. Once it was ready, she added two rather large spoonful of sugar and what seemed like a half cup of milk and sat down on the opposite end of the table from Tom.

He was saying, "So, you guys are sure there was no way anyone was listening on anyone's phones?"

Paige knew Tom didn't tell them they were targeting Detective Coffey specifically. If she was innocent, they didn't want to bring even further mistrust down upon her.

Jerry Bender said, "Positive. Detective Thonton had some spyware on his phone, but it was harmless. Your task force is good to go."

Tom thanked him and Bender gathered up his papers, nodded to her and left the room. When he was gone, Paige got up, shut the door and brought her coffee to sit by Tom.

"Well, I guess that eliminates one possible way they were keeping tabs on us," he said. "The only problem is it only leaves mind control. I'm sorry, Paige. I know you wanted this to be something simple."

She sighed and sipped her coffee. "When is it ever? Let's pray Victor has a quiet evening in the mountains. Where's Linda now?"

"At her desk. She said she was working a new angle. Have you heard from Victor?"

"Not yet. Let's hope that's a good thing."

He nodded his agreement. "What next?"

"I guess we sit and wait. We've got a plan to take care of the demon. We do need to figure out who the other Reader is, but at the moment I don't have a clue how. Did you follow up to see if she was telling the truth about there being no Walmart video?"

"Um, no. I don't know. Let me check."

Tom rolled his chair over to one of the computers, signed in to his department email account and scrolled for a moment. "This isn't good. They emailed me the file. Maybe they just missed it when she asked the first time. Also, still nothing on the DNA from the hair we found on the necklace from the female victim's mouth."

She saw him open the email, then double click a link. From where she sat, she saw a grainy black and white video begin to roll, but most of the screen was blocked by Tom's body. She rested her head on the seat and closed her eyes and searched the Collective for anyone thinking about the Devil's Mark but came up with nothing. She let out another sigh and tried to clear her mind when Tom gasped, and her eyes flew open.

"What?"

He turned his chair around to face her, his face pale and then pointed at the screen. She got up and leaned down next to him and he pointed again at the screen. The camera showed an overhead view of the counter where they sold prepaid cell phones. A woman was frozen in place, handing over her credit card to a young clerk, the prepaid phone laying on the counter in front of her. And Paige knew her.

Chapter Thirty-Four

Victor got up and followed Tank, after motioning for Hawkins to keep watch on the rear of the cabin. Elizabeth was standing next to the window, one delicate finger pulling part of the blind down for a better look, then she snorted a short laugh.

"What?" Victor asked.

"It seems they have sent priests after you, Victor. Dirty priests at that."

Victor walked up beside her, and it was harder for him to see than the supernaturally enhanced former Countess of Blood. He did see three men walking up the road and they were indeed dressed like priests. With the sun behind them, their faces were in shadows, but he saw enough to agree with Elizabeth. Their clothes appeared to be stained, especially the white collars around their necks. When they were a bit closer, he saw their faces and hands were also dirty, their fingernails long and dark.

Elizabeth asked, "Are they here to take your confession, Hand of God? Have you been a naughty boy?"

"Always." Victor let the blind spring into place. "You and

Tank go out on the porch and see what they want. Hawkins and I will sneak out the back and take up positions on the side. Count to thirty then go on out."

Elizabeth and Tank both nodded, and Victor hustled to the rear of the cabin and motioned for Hawkins to join him. Victor snagged his weapons bag, as did Hawkins. Victor opened the door, and the two men went outside, Victor going left and Hawkins right.

While the air was still cool, it was warmer than it had been for several days. The snow was quickly becoming a slushy mess. He got to the front of the house and glanced around the corner to see the three priests stopped, shoulder to shoulder and about two feet apart. He reached into his bag and his hand came up with his MP5.

The one in the middle was completely bald, his scalp splotchy and discolored. The other two men wore shoulder length hair, matted and dull. All three of them gave off the vibe of homeless men who were dressing up for Halloween as Men of the Cloth. Then Victor looked closer, and the bald man seemed off. What came to Victor's mind was he was vibrating slightly, as if the molecules of his skin were moving fast in a short physical space.

Elizabeth and Tank were standing on the porch, the shotgun dangling loosely in Tank's right hand, the Glock tucked into the front of Elizabeth's jeans. She moved forward a step and said, "If you are here to save my soul, I am afraid you are a few centuries too late."

In what looked like a mimic of her movement, the bald priest shuffled forward and said, "Hand over the Spear of Uriel to us and you may leave in peace. Refuse, and face the wrath of our Lord, the Angel of Light."

And Victor knew he was right. Even the man's voice seemed to vibrate, though he had no clue why that was the case. It sounded like his voice was being filtered through a huge vibrato machine.

Tank moved up next to Elizabeth and said, "Fuck it."

He raised his shotgun to his waist, pointed it at the bald man and pulled both barrels. It was then all hell broke loose.

The shotgun roared and the blast hit the bald man's center mass and he simply exploded. He flew apart at the seams and then Victor felt his breath catch in his throat as he realized it was exactly what he did. However, instead of body parts, what exploded into the air were the largest hornets Victor had ever seen, every bit as large as the Murder Hornets now a concern in the Pacific Northwest, and it terrified him. He now knew why the man vibrated: he was held together with hornets, their true nature hidden behind the priest's facade. And hornets were one of his secret fears, one that made his mouth instantly dry.

The hornets rose into the air, gathered into a huge ball, then dove towards Elizabeth and Tank. Elizabeth sprinted forward while yelling for Tank to go back inside. In all his life, Victor had never seen a man that large move so fast as he lunged for the open front door.

Elizabeth squeezed off several shots at the diving hornets and they all concentrated on her. In seconds she was completely covered, and her screams echoed in the mountain holler. He knew they were unlikely to kill her, but she would still feel the pain of thousands of stingers.

She continued to squeeze her gun's trigger even though the shots did not affect the hornets. In her panic, she managed to shoot both the other priests, one in the head and one in the chest. The one shot in the head changed as well, but not like his bald brethren. He seemed to melt, his body turning black as thousands upon thousands of black widow spiders poured onto the ground and surged towards the door.

The other priest also appeared to melt before Victor's eyes too, but this time they flowed into a pile of scorpions, the clicking of hundreds of pincers filling the air, with tails held high and forward, ready to sting.

Sweet, Jesus, Victor thought as he dropped his MP5 into his bag, grabbed the straps and ran to the backdoor. Hawkins reached it the same time he did, the younger man's face was pale, and he was swallowing hard. Hornets, spiders and scorpions are hardwired into the human brain to cause fear and they were clearly doing it for both men.

Victor heard Tank whimpering as he hit the floor on his stomach, turned around and kicked the door shut. Hornets began to slam into the two front windows and tiny cracks began to appear in the panes of glass. The glass started to darken as the spiders swarmed up the walls, the scorpions doing the same.

Victor worked to calm his nerves and think. Then a plan hit him, and it made him want to throw up. Hawkins was spinning around in circles and Victor grabbed his arm and stopped him in place. "I need you to go to the front door and when I tell you, yank it part the way open then run like hell out the back door."

Hawkins started to shake his head and said, "Aw man, I don't think..."

"Listen, you are the fastest one of us. If you don't do this, we all die. Here. Right now." To Tank, he yelled, "Out the back and up the mountain. Run like your fat ass depended on it."

Tank didn't even hesitate. He got to his feet and took off.

Victor turned back to Hawkins. "Give me your rifle and when I go out the back count to five, crack the door and run like Satan himself is chasing you."

Hawkins jaw muscles worked like he was trying to crack

walnuts, but he shoved the gun into Victor's arms and ran to the front door. The cracks in the windows were widening and the spiders were beginning to come under the door, as Hawkins tried to stomp each one. Victor ran for the rear door and heard Hawkins scream, "Hurry. Oh, God, they're coming."

Victor ran about twenty feet up the mountain, with Tank crawling his way upward in front of him. Victor reached into his duffle, took out two huge flares, popped them and after they broke into flame, tossed them to the base of the propane tank and raised the gun to his shoulder and took aim. He counted in his head and then Hawkins came flying out the door, slapping at his clothes as dozens of black spiders crawled all over him, and he ran straight for Victor. Through the door he saw a cloud of hornets, spiders and scorpions chasing him.

He gave Hawkins a couple of steps and then pulled the trigger and shot the propane tank right above the two flares. The 7.62 mm round punctured a huge hole in the tank and when the gas hit the flares, the tank exploded. The force of the blast knocked Hawkins face first into the snow where he lay, not moving. Victor felt the wave of heat hit him like an open furnace and he threw an arm over his face to protect it.

He glanced up and saw his cabin was gone and watched as debris rained down around them. The fiery blast obliterated nearly all the hornets, spiders and scorpions as the fire consumed what was left of the old structure.

Victor slid down the hill to Hawkins and knocked off the remaining spiders, then smashed them with a rock as they tried to attack him. Hawkins was breathing, but his exposed skin was covered with tiny red dots from the bites of the black widows and his breathing was labored.

He checked on Tank and saw him leaning against a tree as he stared at the spot where the cabin had been, his shotgun clutched tight to his chest in two meaty hands, the muzzle pointed towards his chin. Victor said, "Tank, drop the gun and get down here and take care of Hawkins. I need to get to Elizabeth.

Victor slid down the mountain and skirted the debris of his former cabin. He saw Elizabeth lying on the ground, her body swollen from all the hornet stings. There were still a few scorpions and spiders on the ground with hornets hovering above Elizabeth. Victor made a dash to the rear of the van and he skidded to a stop and threw open the rear doors.

The remaining creepy crawlies, along with a few hornets, made a mad dash in his direction. When Victor came around the rear of the van to confront them, he held his flamethrower in his hands, not having time to strap it on his shoulders. He made the device himself a few years ago in order to kill hellhounds and other creatures from the depths of Hell.

He turned on the valve and squeezed the rear and front triggers at the same time just as the wave of hornets reached him. A huge plume of flame erupted from the nozzle and he made sure to keep it away from Elizabeth and incinerated the remaining insects and arachnids. When he was sure he'd gotten them all, he dropped the flamethrower onto the muddy ground and ran to the Infernal Lord.

Her face was so swollen her eyes were completely shut and her lips were nearly three times their normal size. Every inch of exposed skin was covered in huge angry welts, some with the broken tips of stingers visible.

Victor dropped to his knees, lifted her and cradled her head in his lap and she let out a low moan. He carefully brushed the hair out of her eyes and stared at her, his anger growing, feeling it become a hard stone deep down in his soul. He would destroy the demon Aamon, then find the Reader responsible for hurting so many people and rip her apart with his bare hands.

Elizabeth broke his thoughts when she whispered something. He raised her gently so he could hear her better. "What? I didn't hear you," he said.

She spoke so softly he barely heard her whisper, "How do I look?"

Despite it all he laughed, then said, "You look marvelous," then more seriously, "We need to get you to a hospital."

She shook her head and croaked, "You know better. No hospital."

She was right. He wasn't thinking clearly. There was no way he could take an Infernal Lord into a hospital. Their bodies did not follow normal mortal scientific rules and any doctor who tried to treat her would be in for a rude awakening. She would have to heal on her own.

"Right. Sorry. Listen, let me get you into the van and get Hawkins so we can get out of here."

He picked her up and he noticed how light she felt. He carried her to the van, opened the big side door and laid her carefully on the second-row bench seat. He reached into the rear compartment and got a blanket and laid it across her carefully.

Victor shut the door and looked across the ruins of what used to be his cabin and saw Tank sitting against a tree, holding Hawkins in his lap, the younger man still out.

Victor shouted, "Is he alive?"

"Yes. Barely. Man, needs a hospital in the worst way."

Victor jogged through the snow and mud and helped Tank get Hawkins to the van and belted into the front seat. Hawkins' breathing continued to be labored. Then Victor went and gathered up the two weapons bags and tossed them in the rear of the van along with the flamethrower. Victor hopped behind the wheel and looked over his shoulder at Tank, who now sat with Elizabeth's head cradled in his lap, tears in his eyes.

He saw Victor staring at him and said, "McCain, I want names. I want to know who did this and then I'm going to fucking bring Hell to their doors. You hear me? I'm going to fucking kill every one of them."

Victor gave him a short nod. "You got it, Tank. Hell is coming and there will be no prisoners. This will be to the death."

Victor threw the van into drive and started down the muddy trail to the main road. He needed to get Hawkins to the hospital, if not Elizabeth. And he had to call Paige. He prayed the bad guys found out where he was because Linda's phone was tapped, but he knew it wasn't. She was being controlled by the Reader and Victor was going to find the woman and then kill her.

Hell on Earth was here.

Chapter Thirty-Five

Paige felt her breath catch in her throat. The Walmart customer wore a business suit, with dark hair, cut to shoulder length. And on her hip was a gun and a badge. The woman was Detective Linda Coffey. No doubt.

Tom looked puzzled. "This can't be. Why would Linda buy a prepaid phone to call herself?"

Paige knew he knew why but didn't want to say it.

"Because she wasn't doing it of her own volition. The other Reader has been planting suggestions in her mind. The big question is, what other things has she "suggested" Linda do?"

"Oh, no. You don't think…"

Paige felt the bottom fall out of her stomach and offered a weak nod. "Yes. I do. We have to at least consider if she's involved in the murders. We know the men have a connection to the demon, but we've been unable to find one to the women."

"And you think Linda is the connection and has been killing them? Again, why?"

"Maybe when we find the Reader, we will find a connection to each of them. Or maybe there's a connection to Linda. Or maybe she's not involved in the actual killings. Who knows? But now we have a possible way to find the Reader."

Tom asked, "Tail Linda and see if they hook up?"

"Yes. It's a start."

"How do we do this? If we use cops, they will want to know why."

Paige paced back and forth and then said, "We don't want to do that, not yet. If Linda is doing this against her will, then she's an innocent." Paige then remembered Jay. He shot her. Almost killed her. And now he lay in some strange coma in the hospital. All because he was being controlled.

"How then?"

"McCain. He has assets we can use. It won't be easy. She's a cop and she's good. But it has to be done. They have a thing going. That may help influence ... You said she was at her desk, yeah?"

"Yeah. She's working on a lead. At least that's what she said."

Paige went out to the detective's area, but Linda was not at her desk. She checked the women's bathroom and came up empty. She then went outside and saw Linda's car was gone. Paige slipped her phone out of her pocket and dialed the detective's number. It went straight to voicemail. She rushed inside and to the conference room.

Paige said, "She's gone. I called, but it goes straight to voicemail. Something's up."

"You think she's onto us?"

"Like I said, she's good. It's possible she saw through the cyber security ruse. Look, I'm going to get out of here and call McCain. I don't want to call him from the station."

"I'll go with you."

"No. I want you to stay here and see if there's a way for you to check the GPS history for her cruiser. And do whatever it takes to get those damned DNA results."

Paige knew each of the detective cars provided by the department had a GPS tracker built into a little black box located under the hood of each car. It recorded all sorts of data, from the car's speed, braking, and where the car traveled during a defined timeframe.

"Those GPS results might be tough to do without alerting some folks."

"Do what you can but try and keep it under the radar. Got it?" Paige demanded while Tom nodded his head.

Paige left the station and got into her car, lost in thought. How would McCain take the news his girlfriend was involved in multiple murders, at least tangentially. She knew he possessed the capacity for extreme violence. She'd watched him kill four men with a precision and ruthlessness few could match.

Then again, she'd killed four men with as little remorse as he did. Granted, she'd used coyotes to do it instead of a sword, and the men planned to kill her, also no doubt. Yet she'd lost sleep over the encounter. She was sure Victor had not.

For a moment before she moved her car, Paige closed her eyes and drifted into the Collective Conscience. She tried to locate Victor. Anyone to try and see what was going on. She gleaned a quick image. Spiders? The image faded as quickly as it came.

Returning to reality, she put the car in reverse, backed out of her spot and then dropped in drive and headed away from the station, with no real destination in mind. She drove through downtown Louisville, past Actors Theater, the Kentucky Center for the Arts and then the Slugger Museum. She was stalling and she wasn't sure why. As a homicide detective she often was tasked with contacting the next of kin and delivering the devastating news a loved one was no longer coming home.

But this was different. This time, while there was no dead body, there was an otherwise innocent woman who was going to find her life turned upside down by the video she'd just watched. A huge twinge of pain pulsed through her stomach. It was just like her. When Shepherd convinced her she had murdered her own family. With a sigh, she finally dug out her phone and hit the button to call Victor McCain, the Hand of God, the lover of Linda Coffey. A man who she was sure would never be the same.

Chapter Thirty-Six

Victor sat in the waiting room at Harlan ARH Hospital and talked to the ER doc taking care of Hawkins. Dr. Hayes was north of sixty-years-old, slim, and sported a handle bar mustache. He looked like many ER docs Victor had seen over the years: tired and over it.

"We are in the middle of winter and you're telling me Mr. Hawkins was helping you repair the attic in your cabin when a nest of Black Widow spiders fell down and began to bite him?"

"Yes sir, that's pretty much how it happened," Victor replied.

"I thought Black Widows were solitary spiders. They aren't known to nest."

Victor raised his hands. "I don't know what to tell you, doc. I'm not a bug guy. What I can tell you is it scared the bloody hell out of me. How's he doing?"

"He's lucky you got him here quickly. One bite is no big deal to a man of his size. But I counted over forty bites. We had no other choice but to give him a shot of anti-venom, in

192

addition to the muscle relaxers and pain meds. He will truly feel like hell for several days."

"Man, that's harsh. When can we take him home?"

"Because of the anti-venom, we will need to keep him here for observation for at least eight days."

Victor stood quickly, forcing the doctor to retreat a few steps.

"Eight days? Doc, he can't stay here that long. Can we get him transported to Louisville?"

Dr. Hayes rubbed a finger across his mustache a few times then said, "Yes. But it won't be cheap. An ambulance ride across the state will be quite expensive."

Victor could tell the doctor took one look at him and figured him to be on the lower end of the monetary scale. Little did he know Victor was worth millions in stolen Satanist money.

"Doc, I'd like him transported to University of Louisville Hospital as soon as we can. Who do I talk to about it?"

Hayes considered him for a few seconds, and it was almost as if Victor could see the doctor's mental shrug and his decision that he didn't care.

"They will make arrangements at the front desk. Best of luck to your friend."

With that the doc turned and walked through the double doors to tend to his other patients waiting in the emergency room. Victor was about to head to the main desk when his phone rang and he saw it was Paige.

He punched the answer button and said, "Hello, Detective. What's new?"

"Where are you?"

Victor filled her in on the fight at his cabin and the injuries to Hawkins and Elizabeth. "Guess this tells us for sure Linda has been compromised somehow. What did you guys learn during the cyber sweep?"

There was a pause and for a moment Victor thought he'd lost the connection and checked the bars on his phone, but saw they were at full strength. "Paige, are you there?"

"Yes. I'm here. Listen, the cyber sweep turned up nothing. But there are other developments and I don't want to talk about them over the phone. How soon can you get back here?"

"About four hours. I have to arrange to get Hawkins to Louisville. How bad?"

"We will talk when you get here. When you guys are close, call and we can meet at the Riverside Inn."

Victor heard the strain in her voice. "That bad?"

"Call when you're here."

She ended the call. It took all the control he possessed not to crush his phone in his hand. He closed his eyes and drew in several deep breaths and then went to the front to arrange for Hawkins to be transported to Louisville. The doc was right, it was expensive, but that was what his platinum American Express card was for.

After getting Hawkins squared away, he found Tank sitting right where he left him, sitting next to Elizabeth, with her head in his lap. Her eyes were closed and Victor saw she was sleeping. The swelling was beginning to go down, her supernatural regeneration making quick work of the hornet stings.

Victor quietly slipped into the driver's seat and turned around to face Tank. The fear of what happened at the cabin was no longer visible. Instead, Tank's face was completely calm, and it scared the hell out of Victor.

Softly he asked the biker, "How you holdin' up?"

Tank glanced at Elizabeth and then raised his eyes to Victor's. "How am I holding up?" He shook his head and let out a deep breath. "When I ran out of the cabin with all them hornets and things chasing after me, I knew I'd never get far enough up that mountain to be safe. That's why I had the gun under my chin. If they rolled out of the cabin and made it to me, I was going to blow my fucking head off."

Victor said nothing. He knew how the biker felt.

"I'm a bad man, McCain. I know it. I'm never going to be a saint. Some might even consider me evil. But nobody deserves to die the way they wanted us to die. Up to this point in my life I thought I knew where I stood on the ladder of life. I had no fucking clue."

"Is this your way of telling me it scared you straight?" Victor asked.

Tank's laugh was bitter and without humor. "Just the opposite. When I find the people who did this, I plan to see to it they suffer a long and slow death over many, many days."

"No, you won't." Elizabeth's voice was soft but both men heard her clearly.

"Elizabeth, listen you don't--"

She placed a hand on his lips to quiet him. "I've been to Hell, Cletus. You don't ever, ever want to end up there."

"I ain't ever going to be no angel, Lizzy. You know that," Tank said.

Lizzy? An Infernal Lord with a nickname? Who knew?

Victor said, "She's right, Tank." He saw the biker was going to argue and he held up a hand to stop him. "I don't want you to be an angel either. We're going to find who did this and put them in the ground. But we won't torture them. Killing these things is a righteous thing. You will be saving lives by destroying them. But we will do it the right way. You hear?"

He hesitated and Elizabeth sat up, with some difficulty, and turned to face him. "Your only answer is, 'Yes, Hand of God.' I have done enough over all these many years to earn an eternity being punished for my sins. I will not have another person suffer on my behalf. If you cannot do as Victor has asked, then you need to get out of the van. Now."

Tank reacted as if she'd slapped him, though she didn't even raise her voice. He swallowed a few times then broke her gaze, staring down at his hands in his lap and said, "Fine, Victor. We will do it your way."

Elizabeth nodded once, laid back down with her head in his lap, pulled the blanket up to her chin and immediately fell asleep, her breathing now closer to normal.

"Damn, straight," Victor said. "Tank, I'm going to need you to stay here at the hospital with Hawkins until they bring him to Louisville tomorrow."

"I'm not leaving Elizabeth."

"Look, I'll take care of her, but I have to go back and right now. I can't afford to leave him alone."

Tank raised a finger and dug out his cell phone. "I've got a couple of boys here in Harlan. I'll call them and have them keep watch. Good enough?"

"That'll work. But no light weights. We don't know if bad guys will come after him, but we have to prepare for the worst."

"These guys will do the trick. Trust me," Tank said.

"Okay. I do."

Victor straightened up, started the van, and began the long trip home while Tank made the call. He thought about calling Paige again and forcing her to tell him what she knew, but then dropped it. She obviously wanted to deliver the news in person, and he should respect that. Instead, he hit the speed dial for Linda, but it went straight to voicemail which he knew was not a good sign.

He turned off his phone and tossed it on the dashboard. He glanced at Tank and Elizabeth in the rearview mirror. She still slept and Tank, his call finished, now had his own head against the window with his eyes closed. Good. Victor was not in the mood for talk. He didn't even turn on the radio. He simply drove the old country road and let his mind empty of any thoughts, any emotion. He let the quiet wrap around him while he listened to see if he would hear the word of God, like Brother Joshua seemed to do.

He didn't.

Chapter Thirty-Seven

When Victor turned off the van's engine in front of the River-side Inn, Detective Aldridge's car was already there and empty. Tank rocked awake when the motion of the van stopped and he did so as if from a long dream, with Elizabeth's name mumbled on his lips. Tank shook off the cobwebs and found Elizabeth staring up at him, a slight smile creasing her face which was almost fully healed. Strike up another good part of being supernatural.

She sat up and stretched and winced, showing even she was not fully her old self. She said, "Tank, I need a shower and someone to pull out all these stingers from my body. Let us go inside and take care of things, shall we?"

"You got it, Lizzy."

Tank slid the door open and hopped out. As Elizabeth moved to follow, she glanced at Victor and he mouthed, "Lizzy?" and she winked at him and followed Tank inside. Victor shook his head and laughed a bit and then got out, locked up the van, and joined them.

Tank and Elizabeth disappeared into the back and the rest

of the inn was empty other than the bartender, Saray, and Detective Aldridge sitting at a table near the pool tables. She was twirling a glass and from the color it looked like bourbon. Victor motioned to Saray he wanted the same thing and he joined Paige at her table. Neither said anything until the bartender sat his glass in front of him.

Saray asked, "Hungry?"

Victor started to say no when he realized he was famished. "Yes please, Dealer's choice, or in this case, bartender's choice."

She gave him a wink and walked into the inn's kitchen and Vic realized women seemed to always be winking at him. It didn't suck. He raised his glass, tipped it in Paige's direction and took a sip

"Okay, Detective. Time to give me the bad news. What's wrong?"

Paige took a deep breath and let it out slowly. "There's no easy way to say it, so, here it is, not only is Linda under mind control, but she's also involved in the murders of the women with the Devil's Mark on their bodies."

"Tell me and don't leave anything out," he said.

And over the next few minutes she told Victor more about the cyber sweep and her orders to Tom to go over everything Linda worked on since she became involved in the cases, and about the video from Walmart showing Linda buying the burner phone.

Paige said, "And now she's dropped off the grid. Her phone goes straight to voicemail. I've got Tom trying to find her car with the GPS the force has in every car, but no luck so far."

Victor listened without interrupting and when the detective was finished, he said, "I tried calling her as well, same results. But I can find her. Give me a sec."

Victor retrieved his phone from his pocket and asked it to call Kurt.

"What's up Big Guy? What do you need?"

"Kurt, Linda has gone missing, and I need you to pinpoint where she is and send it to my phone."

"Dude, I hope she's alright. Give me a few seconds and you'll have it."

Kurt hung up and Victor sat his phone on the table as Saray brought him a turkey club sandwich the size of a large brick, some onion rings and their special dipping sauce, along with a Guinness they stocked just for him. He also heard the shower start running and he did his best to banish the image of a naked Tank Bone in the shower with Elizabeth from his mind.

When she left, Paige asked, "How's Kurt going to find her?"

As if anticipating the question, his phone dinged and while taking a huge bite of the sandwich, he glanced at the screen and nodded in satisfaction.

"A few years ago, Kurt was kidnapped and buried in a coffin in Hawaii. Thankfully for him, we found him and saved his life. When things calmed down, we racked our brains for a way to always be able to find one another. We decided to inject a tracker under the skin at the base of our necks, under the hairline. You would never know they are there. Now, with a few mouse clicks, we can pinpoint where each of us is at any given time. Once Linda became more involved in what we do, she agreed to have a tracker injected."

Paige looked a bit shocked. "That sounds so, so..."

"Big Brotherish?"

"Well, yeah," Paige said.

"When you're in my line of work, there are things you are

willing to do to stay alive. The other side does not play fair and the way they kill members of the good guys is never pleasant."

"Can Linda use it to keep track of where you are?" Paige asked.

"No. The only one who knows the website and password is Kurt. And if Kurt goes missing, I have the instructions in a safety security box at my bank."

Victor grabbed an onion ring and dipped it in the sauce. The stuff was pure heaven. He motioned to Paige, and she selected one of her own, dipped and ate it. She swallowed and said, "I guess it's as good a plan as any, considering what you do. Where does it say she is?"

Victor put down half of the sandwich still left, wiped his hands on a napkin, opened his phone, and made a few clicks and swipes, and then enlarged the screen with two fingers to see a tiny map.

"Bloody hell," Victor said.

"What, where is she?"

"Zachary Taylor Cemetery. In the back. Near where Aamon climbed out of his rather large iron box."

"That can't be a coincidence."

"Nope," he agreed and took another bite of his sandwich.

"What do you want to do?" she asked.

"Finish my sandwich and bourbon."

"And about Linda?"

Victor shrugged a large shoulder and took another bite of his sandwich.

Paige's eyebrows pulled down in a frown. "I have to admit you seem to be taking this a lot better than I thought you would."

Victor finished the sandwich and rubbed his hands this time on his jeans. "Look, it seems obvious she's being mind-controlled, so I don't blame her for what she's doing. Up to this point we've been dancing to their tune. All we've been doing, other than rescuing Hawkins and Muldoon, is react to what they are doing."

"Agreed."

"So, now I think it's time we did things on our schedule. They are obviously hoping we rush right out there, guns blazing. I plan on making them wait."

"How long?" Paige asked.

Victor picked up his phone and glanced at the time, then set it down. "It's about 11 p.m. now. If it says she's still there at 3 a.m. then I'll head out there and take a look."

"And you plan to stay up until then?"

"Hell, no. They have some cots in the storeroom, and I'll grab one, get Saray to turn down the lights and bunk down here."

"Then get two cots. I'm going with you."

Victor didn't argue. After seeing Paige in action, he knew she could hold her own. He went to the bar and told Saray what he wanted, then followed her to the supply room and a few minutes later he returned with two cots under one arm and an armful of blankets in the other.

The two of them set up the cots and blankets and stretched out as Saray turned down the lights. Victor set an alarm for 3 a.m. on his phone then turned it off and sat it on the floor next to his cot. The only light still on was a blue neon Pabst Blue Ribbon beer light over the bar.

They laid there for a moment and then Paige said into the near darkness, "What's the plan for 3 a.m.?"

"Find Linda, break the mind fuck, then find the Reader and kill her."

Paige asked, with a bit of humor in her voice, "In that order?"

"Nah, I'll settle for killing the Reader first. That ought to end the mind control pretty permanently."

"Yes it will." Killing a Reader would help reset the balance. Make it start over. Paige liked the idea. Then hated herself for it.

Neither one of them said anything more and as Victor slipped off to sleep by the light of a proverbial neon moon, he found his thoughts drifted to the woman lying next to him instead of Linda and he wondered what that meant.

Chapter Thirty-Eight

The alarm went off and Victor awoke from a deep sleep and momentarily wondered where he was. Wisps of a dream began to race away from his memory, and he tried to catch the fleeting thoughts and the feeling of dread that went with them.

When he'd told Paige earlier in the evening he wasn't worried about Linda because what she did wasn't her fault, he'd feigned nonchalance about Linda's situation. He knew it was a lie. He told himself it would be okay, knowing deep down it wouldn't. It was clear she was involved with the murders of several women. Was she simply a bit player or was she the one doing the killings?

Even if she was the murderer, he wouldn't lose any sleep over it if she did under mind control. Linda, however, would not feel the same way. She was a true law and order kind of gal and Victor knew the fact she was involved at all would destroy her. Aamon threatened to kill her if he did not do as the demon asked. The Reader may have already hurt her more deeply than the demon ever could.

He sat up and swung his feet over the side of the cot the

same time Paige did. Her hair was mussed, and he watched as she used the back of her hands to wipe away the sleep from her eyes.

Victor said, "You've got pretty nice bed hair."

She shook her head in amusement. "And your bed-beard hair isn't half bad either."

They both stretched a bit and Paige asked, "What's the verdict? Is she still there?"

Victor tapped his phone and then let out a small sigh. "Still there."

She offered a weary nod. "Then I suppose we must be off."

Victor stood and offered her a hand up, which she took. When their hands touched, her palm felt cool and her grip was strong. He felt a jolt of electricity go through him and from the looks of things, she felt the same thing.

He let go of her hand and cleared his throat a couple of times, while she turned quickly to fold her blanket and lay it carefully on the cot, making a point of not looking at him and it made him laugh.

She turned and looked at him and asked, "What's so funny?"

"You and me acting like high schoolers. Here we are on our way to fight who knows what big bad and ugly and we are both acting nervous over some personal contact."

She joined him laughing. "Well, that's true. We need to keep our focus on the job at hand."

"Yes, Detective," Victor said. He picked up his bomber jacket and slipped it on and said, "I'll go warm up the car. Give me a few minutes to get it warm and come on out."

"Ever the gentleman," Paige said.

"I have to be. I'm afraid if I don't my father will walk up and slap me upside my head."

He left her snickering and walked out to his car, got

inside, started the car and cranked up the heater to melt off the thin film of ice on the windows. While the car heated up, he pulled out his phone and called Linda. Immediate voicemail.

He put the phone away and did his best to let his mind relax and clear before he and Paige rode off to the cemetery. Nothing was yet settled and yet he was already feeling a deep sense of loss. He knew this whole thing was weighing on him unlike most other battles he'd fought against Satan and his minions. The closest thing was when he was forced to shoot Samantha and he looked for all his answers in the bottom of a bottle.

His drinking was now under control, but it was moments like this one where he felt the pull of the bottle. He knew he would never give up that kind of control ever again, but it was still a fight.

Paige came out and got into the passenger seat and held her fingers in front of the vent pouring out the heat. She'd spent the night sleeping in a bar, but the scent of her hair smelled like eucalyptus and mint, as fresh as if she'd just stepped out of the shower. How did women do that?

"Alright, Big Guy, how do you want to handle this?" she asked.

"You've been listening to Kurt in your ear too long. There's a subdivision that runs behind the cemetery. We'll park on one of the side streets then walk in from the back."

"Sounds good to me," Paige said as she buckled the seat belt. It felt strange to be following someone else's orders right now. Especially the Hand of God's.

He put the car in gear and started towards the cemetery and his thoughts ran to another time he found himself in a cemetery with Samantha Tyler and the death of a friend of hers. It was the night he started on the path to losing his soul and becoming the Hand of God. Cemeteries. He was not a fan.

He drove by the cemetery entrance and then turned into the subdivision next to it and worked his way around behind the spot where Aamon climbed out of his earthly prison. He parked on Apache Road under a huge oak tree away from the houses just up the street. He turned off the car and, despite the cold, rolled down his window and sat and listened.

Paige knew what he was doing, and she did the same, her brows pulled down in concentration. They both heard the occasional sound of a car driving down Highway 42 on the other side of the cemetery, but nothing else. He rolled up his window and turned in his seat to face Paige. He got out his phone and checked the tracking software.

"It says she's still here. With any luck she's waiting in her car. It's too cold for her to be out here this long otherwise."

Paige said, "I hate to ask this, but what if she's been in one spot this long because she's..."

"Dead? Then it won't matter, will it?"

Surprised by his question, Paige replied, "No, it won't."

"Anyways, there's a low wall running around the entire cemetery. I have Hawkins' sniper rifle and I suggest we load up, go to the wall and let me look around with the LIDAR scope to see what's what. If it looks okay, then we head over to where it says she is."

Paige said, "Sounds good."

Victor once again turned off his dome light and they got out of the Chevelle and closed their doors as quietly as they could. It was now about three-thirty in the morning and there was no traffic. Victor knew the only problem would be if a cop drove by, but one of the few perks of being the Hand of God was never being arrested by the cops while he was working.

They went to the trunk and he opened it with his key. She

flipped aside the tarp and they both loaded up: com links, the Katana and sniper rifle for Victor, an extra Glock 20 for Paige along with several magazines, and LIDAR goggles for both of them.

They put the com links in their ears, put on their goggles and walked carefully towards the rear wall. It was a moonless night, the air clear and crisp. Victor motioned for Paige to wait. She stopped as he asked. He slipped off the goggles, raised the sniper rifle with its night scope to his eye and bending low, ducked and walked to the wall. The wall was made of creek rock and hit him about waist high. He dropped into a crouch and rested the sniper rifle on the wall, dropped his goggles around his neck and brought his eye to the scope and scanned the cemetery.

The first thing he noticed was Linda's car was nowhere in sight. He knew the cemetery closed at sunset, but Linda could use her badge to keep the place open if she wanted. He glanced at the front of the cemetery and saw the gates were closed.

He got out his phone and took a quick glance at the tracking software. It said she was still here. He put the phone away and then returned to scanning the cemetery, taking his time but seeing nothing.

He summoned Paige with a wave. She hurried over and knelt beside him. Victor said, "Her car is not here, but the tracker says she is. I don't see anything in the cemetery, and I've looked around the perimeter carefully. I don't see anyone. I don't think we have any choice but to go in and look."

"Then let's do it," Paige said, hand on the gun on her hip.

"A woman of action, I love it. And again, remember, shoot first and worry about it later."

She nodded and they both scooted across the wall and instinctively moved about six feet apart, making them a harder target. Aamon's open grave site was about fifty yards away. It was surrounded by caution tape and there was a tarp covering the open grave. Just beyond the demon's grave, row after row of small white headstones stretched off into the distance. Victor always felt weird when he walked on someone's burial site and now he was creeping over one after the other.

Paige constantly checked behind them while Victor led the way. When they got to the caution tape around the demon's burial site, he got down into a crouch and once again pulled out his phone and checked the tracking software. It said they were within ten feet of Linda and the bottom of his stomach dropped away.

He showed his phone to Paige and nodded to the tarp. She knew what he was suggesting and rested a hand on his shoulder. Victor put the phone away and put his mouth right next to Paige's ear, the smell of eucalyptus and mint strong.

"I want you to flip back the tarp and I'll have the rifle ready."

She nodded and moved by him, under the caution tape and took the corner of the tarp in her hand and then looked at him and mouthed, "Three, two, one." She then yanked the tarp off and away. Victor lunged forward and brought the rifle to his shoulder. Through the night scope he saw the dead body of a woman with long hair, swearing a pantsuit, her neck turned in an impossible direction.

"Oh, no. Linda," he moaned. He tossed down the rifle and yanked a flashlight out of his pocket and turned it once, the beam instantly illuminating the woman lying atop the iron demon coffin and he let out a sob of relief. It wasn't Linda.

Paige took off her goggles and said to Victor, "Thank God it's not her. Here, give me a hand and lower me down."

Victor did as she asked, and he helped Paige over the side and into the grave. She took out a flashlight of her own, along with a pair of latex gloves. In the twin flashlight beams, Victor saw the woman was somewhere around forty years old, with brown hair flecked with streaks of gray. Her neck had been broken and the back of the woman's head rested on her chest. On her forehead, the Devil's Mark.

Victor watched as Paige gently pried open the woman's mouth and she saw a cross forced in upside down. Then she bent down closer and fished something else out of the woman's mouth, and held it up to Victor.

"Is this what I think it is?" she asked.

Victor leaned over and took it from her and held it in the palm of his hand. It was small, about the size of a Tic Tac, and covered in blood.

"Yes. It's the tracking device. Someone dug it out and left it here for us to find."

"Do you think she's dead?" Paige asked.

"No. If she were, they would have left her instead. But it means they know we're after her."

"I wonder how. We didn't even know we were after her until--"

Paige broke off and then began to swear under her breath.

"Until?" Victor prompted.

"Until we saw the Walmart video. In the conference room where the task force meets. We were so intent on searching for a bug on Linda's phone, we never stopped to consider if she might have bugged the room to hear what the task force talked about."

"Bloody hell," Victor said.

Paige motioned for Victor to help her out and he did. She said, "Look, I'll need to call this in. Take me to my car at the Riverside Inn and I'll call in the cavalry and get started on figuring out who she is. I'll keep you out of it."

Victor could only nod and then the two of them started

the trek to his car. While they walked, Paige put her arm around his waist, and they made their way to the wall in silence.

Victor knew his life was never going to be the same and when he found the Reader causing all the trouble, it would be hard for him to follow the advice he gave Tank to not make the woman suffer.

And he knew he didn't care.

Chapter Thirty-Nine

"Her name was Mary Fitzpatrick. She is, or was, forty-two years old and worked at Starbucks over in Prospect."

Victor sat in Paige's living room at one end of a long couch, while Paige sat on the other end and filled him in on last night's murder victim. They decided to meet at her place rather than at the station or the Riverside Inn so Paige could go straight to bed when they finished.

In the brief time he'd known her, he had never seen her this tired. Then again, she'd been up all night while he'd managed to get a few hours sleep. It was now 10 a.m. and they both held hot cups of coffee the detective made from the Keurig in her kitchen.

"Any connection to the other women?" Victor asked.

"No. Nothing obvious anyway."

"Of course there's not. Why make things easy for us?"

He stopped talking when a door opened and a woman walked out of what he saw was a bedroom. She was a black woman around thirty years old with a slim build. She wore a long purple dress and more necklaces than he could count. There were several rings on each hand

"You must be Victor McCain," she said and walked over to him and offered her hand.

Victor stood and took it. "What was your first clue?" he asked.

"Tall, dark and brooding. Just like Paige's description of you. And just as handsome."

Victor glanced at Paige, who blushed, and said, "And you are?"

"Visette."

Visette glided over to an armchair and sat with her legs curled up under her and Victor felt, what? Some kind of power, but not like a Fallen Angel or demon. *It was her eyes*, he thought. When their eyes met, the power hit him like a hammer. This was not a woman you wanted to mess with.

Victor tore his gaze from Visette and turned to face Paige. "Look, you are worn out. I should be on my way and let you get some sleep."

He started to get up, but Paige waved him to his seat on the couch. "Don't be silly. I'm good for a bit longer." Paige nodded at Visette and continued.

"And don't worry about Visette. She's like me. In fact, she trained me. Well, to a degree," she said and winked at Visette.

To Visette, Victor said, "You're the one helping to trap the demon. You really think you can get him into a little bitty bottle?"

"Absolutely, Hand of God. All I need is a bit of your blood and I know I can trap him."

"Fair enough," Victor said. "Any ideas on how we can trap the Reader we all want to kill?"

"Trap, no. But I may be able to help find her. Paige has

never gotten a look at the woman, but she tells me you have. Is that correct?"

"Yes," he replied and then told her about the incident on the bridge and him seeing the woman in the Porsche and described her. "But how does this help?"

"I'd like to do something that will actually give us an excellent image of her, if you are willing."

Victor looked at Paige and she nodded he should. Victor shrugged his shoulders and said, "Why not. Are you going to try some Reader voodoo on me?"

Visette laughed and said, "Witchcraft, actually."

Victor froze and said, "You're a witch? A real boiling cauldron, Halloween kind of witch?"

"Well, Shakespeare was not exactly historically accurate, but close enough. But don't worry, I left my broom at home. The eye of newt, too."

Victor grunted a laugh. "What do you need me to do?"

"Give me a moment," Visette said, and she went into her bedroom and disappeared from sight.

Victor asked Paige, "She can't change me into a frog or something, can she?"

"A frog? No," Paige said.

Before he could ask any other questions, Visette returned carrying five candles, a large mat rolled up under one arm and a large sketch book under the other. She sat the candles off to one side and then rolled out the mat and Victor saw it was about eight feet square. Visette had to move the chair and coffee table to get it to lay even.

Victor asked, "Is this a magic carpet kind of thing?"

Visette smiled and said, "It's a fireproof, don't burn down the house, kind of thing. Candle wax can be bad for the carpet."

Victor felt a bit stupid and kept his mouth shut while

Visette went about setting up the candles in a pentagram, and then lighting them from a lighter she pulled from one of the candle bases.

When this was done, she said, "I hope the Hand of God doesn't mind sitting in a pentagram. Don't worry. It's right side up. Victor, please sit here on the floor and be careful not to knock over the candles."

He did as she asked while wondering how a circle could be right side up. He lowered himself down carefully and sat cross legged while trying not to bump the lighted candles, not an easy task considering he took up much of the mat.

Visette picked up the sketch book and handed it to Paige.

"Paige, please hold this out to where I can see the blank page."

Paige did as she asked and then Visette sat opposite Victor and said, "What I'm going to do is much like what Spock would do in Star Trek when he did a Vulcan mind meld."

Victor said, "You can't be serious?"

"Victor, I am a paragon of seriousness."

Victor began to think Visette was having a bit of fun at his expense considering the twinkle in her eyes, but what the hell. "Fine by me."

"Excellent. First, I want you to close your eyes and listen only to my voice. Please do not open them again until I tell you to do so. Do you understand?"

"Yes," he replied and then closed his eyes.

Visette lit something that produced a lot of smoke. Victor thought it smelled a bit like pot. Or maybe oregano. He waited as Visette slowly moved around him. He could tell she blew the smoke toward him as she went. She almost hummed as she worked her way around the circle.

Once finished, she knelt in front of him. "Good. Now I want you to relax and clear your mind. Picture one of these candles in your mind and then stare at the flame and let your mind empty. That's it."

He did as she asked and almost instantly the candle burned bright in his mind's eye, brighter than any dreamed image should be. The flame flickered and he saw different colors alternating inside the flame, first blue, then green and then red, and then a repeat. He felt all the tension leave his body and he floated there, watching the candle.

When Visette next spoke, it felt like she was in his mind with him. She said, "I'm going to lightly touch your temples with the tips of my fingers, so don't be startled."

He offered up a brief nod and then felt the cool touch of her fingers and a tingle ran down his spine and goosebumps popped on his skin. The flame in his mind seemed to grow brighter, bigger, like the flame was trying to fill his entire vision.

Visette spoke in his mind again and said, "I want you to imagine you are on the bridge and the battle with the men on the bikes is over. You are on the phone calling the police and turning around you see her. Do you see her, Victor?"

"Yes. She's watching me. Through binoculars."

He saw the scene in the candle's flame, and he was back on the bridge and not sitting in Paige's living room. He felt her fingers increase their pressure on his temples and then the flame fell away, and he *was* on the bridge. He saw the four men who attacked him lying at his feet, felt the breeze on his face, and smelled the scent of the river below him, then turned and saw the woman watching him. Saw her lower the binoculars, felt himself running towards her.

Visette said, "Her face. Do you see her face?"

"Yes," and this time, in his mind, he growled his answer. "I see her."

He ran faster and felt his anger grow. He now knew she

was the reason for all that was happening to Linda, for the women who died wearing the Devil's Mark. He was going to catch her and then kill her.

"Let your anger grow, Hand of God," Visette whispered in his mind. "Channel your anger towards her and let it burn her image in your mind."

Victor heard himself growl again, a deep, primordial sound. This woman needed to die. And he would be the one to do it. He felt his jaws clench so hard he was grinding his teeth and the growl continued. And this time when he saw her face, it was only a few feet from his own and he saw the woman's eyes go wide, first with shock, then with fear.

"That's right, bitch," he snarled. "I'm coming for you. And then I'm going to seize that pretty little neck of yours in my two hands and then I'm going to break it and watch the life drain from your eyes. I'm coming for you, bitch. And I'm going to send you straight to Hell."

Victor heard Paige gasp at the same time Visette dropped her fingertips from his temples and she told him to open his eyes. He did and realized he was still growling, and his hands were outstretched as if he were reaching for the Readers neck, his chest billowing in and out great heaves of breath like he was running as hard as he could. Visette was only inches away from his grasp.

He snapped his head around to look at Paige and saw she was not looking at him, but at the sketch pad. Wisps of smoke rose from the pad and then she turned it around so Visette and he could both see what she saw. The face of the Reader in full color as if Leonardo DaVinci himself had painted her.

"How in the hell?" Victor murmured.

Paige asked, "Is this her?"

Victor nodded. To Visette he asked, "How did you do this?"

"I didn't do this, Victor, you did. I was simply a conduit. The more intensely you remember the image, the better the quality of the drawing. Your anger for this woman fueled quite the result."

Paige sat in silence. The woman looked vaguely familiar.

"But the memory wasn't exactly like the day it happened. It seemed like she could hear me, see me," Victor said.

"That's because she did. You made a strong psychic connection through the spell. For a brief moment the two of you were linked. She heard what you were saying as clearly as if she were sitting here next to you. Heaven help her when you do catch her."

Victor said, "Heaven won't lift a finger. I *am* Heaven's response." To Paige he asked, "Now that we have an image, what's next?"

Paige was taken aback by his response to seeing her during Visette's spell. "We treat it like any other murder case. We are looking for a connection to the women. I think we take a picture of this image with my phone and then head to the art gallery, show her face around and see if anyone recognizes her."

Visette rose to her feet and began to put out the candles. Victor got up and helped her and then he rolled up the mat and handed it to her.

"Thank you for your help," he said.

"You are most welcome, Hand of God. But be sure to channel your anger properly. Such anger has been the undoing of many."

Victor only nodded.

Paige said, "Give me a minute and I'll be ready to go."

"No way, Jose," Victor said. "You're running on fumes. You need a nap first."

She began to protest and Visette jumped in on his side.

"He's right. Go lay down for a few hours and I'll entertain Victor until you get up."

Paige let out a deep sigh and said, "You're right. I do need at least a cat nap. Make sure you don't bite him while I'm asleep."

"Wait. What? She bites?" Victor stammered.

Both women laughed and Paige disappeared into her own bedroom and closed the door. Visette said, "Don't worry. I won't turn you into a frog."

Victor let out a sigh of his own and thought, *Witches. Of course, there are witches.*

"Do you really have a broom?" he asked.

"Several," she replied.

Witches.

Chapter Forty

"What did you think of Visette?" Paige asked Victor on the drive over to the Giancarlo Altezzoso Gallery.

"We spent the time you were asleep trading war stories. I'm happy she's on our side. I'm still working hard to get used to the ideas of witches. Does that mean you're a witch too?"

Paige laughed. "I'm afraid not. I'm just me."

"Believe me, Detective, you are not 'just me'," Victor said. "When you started the investigation into Brenda Mazza's death, did you interview anyone at the gallery, or did you have someone else do that?"

"It was another detective, a guy named Walker. But they didn't know anything. Brenda was supposed to open that morning. The employees park in the rear of the building. That's where she was found, a bit down the alley away from her car."

"Any video cameras," Victor asked.

"There's a Ring Doorbell on the rear door. It showed her getting out of her car, then walking out of view of the video camera. She never walks back into the camera's view. She stops and turns to look down the alley like someone called to her."

"Any chance the Reader was doing her mind mojo on Mazza?"

"I don't think so," Paige replied. "Her actions were more appropriate to her reacting to someone else in the alley. Not a focused action like she was on a mission."

Victor offered a grunt in reply and nothing else until they parked in front of the gallery. Then he asked, "This is your kind of thing. Would you rather me wait out here while you do your detective thing? And are you sure you don't want Tom here?"

"I'd rather have him trying to find Linda. Besides, I pointed out you were more than capable as a bodyguard."

"Damn straight. Then let's go inside and detect stuff."

They walked inside and a bell over the door announced their entry.

"Every time a bell rings, an angel gets its wings." Paige said quietly.

"Not true," Victor said as he positioned himself behind her.

The gallery was small, about fifty feet wide and forty deep. The gallery mainly focused on Louisville area artists. Paige walked to a series of paintings on the far right of the gallery of racehorses by Michael Prather. Her favorite was one of American Pharaoh, the Triple Crown winner.

Victor walked up beside her and said, "I get why people want to buy something like this. I do. But that stuff?" Victor jabbed a thumb at a group of paintings more modern in style. "Hell, I've seen grade schoolers do better than that and have you seen the price tags?"

From behind them a voice said, "That's why they say art is in the eye of the beholder."

They turned and found a thin woman who looked to be in her mid-sixties, dressed in an all-gray pantsuit which matched her hair. She wore large black framed glasses and a warm smile on her face.

"If you ask me," Victor said, "the artist of some of these paintings had something in their eye while they were painting."

"Honestly? I don't disagree with you." She extended a hand. "Let me introduce myself. I'm Zoe Sullivan. How may I help you?"

Paige shook her hand while holding up her badge at the same time.

"I'm Detective Paige Aldridge and this is my associate Victor McCain. We wanted to ask you some questions about the murder of Brenda Mazza."

One of Sullivan's hands went to her throat, and she closed her eyes. "That poor girl. I've had nightmares about it since it happened."

"Nightmares? They haven't included dreams about demons, have they?" Victor asked.

"Demons? Why on earth would you ask such a thing?" Sullivan exclaimed.

Paige cleared her throat and said, "Ms. Sullivan. I'd like you to look at a picture and tell me if you recognize the person."

Paige removed her phone from her back pocket, clicked to her photo app and showed the picture of the Reader to Sullivan.

After casting another glance at Victor, Sullivan squinted at the photo and said, "That's an incredibly well-done painting. It looks like Ms. Sampson. Who did the portrait?"

Paige said, "An artist friend of mine. What can you tell me about Ms. Sampson? Do you have a first name?"

"Margaret, though we all call her Mags. Surely you don't think she had anything to do with Brenda's murder. I thought she was killed by a Satanist cult."

Paige saw Victor was gearing up to ask another question and she quickly said, "Right now she's simply a person of interest. She may have information we need. How do you know Ms. Sampson?"

"She's a regular customer. In fact, she's a fan of the modern art Mr. McCain seems to not like."

"That's how you know she's evil," Victor said.

Paige shot Victor a look to stay quiet and he wandered off and pretended to be engrossed by the modern art paintings. Paige turned to Sullivan and asked, "Did she have any issues with Brenda? Any problems?"

Sullivan frowned a moment and then said, "You know. She did. It was about two months ago, right before Christmas. Brenda came to me and said Mags yelled at her for not knowing the price of a painting by Leah Walton. A real up and comer in the art world. We had just hung three of her works but had yet to add the price tags. Brenda said Mags gave her a lot of grief for not knowing the prices by heart."

"When was the last time Ms. Sampson was here at the gallery?"

"Not since that day, I'm afraid. She's bought quite a few things from us over the last year."

Both women stopped their conversation when Victor broke out laughing at one of the paintings. He gave them a sheepish look and said, "Four grand? For that?"

Paige saw the muscles in the side of Sullivan's face start to twitch and knew she was close to losing her temper. Paige asked, "Do you happen to have an address for Ms. Sampson?"

Sullivan's expression turned from anger at Victor to one of worry at Paige's question. "Um, Detective, I'm not sure I should be handing out the private information of my clients."

Victor walked over from the art and towered over the gallery owner. "Lady, we are trying to find out who murdered your employee. Savagely murdered. Coming to work for you."

Sullivan swallowed hard a couple of times, nodded her head once, and walked over to desk with a computer, sat down, tapped a few keys, then hit a button and a printer came to life on a small table behind her and spat out a single sheet of paper. She grabbed the paper, returned to Paige and handed her the paper.

"Her address, phone number and email address. I hope this helps you, Detective."

She said all this while making a point of not looking at Victor.

"Thank you, Ms. Sullivan. And I'd appreciate it if you don't discuss this with anyone else." Paige was impressed. She was prepared to use a little mind persuasion to help Sullivan provide the information. Victor could be quite handy in more ways than one.

"As you wish, Detective."

Paige and Victor went outside and got into the Chevelle. Victor started the car and turned up the heat.

She asked him, "Do you always act like a five-year-old?" She remembered when Jay used to say Paige acted like one. A sharp pain of emotions swept through her. She missed Jay.

"Only on days ending in Y. So, we have a name and address. Did you recognize the name?"

"No. But that's not a surprise. It's not like Readers are all members of a club."

He smiled. "Kind of like being the Hand of God. Imagine

my shock when I found out there are another 11 just like me around the world."

Paige feigned mock shock. "Just like you? Please tell me the fate of the world when it comes to Satanic influence does not rest in the hands of twelve Victor McCains.

"Actually, they are all different from me, including several women. They all kick ass."

"And there are six Readers, of which Visette and I are two. One day, when this is over, you are going to have to tell me all about the world you live in. I am both fascinated and scared to death to think about what your existence means for the world."

"That makes two of us. What's next?"

Paige thought a minute. "I think I now have enough to get us a warrant. I'll call a judge I know and ask her to sign off on a warrant then we get a team together and hit her home."

"Getting a crew to hit the house is a bad idea," Victor said.

Paige frowned and asked, "Why is that a bad idea?"

"What if little miss mind screwer is home and jumps into the heads of one or two of the cops going in the door? Can't she suggest we are the actual bad guys and have them shoot us?"

Paige had to admit he was right. "Yes. I suppose she can. I'm guessing you are suggesting you and I go instead?"

Victor tapped the stone under his shirt. "According to you, she can't touch us because of these things. And between the two of us, surely we can handle her."

"And Tom. I made one for him too. Let me call the judge and get our warrant then the three of us will pay Ms. Sampson a visit."

"I call dibs on breaking her neck first," he said.

"Five-year-old. You're a frickin' five-year-old," she replied.

"Whatever. Hey, pull my finger."

Paige laughed and shook her head. "You're incorrigible."

"Damn straight. Hey. What does that mean?"

"Drive to the station while I call the judge. And please, keep quiet."

Victor winked at her, and she guessed it was fifty-fifty he would.

Chapter Forty-One

It took Paige about a half hour to get the warrant issued and then she and Victor picked up Tom in her unmarked car, stopped by the courthouse to pick up the signed document and then they drove over to Margaret Sampson's house.

Sampson lived in a well-to-do subdivision of upscale homes in the far east end of Jefferson County near Valhalla Golf Course. Each home was over a million dollars in value. They stopped up the street from Sampson's home and watched it while they discussed how they would approach the home.

It was a two-story brick, with a three-car garage attached on the side, and a circle driveway in the front. Victor figured it was well over four-thousand square feet in size. "I guess being a bad guy really does pay."

Paige said, "Well, when you can suggest someone empty their bank account and give it to you, and then tell them to forget they did it? Yes."

From the backseat Tom said, "No car in view and no way to know if she's home other than to go up and knock."

Paige agreed. "When we pull into the circle driveway, Tom, you go around back and make sure she doesn't take off if she's home. Victor and I will go to the front."

"How do you want to handle it if she doesn't answer?" Tom asked.

Victor said, "You guys have a warrant. If the doors are locked, we kick them in and go inside. Time to cowboy up, Tom."

Tom shook his head. He wasn't sure he was very fond of McCain. Hand of God or whatever. "We can't always do the bull in a china shop approach, Vic. Sometimes we need to be more subtle. What do you want to do, Paige?"

She looked between Tom and Victor and said, "We have a warrant, so we kick the door down and go inside."

Tom nodded towards Victor and said, "He's a bad influence on you."

Victor said, "Don't worry, Tom. I tend to grow on people."

"Call me skeptical," Tom asked.

Victor laughed and winked at him and the LMPD officer offered him a smile in return. Paige hoped the two men would become friends. If they all lived.

Paige put her car in drive, hit the gas and quickly turned into the circle driveway. Tom was out and moving towards the rear of the home before she got the car stopped. Victor was only a step behind him, and he rushed to the front door and hit the doorbell. Paige got out and joined him, standing on one side of the door with him on the other. Paige glanced around the neighborhood to see who may be watching. Feeling sure no one would be hurt, she pounded the door with her fist and shouted, "Louisville Metro Police. We have a warrant. Open the door."

No one answered. She pounded the door a second time and repeated her orders, but still no one answered. She nodded to Victor, and he started to kick the door in. But then he stopped and instead used his elbow to break one of two panes of glass which flanked each side of the door. He then reached in and turned the dead bolt and opened the door an inch.

"What happened to kicking in the door?" she asked.

"Heavy duty security door. Not sure it would work. But breaking the glass and turning the lock almost always does the trick. I never knew why people put the two together. Doesn't make sense. Ready?"

Paige took out her gun and he nodded and pushed the door open and immediately someone started shooting, splinters of wood flying off the frame as several shots exploded into the door frame.

Victor drew his Glock and Paige said, "Victor, you can't use your gun. You are not supposed to be here. Put it away."

He did as she asked, but she knew he didn't like doing it.

She shouted, "Police. Lay down your weapon and come out with your hands up."

She tried taking a quick look inside and another two shots were fired from inside. Victor did the same thing, looking around the door frame with the same results: shots hitting close to where his head had been a moment before.

"Jesus, it's a kid. He can't be more than fifteen years old and he's sitting on a couch in a living room off to the left. I only got a quick look, but it's a kid."

Paige asked, "Sitting on the couch? Not in a defensive position?"

"Sitting like he was watching TV and decided to shoot the door. That's not right. He has to be mind-fucked."

Paige shouted to the teen inside. "Look, we don't want to hurt you. Put the gun down. Please.

Paige's phone rang and she saw it was Tom and answered

and filled him in on what was going on and told him to hold tight at the rear door. She put her phone away and said to Victor, "Suggestions?"

"Yeah, but you won't like it. Cover me while I go inside."

Before she could object, Victor ducked down low and dove inside the house, doing a tumble of which any gymnast would approve.

Paige stuck a hand around the door and fired a couple of rounds, aiming high to miss the kid. The teen squeezed off a shot to hit Victor but missed him. It gave Paige a chance to switch to the other side of the door where she could get a look at him.

Victor was right. He appeared to be about fifteen years old, and wore a white T-shirt, jeans and Nike tennis shoes. His hair was brown and curly, and he sported the first shadows of a mustache on a trembling lip. In one hand he held an older model Glock and something in the other hand she couldn't quite see.

"Victor, did you see what was in his other hand?"

"No. Let me check."

He whipped his head around the entrance to the living room and back fast enough to avoid another shot. After he did, he dropped his chin to his chest and then breathed in deep and let it out slowly, then turned to look at Paige.

"What?" she asked.

"It appears he's holding a bomb detonator."

Paige felt her own eyes go wide and she hissed, "Get out of there. Now."

"We leave and I bet the kid dies," he replied

"We stay and he likely dies. Us with him. You can't stay. You have to get out."

Victor drew in another deep breath then straightened.

"Detective Aldridge, I need you to try to get into his mind and short circuit the other Reader. I need you to do it now."

With that the Hand of God disappeared down the hallway to the kitchen and then turned left and out of sight. Paige let out a string of swear words and then closed her eyes and searched for the teen in the Collective. She found him easily enough as he was the only one thinking about the bomb. She reached out to him and hit a mental wall, one erected by the other Reader and her control was incredibly strong.

Mentally she beat against the mental barriers with her own will. She searched for a way to get around the walls, under them, over them, all without success. Having no other option, she used her own will like a sledgehammer and began to methodically break down the other Reader's wall. This reminded her of fighting with Junna against Shepherd in the Collective Conscience. She wished Junna was here to help. She then reached out through the Collective Conscience to try and reach Visette. No luck. Visette must have been wearing an Abet stone as well and Paige didn't have time to call.

She sensed the teen's thoughts becoming confused as he fought to understand what was happening to him. Her own thoughts were not getting in, but one of his finally found a way out: *help me.*

She dug down deep and thought about what Visette had told Victor during the spell to create the image of the other Reader. *Let your anger grow and use it to sharpen the image.*

And that's what she did. Her anger at the other Reader blossomed and turned her sledgehammer into a battering ram. She allowed her sorrow at the deaths of the men and women to become a part of her anger. The final push, she let the anger of someone controlling Jay to try and kill her give her the final boost she needed. Her anger then grew so large the battering ram became a guided missile.

She felt the other Reader's walls collapsing and then she felt the other woman scream at the teen to push the button on the detonator. Paige screamed just as loudly for the teen to put the detonator down. Her physical self heard the teen howling in frustration as his mind was being torn apart by the battle being waged by the two Readers using his mind for the battlefield.

And then it stopped. All of it. Her connection to the teen's mind disappeared from one heartbeat to the next like the flipping of a light switch. Her eyes flew open, and she risked a glance at the teen and saw Victor McCain standing behind him. McCain held the detonator and Glock in one huge hand while his other hand held the teen steady on the couch. She started to wonder how when her mind caught up to her eyes and she saw Victor's Abet Stone now hung around the teens neck and it glowed a bright orange. Victor had used the stone to end the Reader's mind control.

She shouted her own mental challenge to the other Reader in the Collective. She knew it was unlikely the Reader would be able to read her thoughts, but she didn't care. They'd saved the teen's life and she felt a surge of triumph course through her.

She put her gun away and walked to the teen and knelt on the floor next him. He was sobbing now, his pain and anguish racking his body. He kept saying, 'I'm so sorry' over and over.

She took one of the teen's hands in hers and said, "You're going to be okay." She raised her face to Victor and mouthed, "Get Tom." The bounty hunter gave her a thumbs up and left to do as she asked.

"What's your name?" she asked the boy.

"Caleb. Please tell me I didn't hurt anybody. I didn't want to shoot at you guys, but I couldn't help it. I heard her voice in my head and it told me anything that came through the door but her was a demon and I was to kill it. And if that didn't work, I was to blow up the house to save everyone else."

Victor returned with Tom in tow and Victor asked, "Hey kid. Where's the bomb?"

"I'm sitting on it. It's under the couch," Caleb said.

Both Victor and Tom jumped back a few steps and Paige rose to her feet. She said, "Everyone, out. Now!"

They all left the house and Paige looked at Caleb. "Now, other officers are coming. They won't believe you when you tell them you were mind controlled. We all believe you. We need you to tell them a woman was here, fired the gun and left you on the couch with the detonator. We'll tell them the woman held you hostage, but she got away when we tried to protect you. Got it? I'll help persuade them."

"Yeah, okay," Caleb nodded. Paige would work on his memory after all of this was over. She told Tom to take Caleb to her car and watch over him and Tom led the boy away. She held up a finger to stop Victor from asking any questions while she got out her phone and dialed a number. Someone on the other end answered and she said, "This is Detective Paige Aldridge, badge number 2031 and I need you to send the bomb squad to the following address. We also have an active shooter on the loose. We need a full tactical unit here for a neighborhood search."

She gave them Sampson's address and then hung up the phone as a police car came rolling down the street fast, lights and siren on full blast, and stopped on the curb next to them. Two uniformed officers hopped out, their guns in their hands. One of the cops, an older man with Sergeant's stripes, wore a name tag which read Latimer. The younger cop's read Carter.

Paige held up her badge and identified herself. "I'm Detective Aldridge and the shooting is over, though we have a possible bomb in the house. The Bomb Squad is on the way. You can put your guns away.

The two officers did as she asked and then Latimer squinted as he gave Victor a hard look. To the Hand of God, he asked, "Hey, aren't you Victor McCain?"

Victor raised an eyebrow and glanced at Paige before answering. "Yeah. That's me."

"And you're the one responsible for Tommy Wallace goin' missin', right?"

"Wrong. You guys investigated his disappearance for months and you found nothing showing me involved. You know why? Because I wasn't."

Victor knew while technically true, it wasn't totally true as Wallace died at the hands of his brother Mikey.

Both men gave Victor their stony cop face, then started for their car. Before sliding in behind the wheel, Latimer turned to Paige and said, "He's made Detective Coffey a pariah with the force. If you're involved with him now, you're next."

"Gee, thanks Officer Latimer. Any other advice you'd like to offer from the stone age?" When the officer failed to answer, she said, "I didn't think so. Now how about you two go do your job and go block off the end of the street and keep people out of here until the bomb squad can check things out."

Without saying another word, the two men got in their car and sped off to do as she asked, neither one looking exactly happy to be doing so. She turned to Victor and said, "I'm sorry about that. I know you had nothing to do with Tommy's disappearance."

A look on Victor's face made her stop and step closer. "I'm right, aren't I?" she asked.

"Mostly. It wasn't me. It was Mikey."

"Oh, Victor. Tell me it's not true," she whispered.

With new cop sirens heading their direction he explained how Wallace went after Mikey on his own and was no match for an Infernal Lord. "He was simply overmatched," he said.

Paige shook her head. "You should have warned him."

There was a bit of anger in Victor's reply when he said, "I am many things, Detective, but a psychic is not one of them. I had no idea he was tracking Mikey. You suggesting I should have warned Wallace would be like me suggesting you should have warned Caleb before Sampson got to him.

She knew he was right, but it still angered her, and she wanted to say more but was stopped when the bomb squad arrived. She sighed and said, "If anyone asks, you got here working as a bounty hunter tracking down the same woman. Got it?"

Victor offered a curt nod and then walked over to her car, leaned against the trunk, crossed his arms and watched her. She stared back for a moment and saw the defiance on his face. A hard man. She broke off the staring contest and tried to put him out of her mind as the bomb squad arrived. She took control of the scene and walked over to talk to the bomb squad captain. She didn't succeed.

Chapter Forty-Two

Victor watched the bomb squad finish putting up their gear after dismantling the bomb Sampson stashed under her couch to blow up whomever was unlucky enough to come through her front door uninvited. Thankfully for Caleb, the first two through the door were the Hand of God and a Reader, the only two people on the planet uniquely qualified to save the day. And they had.

With any luck, Paige's suggestion the Reader was responsible for the shooting and not the kid will keep him out of jail. Victor was quite sure his prints would not be found on the bomb, and that might get him out of a domestic terrorism charge. No matter what happened, though, the kid was royally and totally screwed. Having multiple people fighting a mental war in your head had to leave some kind of residue.

If there was anything which pissed off Victor the most, it was the innocents who paid the price for the continuous war between good and evil. When the Watchers, a group of fallen angels who were supposed to be buried until Judgement Day got loose and then possessed a bunch of college students, they destroyed the lives of dozens of people. Now Sampson was doing the same thing.

And his mood wasn't being helped by Paige's reaction to what happened to Detective Tom Wallace. He understood, on a practical level, the strength of the Blue Wall, the unwritten rule of one cop supporting another, no matter the circumstance. In the case of Detective Wallace, Linda had tried to reign him in, but he refused to listen, and it cost him his life. He thought she would be more understanding. She knew what it was like to deal with collateral damage their lives always encountered. When she got angry it caught him off guard.

He broke off his internal pity party when a weary Detective Paige Aldridge walked up to him. Tom had long since taken Caleb to the precinct for processing and the only people left were the two of them and the bomb squad techs who were putting away all their gear. It was now late in the evening and most of the neighbors who stood on their front porches or in the street to watch all the action, were all inside their homes.

She stood in front of him, her head down and her arms crossed. He started to say something but got a mental nudge. It would be a good time for him to keep his mouth shut. Something he found hard to do.

Finally, she raised her head and met his gaze and he saw a deep sadness in her eyes. She said, "I'm sorry. I know there was nothing you could do to save Tommy. While I didn't know him well, I do know when he got an idea in his head, there was no stopping him. And if he decided he was going to bring in your brother, well, he wouldn't stop till he did or died trying."

Victor felt all the energy leave his body and deep inside he matched her sadness. "And that's what he did. And I'm sorry, too. Wallace was only trying to do what was right. And he was right, my brother was a real son of a bitch. His only problem was, it was like a puppy trying to take down a Rottweiler."

She nodded and glanced at the house. "We found hair in a brush. We will compare it to the hair we found on one of the victims. The eyeball test says it's similar, but who knows. DNA will tell us for sure. We do have another problem, though."

Victor laughed. "Only one? Lay it on me."

"We searched the house high and low. We found some bills. After Tom got Caleb processed, I had him run a background check on Margaret Sampson. Know what we found?"

"Let me guess, Margaret Sampson only has a credit history that goes back a few years. Am I right?"

"Score one for the former bounty hunter. It goes back just short of two years. It's for sure an alias." Paige noted the concerned look on Victor's face. "Don't worry about Caleb. He'll be alright."

"How do you know that? The poor kid is traumatized and how…"

Paige smiled at him, causing him to stop mid-sentence. "I've got this one. I can clear his mind. Implant a memory of being held hostage only. He'll never remember he fired a shot. I'll set things right in his head shortly. I can also influence the cops' mind. He'll be alright."

"Handy little trick you got there. The power you have."

"I don't use it unless I have to. In this case, well, an innocent would have to go to hell and back. He doesn't deserve this. She does."

"And it puts us right back to the proverbial square one."

"Not quite," Paige said. "The search team didn't find her, obviously, but we've flushed her out and we have her picture out all over the city, including all the hotels. If she tries to book a room somewhere, we will know."

Victor stuffed his hands in his pockets and stared at the ground for a moment, then said, "Look, I'm also sorry you're now being tarred with the same Victor McCain stuff Linda has had to deal with. You don't deserve the hassle."

She punched him on the shoulder. "I'm a big girl, Victor. Screw 'em if they can't handle it. When you're a woman in a man's world, the constant judgement comes with the territory."

Victor scratched his beard and said, "Fine. I think it's time we remove one of the chess pieces from the board."

"The demon?" she asked.

"Yep. Why don't we go see Visette and let's throw big, bad and ugly in his coffin?"

Chapter Forty-Three

Victor was once again awed by the power he felt rolling off Visette. They were sitting around Paige's dining room table. Tom, Elizabeth and Tank had joined them, each of them with a cup of coffee in front of them. Well, everyone but Tank. He was drinking Jack Daniels.

Victor said, "Okay Visette, what do we need to do to get this party started in trapping the demon?"

Instead of answering, Visette got up and walked into her bedroom and returned with a bowl that appeared ancient and a weird looking knife. She sat the bowl down in front of him and said, "We start the party by drawing blood from the Hand of God."

He said, "Uh, why does your knife look like it's made of bone?"

"Because it is."

Tank laughed and asked, "Is it from the bones of one of your enemies? Is it full of magic and shit?"

Victor ran by the inn to pick up Tank and Elizabeth and

on the way over he explained about Visette being both a Reader and a witch. Tank especially loved the witch part.

"I'm afraid not. It is made from the bones of a timber wolf and the only thing special about it is it is extremely sharp." She turned to Victor and said, "Hold your hand over the bowl, please. "

Victor did as she asked, and she took his hand in hers and closed her eyes. She began to chant a spell so softly he could not hear what she was saying. Near the end, without opening her eyes, she used the knife to cut a thin line across his palm. Victor felt the sting of the cut and then watched as his blood dripped into the bowl.

She continued to chant and as Victor watched, the blood began to move in a slow circle around the bowl. As more blood filled the bowl, it moved faster and faster until with a final whispered word it started to settle into a pattern. He bent closer and saw the name Aamon bubble briefly to the surface of the collected blood before it disappeared.

"Magica coloris," Elizabeth hissed in Latin. Victor remembered enough of the Latin the Catholic nuns beat into his brain during his high school days. White magic.

Visette smiled at Elizabeth and said, "Some call it that, yes."

Tank snorted, "Well, it's good to see someone finally draw some blood out of you, McCain. Lord knows I've wanted to for years."

Paige said, "You'll find some bandages in the hall bathroom under the sink."

Victor got up and went to patch himself up and thought about what he just saw. Of all the strange things he had witnessed over the years, seeing his own blood spell out words made his stomach turn. He turned on the cold water and ran it over his palm until the bleeding slowed. He watched the blood swirl with the water as it disappeared down the drain, half expecting it to start spelling more things.

He found the bandages where Paige said he would, doctored up his wound and returned to the table to hear Elizabeth and Visette in a heated discussion.

Elizabeth said, "Witchcraft is the Devil's work. You are putting your soul at risk. You have to know this."

"My powers come from Nature and could not be purer. If the Creator made all we see, then he put the power in Nature for those of us who can make use of it. Magic is no more good or evil than the person who wields it. Magic is a tool. Like the wolf's knife. If I use it in the service of good, then it is fine. Should I wield it in the name of evil, then it is not."

Tank broke in and asked, "Hey, can you make me one of those little dolls and make it look like Victor? Then I can make him do what I want."

It broke the tension as both women shook their heads and smiled. "I am sorry," Visette said, "but that is voodoo and that is not something I can do. Even if I am from New Orleans."

Victor sat down and said, "I saw the demon's name in the blood."

Visette nodded agreement. "I used the spell to bind your blood to the demon. When we are ready, I will release the spell and then the demon will be drawn to the blood like a white hot beacon in the night."

Tom asked, "What's next?"

Paige said, "We find a place to set up our summoning spell to draw him where we want him, then we use Victor's blood to lead him to the bottle trap. Once we have him inside, then we bind him so he can't get out and then bury it somewhere."

"What type of place do you need," Victor asked.

Visette said, "Preferably someplace with plenty of space. You can be sure he will not come alone. You have proven yourself more than capable and he knows you are not likely to be alone. So neither will he."

Victor closed his eyes and thought for a moment and then said, "There's an old train repair depot not too far from the Derby Mission. They used to strip parts out of broken-down engines and box cars to reuse and then what they couldn't they sent to the scrap yard down by the river. That's all green space now."

"Sounds like just the place," Visette said.

Paige drummed her fingers on the table for a moment then said, "We sure could use a few more people. Visette and I will be busy casting the summoning and binding spells."

Tank said, "I can bring some of the guys. Won't be as many as last time, McCain. Word gets around and a lot of the guys feel going out with you is close to a suicide mission."

"I don't blame them," Victor said. "It shows they have some sense. How many do you think you can get?"

"A couple, maybe. Not many."

Paige asked, "How's Hawkins? Is he well enough to pitch in?"

Victor shook his head. "Not yet. Tank got him transferred here to University of Louisville Hospital, but when I called, he was still out of it."

Visette asked, "Is this your friend who was bitten by the black widow spiders?"

"Yep. They messed him up pretty bad. And the anti-venom is a bitch, too."

"I might be able to help with that," Visette said.

Victor sat up straighter. "You think you can wiggle your fingers and make him better?"

"Perhaps," she replied. "Why don't we go find out."

"Why don't we? Tank, you and Elizabeth go round up as many of the bikers who will come along."

"You got it," the big biker said.

Tom stood and said, "Paige, I'll head to the station and see if anything's popped on Linda or the search for Sampson. When you guys are ready to head to the train yard, let me know and I'll be there."

"Thanks, Tom. Plan on later tonight."

When Tom, Tank and Elizabeth were gone, Visette went to her room to pack a bag, and Paige said to Victor, "You know there's a good chance none of us will make it to the morning."

"Sister, in my job, that's the way it is for me every single day. The only time I can sleep easy is when I'm at the Mission and thanks to the Church on the premises, they can't touch me. It's the only place I can sleep, truly let it all go and rest."

Visette returned and said, "Let's go see your Army friend."

———

University of Louisville Hospital was relatively new and the private rooms where they had Mike Hawkins were located on the fourth floor and the hallway and rooms featured a faux wood style. Homey and peaceful.

They found Hawkins asleep in his bed with a nurse checking his vitals when they walked in. The former Army captain's breathing was still labored, and his heart rate was accelerated, even while asleep.

Victor glanced at the board on the wall and saw the nurse's name was written in black sharpie at the top: Sherri. She smiled at them when they walked in and asked, "Are you family?"

"Friends," Victor said.

The room featured a recliner and a bench seat in the

window overlooking the parking lot. Visette and Paige sat on the bench seat while Victor took the recliner.

"How's he been doing," Paige asked.

Sherri said, "About the same. We have to keep him sedated due to the pain of the spider bites." She stared at Hawkins for a moment then said, "I've never seen anything like this. That many spider bites at one time? How awful."

"None of us have," said Victor.

Sherri glanced at a Fitbit on her wrist and said, "Well, time to get to the next patient. Let me know if you guys need anything."

After she left, Victor rose quickly to his feet and leaned against the door to prevent it closed from anyone else entering the room. Paige and Visette moved just as quickly as the two women took items from Visette's bag. A small blue candle, yet another bowl and the same wolf bone knife.

Paige went to the sink in the bathroom and filled the bowl with water while Visette sat the candle on the bedside table next to Hawkins' head. She pulled a lighter from the bag and lit the candle and then waved her hand over the flame while repeating an enchantment three times:

In the divine name of the Goddess
Who breathes life into us all
I consecrate and charge this candle
As a magical tool for healing

As she finished the last word of the enchantment her hand stopped moving and a white light flowed from her fingers into the candle. For a moment the flame took on the same white light, and then faded to a flickering yellow. Victor swallowed hard and did his best not to shout out *bloody hell*.

Visette took the bowl from Paige and then held it over the candle, the flame licking the bottom of the bowl. Then three times, she repeated another chant:

Magic mend and candle burn
 Illness leave and health return

She handed the bowl to Paige and then picked up the wolf bone knife. She began to chant so softly he was not able to hear the words. In one hand she moved the knife back and forth over Hawkins' body, starting at his head and moving down to his feet. Every few seconds, as she did this, she dipped the fingers of her other hand into the bowl and sprinkled drops of water onto him. While he couldn't be sure, it seemed as if each drop of water glowed with the faint white light he saw before.

He watched in awe as Hawkins arched his neck, took in a long deep breath, and let it out slowly. The monitor tracking his heart rate continued to beep, but as he watched, the heart rate began to slow from the high nineties to the eighties and then to the seventies and finally to the mid-sixties. His breathing slowed and became steady, his chest rising and falling as if he were in a deep peaceful sleep.

Visette never stopped her chanting and Paige moved with her as she kept the bowl in easy reach of the witch. When she reached his feet, she moved to the foot of the bed and raised her hands high and outstretched, her own neck arched and with a final spoken word, she collapsed and fell into the recliner, her energy spent.

It was then Victor felt someone pushing and banging on the door, trying to get into the room. He looked at Paige and mouthed *the candle and the knife.* Paige quickly put out the candle, grabbed it and the knife and tossed them into the bag. She sat down quickly and nodded to Victor who moved away from the door.

Sherri came into the room, a frown on her face and she started to ask him a question when she looked at Hawkins and her eyes went wide. Victor followed her gaze and saw him sitting up in bed and stretching. All the red spider bites were gone, his skin unblemished and normal.

Sherri stammered, "W-w-w-hat in the w-w-w-orld?"

Hawkins glanced around the room and said, "Why am I in a hospital?"

Victor walked over and stood next to the bed and asked, "What's the last thing you remember?"

Hawkins' brows drew down as he thought a second and said, "You, Elizabeth, Tank and I were going to drive to your cabin in Harlan. Was there an accident? Am I OK?"

"Brother, I think you're just fine. I'll explain more later." He made a small head nod towards the nurse and Hawkins got the hint.

"Sounds good." His stomach let out a loud rumble and he added, "And man, I'm starving. I think I could eat my weight in steak. Can we get out of here?"

Victor turned to Sherri and asked, "The man would like to leave, and he seems all healed up. Great job. Who do we need to talk to?"

Sherri opened her mouth to reply and then shut it and simply turned from him and walked out of the room. Victor let out a small laugh and then shut the door behind her.

He turned to Visette and asked, "Are you OK?"

She nodded sleepily and said, "I'll be fine. Let me take a

nap until she gets back with the doctor."

She pushed the recliner until the footrest came up, laid her head against the headrest, and promptly fell asleep."

Paige moved to stand by the bed and asked Hawkins, "How do you feel?"

"I feel fantastic. Why do I get the sneaky suspicion I shouldn't?"

Paige looked Victor's way and he said, "Because you shouldn't. You can thank the young lady in the recliner for your wellbeing. Well, you can thank her when she wakes up."

The three of them glanced at Visette asleep in the recliner, softly snoring.

"She's cute," Hawkins said.

"And taken," said Paige.

Hawkins shrugged his shoulders and said, "My loss. Oh. And I'm hungry."

Paige said, "That's likely the result of the healing magic."

Hawkins' eyes bugged a bit and he said, "The what?"

Victor slapped him on the shoulder and said, "Once we are out of here, I'll fill you in."

Hawkins stared at Visette and nodded weakly. Then his stomach growled again.

"Dude--" he started

Victor raised his hands in surrender. "I know, I know. You're hungry. There's a steak place right up the street and when we get you out of here, we will go straight there."

"Now you're talkin'," Hawkins said, and he laid down again and put his hands behind his head and started whistling.

Victor shook his head and said to Paige, "I think when she wakes up, I want one of them healing spells."

"Think it will help you?"

"Sure as hell can't hurt."

Witches. *Bloody hell.*

Chapter Forty-Four

It took another hour or so to free Hawkins from his hospital bed and even then, the doctor wanted to keep him overnight for observation. When Hawkins pointed out he would only stay the night over the good doctor's dead body, the M.D. signed the paperwork and then they were off to find him food. Another hour and a half and one steak dinner later they were all gathered at the Riverside Inn for a council of war. Elizabeth, Paige, Hawkins, Tom, Visette, Tank and two bikers, two brothers named Jack and Colby. Both were nearly as big as Tank and, if possible, gave off the vibes of being twice as violent.

Visette seemed much better after her short nap and swore she would be ready when it came time to cast the binding spell. Her mood improved greatly when Tom showed up and gave her a long hug. Not so much for Victor as not only did Tom not hug him, but there was also still no word on either Linda or Sampson.

"We do now have our connection between the female victims," Tom said.

"Tell us."

Tom took out a pocket notebook, the kind it seems every police detective carries, and flipped down a few pages. "We already knew the connection between Brenda Mazza and Sampson. Mazza ticked off Sampson one day at the gallery. The second victim has been identified and her name is Tiffany Spears. She house-sat for Sampson and her mother said Sampson complained Tiffany let one of her favorite plants die."

"And Mary Fitzpatrick?" Paige asked.

"Sampson was a semi-regular at the Starbucks where she worked and one of her supervisors remembers Sampson crucifying Mary over a latte when the poor girl forgot to put Splenda in her drink. The connections are all weak, but they are there. Now we just need to find her. We have the BOLO out all over the city."

Victor said, "I think hoping we will catch Sampson checking into a hotel is pointless. If she needs a place to sleep, can't she just wiggle her fingers, or whatever it is you Readers do, and get someone to give her a place to sleep for the night?"

Paige sighed and said, "Yes she can, though finger wiggling isn't needed."

Tank said, "If the bitch is smart, she's headed out of town and will stay gone. She's a dead woman walking."

Victor said, "I'm betting she's still here. and if she turns up, don't hesitate. Put a bullet in her brain before she can hop into yours." He asked Visette, "What do you need to set up the binding spell?"

"Once we get to the building you have picked out, I will need a large flat space to prepare the spell. When that is finished, I will drip a drop of your magic imbued blood on your forehead. This will draw Aamon to you. He will come full of rage, as the spell I cast when I drew your blood ties him to you."

Victor frowned. "Tied to me how?"

"Picture being attached to each other by a ten-foot chain. On your end, it is simply tied around your waist. No big deal. On his end, however, it will feel as if he were impaled by large fishhooks and every time you move, they are yanked deeper into his skin. That kind of tie. The moment the drop of blood hits your skin, the link will be activated, and he will want to find and kill you as quickly as possible."

"Bloody hell," breathed Victor. "Lady, you don't mess around. And once we get him here, you're sure you can bind him? I'm still having trouble picturing a huge raven headed demon trapped in a bottle."

"That's because you are only thinking of this plane of existence. Demons can exist on many different planes and dimensions. When he is in the bottle, he will be trapped in a pocket dimension. From his perspective, it will be as if he were trapped in a vast unending desert. From our plane of existence, he will be trapped in a small bottle."

"If you say so," Victor said. "As long as you can pull it off. What happens if you summon him to us and you can't bind him?"

She smiled sweetly. "Then we will likely all die. You first."

Jack and Colby glanced at each other but otherwise showed no emotion one way or the other. Victor said to them, "No shame in backing out now, gentlemen."

Colby said, "I think you are all batshit crazy. But if you're not..."

Jack finished, "Then we want in on kicking demon ass. Tank says you're on the up and up. I guess we will find out."

Paige asked, "Any way to know if Aamon will bring help?"

"I can't imagine he'd risk his ass after what you and I've

managed to do to them up to this point, but who knows? Prepare for the worst and wait for it to get even worse."

Elizabeth snorted. "An Infernal Lord, a Witch, a Reader, a Hand of God and a Tank. Even if he brought one of his legions from Hell, it would not be enough. In fact, I don't believe this Witch will need to bind him. We shall rip out his heart and feed it to the dogs."

"Well, first off, we don't have any dogs. Secondly, if Visette can bind him, it will limit the number of casualties."

Elizabeth sniffed. "I have seen this cop woman use dogs to eliminate her opponents. As for casualties, men were put on this Earth to die. It is how God wanted it. Best to die in battle."

Hawkins spoke up for the first time, "General Patton said *the object of war is not to die for your country but to make the other poor bastard die for his.* Victor is right. Limiting casualties should be our goal. With that said, if this is how we must die, then so be it."

Visette cleared her throat and said, "While I understand the desire for vengeance, if you kill the demon here, he simply returns to Hell. If we trap him in the bottle, he stays there forever, and Hell loses a captain."

Elizabeth pursed her lips and said, "That is true. And my former master will be angry Aamon has once again been hidden from his view. Very well, I approve."

"How nice," Paige said.

Elizabeth's eyes narrowed with a brewing anger and Victor stepped in before the top could blow. "Great. We are all on the same page. Visette, once you prepare the spell, how long will we have to get Aamon to you?"

She put a finger to her lips, thinking. "Not long. No more than an hour. The candles I use are not large, for a reason.

The ideal thing would be to start casting the spell when we know he's arrived, then you lure him to us."

"Okay. Once you drop some blood on my forehead, how long before he shows up?"

She offered a throaty laugh. "Very soon, Victor. He won't have to search. The blood will draw him to us. Finding and killing you will be his one and only objective."

Once again Victor wondered at the sanity of having a high-level Demon Prince from Hell bonded to him, but in the end, he realized he once again didn't give a rat's ass.

"Fuck him if he can't take a joke," Victor said. "Let's roll."

Everyone gathered up their gear and in his mind Victor went over what was going to happen: Set up the spell, piss off the demon, wait as bait, then kick his ass until a witch traps him in a returnable bottle. How hard could it be?

Chapter Forty-Five

Construction on the Louisville and Nashville Railroad began in 1853, connecting, appropriately enough, Louisville and Nashville. Over the next one-hundred and fifty years or so, the rail line expanded throughout the state until it merged with another company and eventually became known as CSX in the early 1980s.

Until the mid-1990s, there was a train scrap yard located along the Ohio River near downtown Louisville. The city reclaimed the acreage, cleaned it up and then opened a park. Much of the scrap came from an L & N facility on Louisville's southside. When CSX bought the operation, the salvage work moved out of town.

The old salvage and switching station was housed in a monstrously large building off Dixie Highway. The three-story brick building sat abandoned like the bones of a long dead animal. Nearly all the windows were shot out by vandals and the inside was covered in the bright paint of taggers. The building was scheduled for demolition in the early part of the summer. Victor figured the city wouldn't mind if they caused a bit more structural damage.

The group made their way into the building using several powerful Maglites, as power to the building had been turned off many years ago. The night was not as cold as the previous evenings, but it was still cold enough for their breath to condense in small clouds as they breathed out. They parked in an empty lot down the street and walked the last half mile or so, not wanting the cars to bring unwanted attention.

Victor, Hawkins, Tank, Jack and Colby all carried large bags filled with the items of modern warfare. In addition to his bag, Colby carried a huge battle axe in one hand. When Colby asked the man why he brought an ax, he replied, "That's what all the guys in the movies use to fight demons."

It made as much sense to Victor as anything else. Paige and Visette both shouldered their own bags carrying the stuff needed to prepare and cast witchcraft. Tom carried his Glock on his hip and a shotgun in his arms. Elizabeth came as she was and was more dangerous than all of them combined.

In addition to the bag he carried, Victor wore his katana in the sheath on his back. When they got out of the car, the blade started to whisper to him, so soft he strained to make out the words and then realized the whispering was in Japanese and was being said in a chant like cadence. He sent a thought to the sword: *what the bloody hell?*

And with what was surely a mental annoyance at being interrupted, the sword sent a thought back: *A war chant. I prepare for battle. Leave me alone.*

Victor pulled up so short Hawkins nearly walked into him from behind, and the Army captain asked him if he was alright.

"Yeah. Great. I thought I heard something, but it was nothing."

Jack asked, "And why must we do this late at night when it's the coldest?"

Visette answered, "Not the coldest, but the darkest. Have you never heard of the Witching Hour? Candle magic is best performed when the flame shines the brightest."

Once inside, everyone followed Visette to a relatively clear area in the far corner of the main room of the building, in a good-sized niche which would give the women some protection from any fighting in the main room. "Vic, would you and the boys help me clear out the space?"

Victor nodded and the other men began to help pick up some wooden debris and a few rocks, clearing out a nice flat space on the concrete floor to make room for the binding spell.

——————

Paige found a graffiti covered concrete column and leaned against it. She decided she would think about the case at hand. Not the demon. Take her mind off the situation for a moment before things become dire.

She remembered setting Caleb's world back to right as much as she could by manipulating his memories in the Collective Conscience. Caleb would still be traumatized, but not as bad as he could have been. She learned Sampson took him while he was walking down the street to go visit a friend and play video games. Just a random happenstance. Nothing connected to anything. More proof Sampson, or whatever her name was, didn't care about anyone. Paige wondered about her motivation. Why was she trying to kill her and Victor? Why kill the women over such petty things? Why was Linda involved? As a matter of convenience? Because she was close to Victor?

Paige glanced over in Victor's direction. She half smiled. Why on earth was she so drawn to this man? In his own way, he scared the living shit out of her. Yet, there was something.

Linda. Paige fired a quick message off to Mariah at the lab.

Please put a rush on the DNA for the hair on the necklace and the hair that came to you today from my crime scene. IMPORTANT!

Paige felt a small pang of jealousy toward Linda, but she was thankful for a few quiet moments alone. She wished she could settle in and do her favorite things. Drink coffee and take a bubble bath.

Closing her eyes, she imagined drawing her bath, stepping in and sliding down into the water so she could lay in the tub, letting the warmth and the lavender bubble bath scent relax her as much as possible.

Her eyes shot open, she held up her phone and looked at the picture of the Reader. If each Reader had to die to fulfill the prophecy, Sampson had to be the first to go. This woman wreaked more havoc than Paige's brother Shepherd. At least Shepherd was only focused on her and Junna. He had controlled a young girl, Hannah, to get close to them. But Sampson, on the other hand, controlled many people and many people died doing her bidding. And from all indications, because she was nothing more than pissed off. Paige swallowed hard. Many people died at the hand of the Hand of God, too.

Paige struggled to come to grips with that. She had to remind herself it was in self-defense, of himself and others. Yet Victor's rage toward Sampson, wanting to kill her in revenge, was not self-defense. Victor was full of rage. And rage was something she was beginning to understand. That scared her. How could she even be attracted to him? She couldn't shake it. She felt connected to him somehow.

Would God really sanction such behavior? Or did Victor get some sort of free pass? Would he really just kill to set things right? It was true the wrathful God of the Old Testament punished the wicked in many ways. The total destruction of the Great Flood. The burning of Sodom and Gomorrah. Victor was dealing out the same kind of Old Testament justice.

Then again, would Paige kill when the time came to do so? That was the task set before her. A prophecy she had to fulfill. The Readers would have to die. Paige would have to die. The weight of the events unfolding around her pressed down on her making her feel like she could sink through the concrete floor and down through the earth. Every ounce of her wished she could.

Paige shook the thoughts from her head and rubbed the Abet stone she still was wearing. Victor had taken his stone back from Caleb as she felt safe enough Sampson wouldn't use Caleb again. He'd served his purpose even though it failed. Besides, she had asked Visette to put a protective spell around him. Visette cast it through her Abet stone. It had to work, right? They didn't have enough to give one to everyone. It would have to be enough.

Paige took a long, deep breath. Don't think. Just rest. Just relax. Just clear the mind. She felt like she was in a nightmare, screaming, but no one could hear her. And a demon was coming.

Victor's voice broker her train of thought. "You okay there, Paige?"

She only nodded and walked away from him to watch

Visette and wonder what she might be able to do to help. Visette handed her a piece of white chalk. "Here, draw a circle, about ten feet in diameter. Then take the salt and pour a solid line of it all around the circumference. I have four more boxes of salt in my bag. Use it all."

Paige nodded and went to work.

―――――

Victor glanced around the large main room and pictured old steam trains being brought into the building and the men who worked on them. Constructing the rails from the East Coast to the West Coast is what allowed the United States of America to flourish. Seeing how far the old building had deteriorated made him sad. While at the University of Kentucky, he majored in history, and it got to him when he saw any part of it pass into nothingness.

He gave himself a mental slap and turned to the rest of their motley crew.

"Here is where we make our stand. To start, Captain, I want you up there." Victor pointed to a walkway which ran the circumference of the building. "I want you to take the high ground and use your sniper rifle to punish those down here. If it gets hairy down here, then feel free to come down and join in hand to hand. But I want you to be out of ammo when you do."

"Roger that," Hawkins said as he walked over to a rickety set of stairs and made his way to the upper level to take his position.

"Tank, I want you and your boys to drag some of the old wooden pallets and other debris to make three crossfire shooting positions. One there, there and there." Victor pointed to three positions where, when the bikers were prepared, would allow them to cover the main entrance to the depot with great shooting angles.

Tank said, "We will cut the mother fuckers to fucking ribbons."

"Fuck yeah," said Colby.

"Damn straight," said Jack.

"You boys have the night vision goggles and com links I gave you?"

Tank pointed to his weapons bag. "I got 'em. Don't worry about us."

And the three men went to get their spots ready.

"What about me?" Tom asked.

"I want you to set up a position near Paige and Visette. If anything gets by us, you will be their only defense while they are performing the spell."

The officer nodded and went to set up his own spot for the coming battle.

"And you and I, Hand of God? What will we do?" asked Elizabeth.

"You and I are the roamers. We go where we are needed and kill every son-of-a-bitch we find."

"So it shall be said, so it shall be done," she said, and wandered off to look around the depot.

It wasn't long and he saw everyone was ready. He did a com link check and each person replied when their names were called. They were as prepared as they were going to be. He went to Visette and waited for her to pause long enough in her preparations to notice him. She motioned him close.

He said, "We are ready. How about you?"

"Very close. Close enough to bring the demon to us. First, I must have your Abet Stone. We need to make a mental connection between you and the demon."

Victor slipped the stone from around his neck and handed

it to the witch. Then she retrieved the bowl holding his blood and held it in both hands while she softly chanted a spell. At the same time, she dipped an index finger into the blood and drew a symbol on his forehead. With a final whispered word, she stepped close, pursed her lips and blew softly on the blood and his world exploded.

The force of the connection between himself and the demon was immediate and crushing. One moment he was concentrating on what Visette was doing and the next Aamon was there. The demon flooded his consciousness and tried to overwhelm him, to control him. The vastness of the demon's existence and the power of his will were like nothing Victor ever felt in his life. And he knew if he lost this battle with the demon for control of his mind, he was done for, and it terrified him.

Then the lizard part of his brain, much like it did when confronting the unknown at the cabin and his battle with the Gray Man, responded and the terror was replaced by a towering anger, and he felt his mental defenses harden. He would be damned if he would let this Hellspawn beat him. He was not some guy off the street, someone easy to take down and kill. He was the Hand of God, God's warrior.

He focused every ounce of mental energy he possessed to a hard point and used it to send his thoughts against the demon and said, "I told you I would rip off your arms and then beat you to death with them. And that's what I plan to do, asshole. Come to me, if you dare, and I will destroy you."

He was rewarded with a shout of rage and a simple reply, "I come and I bring death."

"Whatever, dude," Victor sent back and then found he was able to relegate the demon to a small area of his consciousness, much like a small room. He mentally shut the door on the room and the demon continued to rage but it was like a small itch at the back of his brain.

He realized he had closed his eyes and he opened them to see Visette and Paige both staring at him, worry clear on their faces. He smiled at them and said, "Congrats. Your spell worked. He's coming. And he's royally pissed at having to do so."

Visette released a breath she was holding and said, "We will be ready."

He was going to say something else when Hawkins yelled, "McCain, they're here."

He turned and mumbled, "That was quick."

It only took a moment for him to realize it wasn't the demon, unless they all figured out how to drive cars. Dozens of headlights swung into view outside the depot, their lights casting crazy shadows around the depot through the broken windows. Victor heard dozens of people outside and just as many car doors opening and closing.

Victor reached into his weapons bag and took out his night vision LDRs and slipped them on. He tapped his com link and said, "Hawkins, do you have eagle eyes on the targets?

"Roger that. I'm guessing about forty guys and... wait a sec... some humongously large dogs."

Bloody hell. "Not dogs," Victor said through the com link. "Hellhounds. Careful guys. Not only are they huge but some of them drip acid when they bite you."

"Now you're talking," said either Jack or Colby. He couldn't tell which. Pure insanity.

Tank asked, "Did you bring your flamethrower to melt the pooches?"

"I have it," Victor said, "but I don't dare put it on while there are bullets flying around. Propane tanks and bullets don't go well together."

Hawkins asked from above them, "Want me to light a few of them up?"

"Feel free to terminate with extreme prejudice."

"Roger that."

And then one of the Army's top snipers went to work.

Chapter Forty-Six

Snipers fire literally tens of thousands of rounds to hone their craft. For them, the art of the long-range kill is as automatic as it would be for a regular person to push the button on their fob to lock their cars. Hawkins was not simply a sniper. He was one of the best the Army ever trained.

When he rose into one of the windows completely free of glass, shooting the goons of the Church of the Light Reclaimed at a distance of one-hundred feet was something he could do in his sleep. Victor watched through a small hole in the wall as Hawkins snapped off five quick shots and Victor saw five guys go down. Permanently.

He ducked down as the remaining Church mercenaries returned fire, their bullets mostly hitting the stone wall of the depot, with a few rounds making it through the windows and burying themselves in the ceiling. Hawkins ejected the magazine and loaded another in the rifle, as snipers usually use a small magazine to make it easy to lay low and still. Hawkins used one which held five.

Victor glanced around the room and saw that the bikers

and Tom were ready, as Paige and Visette continued to prepare the spell for the time when Aamon made his appearance. The one person he didn't see was Elizabeth, but he knew she would be ready when the time came.

Hawkins was once again ready and he crab crawled down the walkway another twenty feet or so, rose into a kneeling position next to the window, drew in a long breath and let it out slow and steady, and then swung into the window and fired another five shots faster than Victor was able to think it. Five more down.

This time the return fire was quicker and more on target. Several bullets hit the windowsill next to Hawkins and before he was able to drop down, a large splinter of wood blew off and buried in his cheek. He winced as he pulled the splinter out and tossed it to the ground. Then he once again ejected the magazine and loaded a new one. One tough dude.

There was continuous shouting outside and Victor knew the other men would be inside in short order. He shouted, "Be ready. Here they come."

The main entrance to the depot was thrown open and he saw two objects thrown inside. Flash bangs. He was about to shout a warning when Elizabeth darted into view, corralled both grenades and then laid down on top of them. The twin explosions were strong enough to lift her body off the ground and she let out a moan, but she used her supernaturally enhanced body to mute the effect of the grenades.

When she rose to run out of the way, Victor saw a huge chunk of her stomach was simply pulverized. He knew she would regenerate the wound and heal up, given time, but it had to hurt like a son-of-a-bitch.

He didn't have time to worry about her as right behind the grenades, about a dozen Church mercs stormed inside and then things got incredibly loud as Tank, Jack and Colby opened up. Tank cut loose with a Mossberg Tactical Shotgun from center position, each round booming in the vastness of the depot. Flanked on either side, Colby and Jack let it rip with the semi-automatic choice of bad guys everywhere, the AR-15.

It took only seconds for the three men to cut down the Church goons and litter the floor with dead and dying men. The only one of the good guys to be hit was Jack, who was grazed in the left shoulder by a stray round. "Jesus," he said. "It's not bad but it burns like Hell."

From the shadows Elizabeth said, "I promise you, it does not."

Each of the men were reloading when the two hellhounds charged into the building, moving with a speed any cheetah would envy. The first one through the door made a beeline for Jack, smelling the blood of the biker with its own supernaturally hyped sense of smell. The second headed straight for Tank.

Neither man had yet to fully reload, with Tank in the middle of pushing shells into his shotgun and Jack fumbling his attempt to shove in a new magazine for his AR-15. Jack screamed as the hellhound hurtled the pile of wooden pallets he was standing behind. The huge beast snapped its large jaws into the side of his neck and took the big man to the ground.

Colby screamed his brother's name and raced to his aid. He dropped the AR-15 on the ground, hefted the battle axe and charged the nightmarish creature. To Victor, he looked like an ancient Viking come to life, with his black beard, massive shoulders and the axe held high.

In his peripheral vision he saw Colby swing the axe in a mighty arc and bury it deep into the back of the hellhound. And that was all he saw, as he found himself holding his katana, the blade glowing blue in the darkness, and coming to Tank's defense.

Tank might be a large man, but he can move with the deftness of a much smaller man when the need called for it. And this was one of those times. He timed the leap of the hellhound and as it rose to grab him by the neck, Tank dove down under it and drove the stock of the shotgun into the beast's belly.

The creature let out a bellow, landed and turned around, only to find Victor standing between it and its prey. Victor felt the katana warm in his grip and the warmness flowed up his arms until it enveloped his whole body. Then the sword was moving in forms and defenses not of his making, but of a dead Samurai warrior.

Every time the hellhound lunged at him, Victor moved out of the way with the grace of a ballerina. And each time, Victor flicked the sword and cut the hellhound in a new spot. The beast's growls grew in fury each time it missed biting its tormentor and the howls of pain louder with each new cut. Soon there were cuts all over the creature's body and it started to slow. Victor's mind followed all this like a spectator inside his own head and the sword's chanting not only returned but intensified and he felt his bloodlust rise.

With a final flourish, Victor feinted with the katana and when the beast made a final desperate attack, he spun behind the hellhound and drove the blade deep down at the base of the creature's skull, severing its spinal cord. The hellhound died instantly.

His desire for more blood to spill made him turn to take on the other hellhound but saw it was also down, cut into several pieces by Colby and his battle axe. The biker sat on the ground, covered in blood Victor hoped was not his and held his brother's lifeless body in his arms, his throat torn out by the hellhound. Colby wept silently and rocked back and forth, his eyes closed.

Victor spun on Tank, his sword held high, and the burly biker fell backwards to the ground and tried to scramble away with his shotgun pointed at Victor's chest. He said, "Hold on there, McCain. What the hell?"

Victor pulled up short and fought to wrest control of his mind from the sword. It was a lot like his mental battle with Aamon, only in this case the sword exerted control with almost no resistance on his part.

Victor lowered the sword with an effort and held it at his side and closed his eyes and mentally to the sword, "Stand down, damn you. I'm in control, not you."

They must all die. They are not worthy of us.

A small part of him agreed and it terrified him.

"I decide who is worthy or not. And if you can't accept that, then by this time tomorrow you will be melted down and poured down a drain, do you hear me?"

The sword said nothing.

"I said, 'do you hear me?' A refusal to answer will bring the same result as defiance."

As you wish. I will do as you ask.

Victor felt the demon he'd stuffed into a little mental room stop its ranting and raving and knew he was privy to the mental conversation between himself and the sword and Victor wondered what Aamon was thinking.

Victor opened his eyes and saw Tank was on his feet, the shotgun still pointed at him. Victor sheathed the sword and held up his hands. "My apologies, Tank. I got caught up in the moment."

Tank lowered the shotgun, but Victor noticed not all the way. "First off," the biker asked, "when did you learn to fight like Tinkerbell with a sword, and when did you learn to speak Japanese?"

"Japanese? The only Japanese I know is Shogun. That's it."

"I'm telling you, you were shouting in Japanese."

From the walkway above them Hawkins said, "He's right. You were. You started with "Tenno Heika Banzai", long live the emperor, then followed with a war chant too fast for me to try and keep up. But it was for sure Asian."

Victor glanced over at Paige, Visette and Tom and all three were staring at him. Victor turned to Tank and said, "I guess I've been watching too many samurai movies lately."

Elizabeth walked slowly out of the darkness and into the light of the spell candles. "You are so full of shit, Hand of God. That was Muramasa's sword talking through you. It is said each of his swords possessed part of his soul. You are treading a dangerous path, Victor."

Before he could respond, they heard the opening and closing of car doors, the starting of engines and cars tearing away from the building. Hawkins went and carefully stuck his head around a window to find out what was going on.

"It would seem the remaining members of the Church of the Light Reclaimed have decided retreat is the better part of valor."

Victor drew in a deep breath and let it out slowly. "Good. Aamon should be here any moment." To Visette he asked, "Are you ready?"

"Almost. Another minute or so," she replied.

He walked and squatted next to Colby. "I'm sorry about your brother."

Colby nodded and then laid his brother carefully down on the concrete floor and stood. Victor stood as well. Colby said, "He went down fighting, and that's all he ever wanted to do."

The large man bent over and picked up his ax, rested it on

his shoulder, and said to Victor, "That was the first wave. Demons will be next?"

Victor nodded. "At least one. Time to cast a badass spell."

———

Paige dropped the last of the salt and Visette began to pace around the circle Paige had drawn on the cold floor. She placed four candles along the edge of the circle along with a bowl of water. She then placed the bottle, a cord of twine, a wrapping made of blue and green glass interlaced with small mirrors in the center of the circle. She then put a long piece of red yarn in her pocket. To Paige, the whole scene was peculiar.

Visette said, "We are ready, Victor. We need as many of you in the circle as possible."

"Got it. Hawkins, come on down."

Elizabeth said, "I will not be one of those people. Witchcraft is too close to the work of my former master."

"No worries," Victor said. "Tank, you, Hawkins and Tom jump in the circle and lend a hand."

"No way, McCain. I'm staying out here in case there's a fight."

"And I need you in there in case the fight appears inside the circle. If Visette loses control, then all hell, quite literally, will take place right in front of you."

The biker swore a few times and then said, "Fine. But if I think you guys need my help, I'm jumping in and leaving the circle. You hear me?"

Victor nodded. "I hear ya. I think Elizabeth and Oden here," as Victor pointed to Colby, "and I will be okay."

"Hawkins offered Victor his sniper rifle. "Want this?"

"Thanks, but I've got something better for this fight."

Victor walked over to his weapons bag and pulled out

the flame thrower. He slipped the katana belt off and strapped on the flamethrower. Once all the straps were situated, he picked up the katana and slung the belt over his shoulder.

Visette motioned Paige, Tom, Tank and Hawkins to join her inside the circle, and then she began to cast her spell. "I call upon the powers of the North and all the spiritual and elemental beings associated with the powers of the earth to protect the performance of this rite."

Slowly Visette turned toward the next candle and lit it. "I call upon the powers of the East and all the spiritual and elemental beings associated with the power of air to protect the performance of this rite..." Visette continued to call the rest. "About us, below us, all around us, this sphere encloses about us while we perform this magick rite. Protect us, dear ones. Keep us safe from the evil that comes our way."

After the candles were lit, Visette almost sang, "Divine Goddess and Gods, angels, elementals and spirit guides, I thank you for the beautiful energy of white love and healing you shine upon us. I ask for your help in releasing all that does not have our highest good in mind. I ask you help guide us with cleansing this space so that only beings of light and love may enter here with this demon. I ask to receive a beautiful healing white light of protection and blessings as we trap Aamon for all eternity. Protect us from any and all harm. Allow not our thoughts to escape this circle nor allow anyone else's to enter. For this, I give my heartfelt thanks."

Visette beckoned the mist from the bowl to swirl and fill the room. It moved around the circle of chalk and salt, forming a barely visible shield around them.

"In this night ... with all our might ... give us vision ... give us sight ... In the light of the moon ... within the circle of four ...... come to us power to open the door ... between this realm and the one we cannot see … harm no one and mote it be."

Visette and Paige repeated the chant in unison three times before they closed their eyes. They both took on a light blue glow. Visette leaned over and placed the bottle in the middle of the circle. It seemed to throb in the faint light of the candles. The mirrors on the outside of the bottle reflected the candles so the entire room seemed to sparkle with little lights.

Paige watched Visette take a moment to clear her mind. She spoke to the people inside the circle. "This is the hardest part of any binding spell. We will have to infuse the item to represent Aamon. This means clearing your mind of everything else, as much as possible or the binding will not be as successful or possibly not work at all."

Visette took a deep breath and continued. "Don't focus on the reason we want to bind him. Focus on him. Have a clear image of his raven's head in your mind's eye.

Paige closed her eyes and imagined the demon. She drew the image in her mind much like Victor managed to draw Sampson's image on the page of the notebook. Her thoughts went deeper and deeper until she felt as if the demon was breathing right in her face.

She opened her eyes. Visette looked up at her. "Any moment, now. Be ready."

Everyone took on a battle stance that reminded Paige of a Marvel's Avengers' movie poster. All turning back-to-back, looking around. Ready to pounce on anything that moved.

Nothing. Nothing at all.

The candle at the South location started to flicker. Paige thought it might be a slight breeze. Then the one at the West location joined in the dance. Everyone watched as the two flames danced about. Almost mesmerizing. Then the North and East flames joined in. Each flame getting larger and larger.

Causing the candles to burn up more quickly. Smoke started to swirl around the circle, still no one moved. They barely breathed.

"He's coming," Visette said as she took the cord she had tied around her waist. She wrapped it tightly around the bottle. As she wrapped the bottle she spoke firmly,

I bind you Aamon,
I bind you from doing harm.
By the goddess and this charm,
You will do no harm.
So mote it be.

Visette bent over, picked up the bottle and took it to the candle in the North's position and singed it slightly with the flame of the candle. She then immediately dipped it into the water to prevent the cord from unbinding. She then returned the bottle to the center of the room.

The bottle was now ready and with Visette visibly exhausted, she took a strand of red yarn she held in her pocket and gathered her strength and continued to chant.

With the strand of the crimes
of your own design
I bind your evil
Three times, seven times.

I bind you with your own
Evil Intents Within

And so let this magick
Unfold And spin

She tied each end of the yarn with three secure knots and sealed the spell.

Goddess of bleakest night
Send our enemy and end our plight
Burn them in thy sacred fires
And hold them deep within the pyre!

Everyone waited as the candles slowed their dance.

"Did it work? Was it that easy?" Tank asked.

Visette shook her head. Just as she opened her mouth to speak, a puff of hot air filled the circle like a balloon. The candles went out and so did their Maglites.

It was completely dark.

Visette began again.

I bind you Aamon,
I bind you from doing harm.
By the goddess and this charm,
You will do no harm.

. . .

Something hard hit Tank on the head and he nearly went down. He swore he could see stars as he grasped his shotgun tightly. "He's here! But where? I can't see."

Visette waved her hand in the air and immediately all the candles lit again. Just outside the circle, surrounding them, there was a hoard of demons.

Paige could hear a voice as if it were circling her. It repeated, "You suck. Everyone hates you and thinks you're a fucking loser. You don't deserve to be alive. You could save the world if you would just die. Now go kill yourself like the worthless piece of shit you are."

She felt the hand on her gun try and turn toward her head. She fought back. It was strong. She felt the stone burn her skin through her clothing. "No!" Paige said out loud.

"You are a fucking loser," the voice repeated. All at once, she envisioned Shepherd standing over her all those years before. Watching as she killed cats at his bidding. She remembered how it felt to be controlled by him.

"No!" She said again more loudly and shook her head. The voice stopped as she felt the air move away from her and towards Tom. "Tom, he's coming toward you."

"I, I can't see anything," Tom's voice shook.

Dark figures emerged along the outside of the circle, barely visible as if their bodies were made of a finer material than anything else ever seen. Hundreds of them. Most of them resembled birds. Winged beings with red eyes glowing dimly in the dark.

One of the larger demons moved closer to the shield protecting them. His head was large and looked like a lion. His lips curled and revealed teeth that looked like that of a donkey. His chest was bare, but he had a hairy body, and his hands were stained with blood. Long fingers and fingernails curled around his large hands. His legs bent like that of a satyr.

Visette spoke again. This time more forcefully.

I bind you Aamon,
  I bind you from doing harm.
  By the goddess and this charm,
  You will do no harm.
  So mote it be.

From somewhere inside the depot, the demon Aamon laughed.

Another large demon approached the circle. He had the face of a dog with abnormally bulging eyes. Instead of fur, he had a scaly body like a lizard and a large snake-headed penis that writhed in front of him. His hands were perched on wings like a bat and had the talons of a bird. He placed his hand on the protective shield. It ripped like a sword went through a thin lace curtain.

And then Hell on Earth really broke out.

Chapter Forty-Seven

Victor positioned Elizabeth and Colby in opposite corners of the main room of the depot, while he took another corner. The three of them tried to watch the room at the same time they watched Visette cast the binding spell. He kept the barrel of the flame thrower up and ready, his finger resting next to the twin triggers, one to send the propane down the barrel and the other to light it up.

He watched Paige standing across from Visette, at times joining in on the spell chanting and other times watching intently. He found himself watching how she moved, how she talked, and he was mesmerized. She was beautiful, sure, but there was more to it than that. Maybe it was the fact she was different, like he was.

He shook his head and told himself to give it a rest and concentrate on the task at hand. Damn love-struck schoolboy indeed. He started to laugh but stopped when all the candles went out at once. He scanned the room with his LIDAR goggles and saw Elizabeth and Colby both tense, but nothing else. Then Visette made a motion with her hand and the candles once again came to life. And when they did, the room was full of demons. One moment the area was empty, the next breath it was full of demons. There were fifty at least, with two much larger than the rest. One had the head of a dog, the other a lion and both were moving towards the spell casters.

And then from somewhere deeper in the room he heard a laugh. Aamon.

He tapped his com link and said, "Elizabeth and Colby. Hit the two big ones. I'll flame the riff-raff."

Victor waited only long enough for the Infernal Lord and the biker to move towards the candles and then he opened up with the flamethrower. One of the things the denizens feared more than anything short of Satan himself, was fire. It seems spending an eternity in Hell makes fire on the top of your hate list.

He shouted, "Hey birdbrains, over here."

A large group turned to face him and then they disappeared in the plume of fire pouring out of the flamethrower. The fire plume was about the size of a semi-truck trailer and in an instant dozens of demons were turned into crispy critters. They howled first with rage, then with terror, then pain.

Several of the demons tried to fly over the top of the fire and it forced him to raise the flamethrower's barrel higher to fry their asses. The moment he did, something grabbed the tanks of the flamethrower and threw him hard against the wall behind him. When this happened, instead of simply catching the flying demons, the fire plume strafed the ceiling. And while the walls might be made of stone, the rafters and roof were made of wood. Old, dry wood. The flames took hold in several small spots, and then the spots grew.

The force of being thrown into the wall knocked the air from his lungs. He laid there for a moment, looked up and realized he just set the roof on fire.

Great.

Yet that was not his more immediate problem. Towering in front of him was Aamon, demon and a captain of Hell. The leader of an entire legion of demons, in full demon form, his raven head with wolf's teeth on full display.

"It is time for you to die, Spear of Uriel."

Victor shrugged off the flamethrower and let it slip to the ground. Fireworks are great against lesser demons, but the flames are no concern for the more badass denizens of Hell.

He stood wearily and unsheathed the katana, the blade in full blue blaze mode. In his mind, the blade spoke to him.

Is this one worthy of death?

Despite being in a burning building, with a major frickin' demon in front of him, his friends in danger of losing their lives and his own death more likely than not, Victor laughed.

He thought back, "Yeah. This one is worthy of death. Have at it."

He once again felt the warmth of the blade flow deep down into every fiber of his body and the weariness fell away. His movements became fluid and easy. He was ready.

To the demon he said, "Time to die, Mr. Bond."

Aamon cocked his head to the side, as a real raven might do, and said, "That is not my name, human."

Victor guessed they didn't get James Bond humor in Hell. Such is life.

"Whatever. It means I'm going to kick your ass."

Aamon responded by saying a word he didn't know and then a flaming sword appeared in his hand. The flames flicked between a red and a blue and the blade was several inches longer than his own blade. The demon was about a half foot taller than he was and it gave him a longer reach.

Victor asked the blade, "Have you got this?"

It is a good day to die.

"A little more confidence please."

Bonzai!

And with that, Victor McCain, the Hand of God, went to war with a demon.

Paige watched the demon rip apart the shield spell like it was made of tissue paper and she knew it would kill them all if they gave it half the chance. Without even knowing if it was possible, her mind flew to the Collective Conscious, and she searched for anything thinking about her and it was there. The demon's mind was there. She knew what it was the second her mind found it. First coyotes, and now demons. Paige wondered if the other Readers were able to do such a thing.

Unlike the animals, the demon's mind was not made up of images. Nor was it made of words in thoughts like a human. Instead, it was filled with emotions. Fear. Terror. Anger. Betrayal. Excitement. Bloodlust. Paige had never felt emotions in the Collective Conscious before. It wasn't supposed to be possible. Yet, she wondered why demons had emotions at all.

Without thinking about it she knew it made sense. A being who spent their entire existence in Hell, would not be thinking about rainbows and unicorns. There would be no happy emotions like love or loyalty, friendship or humility. They were consumed with all that was negative. It was so strong. She couldn't help but feel it.

What there was, though, was something she could work with. She seized on betrayal and sent the thought into the demon's consciousness that the demons behind him were going to betray it and attack it from behind. They wanted to take over his position in Hell. To bring him down.

She saw the creature's bug eyes get even larger and it

wheeled around and roared in fear and struck out at the two closest winged demons. It snatched each one by the throat using the claws at the end of its wing. And with two quick movements, snapped their necks. Without stopping, it then moved on to the next demon and attacked it the same way. Before long, the demons were attacking the dog headed one in mass. They were, for the moment, not a problem.

She returned to the spell casting and prayed they would finish in time.

———

Elizabeth searched the area around her and saw a piece of rebar sticking out of the wall. She seized the metal in both hands and yanked it out of the wall and saw it was about four feet long. It would do.

She saw with satisfaction Victor was laying waste to the mass of demons using fire and not Muramasa's katana. There would come a time soon when she would need to take the sword from him for his own good. If he was not careful, he would suffer the same fate as the former Infernal Lord and go mad. Today, however, was not that day.

She strode towards the lion headed demon but was intercepted by a group of four lesser demons. They spread out to block her path and one of them hissed at her and said, "The Lord of Light wants you back in Hell, bitch. He has great plans for causing you pain and agony."

Much like Victor could sense a Fallen Angel, demons could sense an Infernal Lord and she knew every one of them in this room would want to be the one to kill her on this plane of existence and to send to her punishment with Lucifer. It would be their undoing.

"You first," she said.

Her attack was as brutal as it was fast. She spun the rebar in one hand like a baton, drawing their attention and then spun, low and hard. The rebar caught the first demon in the midsection and the force of the blow broke its spine and sent it flying into one of the others, knocking it backwards. She reversed and drove her fingernails deep into the chest of the third one, her nails as sharp and hard as a bear's claw. She seized the demon's heart and ripped it from his chest, still beating. The fourth demon, seeing this, stood frozen in place and it was the last mistake it would ever make.

With a flick of her wrist, she drove the rebar through one of the demon's eyes and out the other side of his head. It fell to the floor of the depot, spasmed, and then was still. She moved towards the demon left before her. It screamed and fled away, knocking aside other demons to get away from the Infernal Lord. She let it go and turned her attention to the demon with the lion's head.

Tank slowed the thing by emptying his shotgun into the creature's body and it was forced backwards with each shot. But shooting a demon was not the way to kill one. She took one huge step and then leaped into the air and covered thirty feet in one jump. She came down and drove the rebar into the top of the lion's mane of hair, the metal piercing the thing's brain. The force of the attack took the demon to the ground. She yanked the metal out of the creature's skull and with several swings, severed the demon's head.

Tank said, "Oh my God, Lizzy. Thank you."

She winked at him and said, "Not God, lover boy. I'm better."

She glanced at the ceiling and noticed it was on fire and the fire was spreading fast.

She said, "If you guys don't bottle up Aamon in the next minute or so, then you will never do it."

Tank followed her gaze up and said, "Holy shit, that's not good."

————

Colby knew he was about to die. Victor may have cleared out a huge swath of demons, but there were too many left. He waded into a large group of them and laid waste with his axe. He cut several clean in half, others lost wings. But the blows from the demons started to land more often than they missed. Their claws felt as tough as diamonds and they ripped huge gouges on his arms, back and legs.

The area around Colby was slick with blood. He began to tire from the fighting but managed to hack off the head of a larger demon. He over swung and slipped to one knee. The moment he did so, several demons slammed into him, driving him to the ground. He tried to roll over, but the mass of demons pinned him on the floor.

One of the demons drew a fingernail across his neck and sliced him open as easily as a surgeon's scalpel. The thing leaned down and hissed in his ear, "I will drink your blood before I kill you, mortal."

Colby felt the rough texture of the demon's tongue as it ran across the wound on his neck. Colby knew it was time to take out as many of them as he could. He managed to get his hand inside his front jeans pocket and wrap his fingers around one of the things he took from Victor's weapons stash in his trunk: an M67 grenade.

He brought the grenade to his teeth and pulled the pin. With a mighty effort he heaved up one shoulder and snaked his arm around the demon's own neck and pulled his face close to his own.

"Eat shit and die, mother fucker," Colby snarled.

He released the pin and then shoved the grenade into the mouth of the demon, clamping his hand under the thing's chin and holding his mouth closed. Colby was laughing when the grenade went off.

———

A huge explosion rocked the room where Colby was fighting a group of demons and Paige barely noticed. She stood in awe and watched the sword fight between Victor's blue blade and Aamon's flaming sword. She was a huge fan of fantasy movies and particularly loved any which involved sword play. The fight in the *Princess Bride* between Wesley and Inigo was one of her favorites. And watching Victor's sword play, he was better than any she had ever seen. Despite his massive size he made thrusts and parries any sword master would be hard pressed to make. He was perhaps, in this moment, the best swordsman on the planet.

And he was losing.

Aamon seemed to be almost toying with Victor. He parried every attack the bounty hunter made, and constantly moved, making Victor do the same, and Paige saw Victor was getting tired. The demon's superior strength was also wearing him down.

While she watched, Aamon changed tactics and instead of moving, the demon slammed the fire sword down in great overhead swings. Victor parried the best he could, but one parry was a fraction of a second too late and the demon's sword slipped past the move and nicked Victor in the shoulder.

While he did not yell out in pain, it was evident on his face how much the blow hurt, and Paige knew he would not last much longer. She whirled to Visette and said, "You have to do it now. Now!"

Visette stepped up next to her and handed her the bottle to be used to trap the demon. In her other hand she held the bowl containing Victor's blood. She said to Paige, "Hold the bottle close, please."

Paige did as she asked and held the bottle next to the bowl. Visette then closed her eyes and chanted:

Powers of the wind surround him
  I ask for the gift of invisibility
  When those who look turn around
  His face, his body can't be found
  In this place he will no longer be
  To anyone with that can see
  So mote it be

On the last word she flung her arm towards Victor, her hand outstretched spread wide and then from one heartbeat to the next, Victor disappeared. Aamon, his blade raised high for a killing blow bellowed in rage and began to search the area for the Hand of God. Visette then dipped a finger into the bowl of blood until the tip was covered. She moved the finger over the bottle and one single drop of blood fell inside and the world changed.

———

Victor felt the heat of the flame sear the flesh on his shoulder, the pain immense and all consuming. He bit back a scream, not wanting to give the Hellspawn the satisfaction of knowing how much it hurt. He knew Aamon was going to beat him from sheer strength. He searched his mind trying to come up with a way out but found none.

He decided if he was going to die, then so be it. It was time to go full kamikaze on his ass and do his best to wound the demon. And with any luck, Elizabeth and the rest would finish him off.

He began to make a feint when an opaque wall appeared between himself and Aamon. Through it he saw the demon bellow in rage and start to search for him, looking from side to side.

What the bloody hell?

He turned and saw Visette with her hand pointed at him and knew this was her work. Somehow, she'd made him invisible to the demon. How long the spell would last, Victor had no way of knowing. He took the moment to catch his breath and then saw Visette dip a finger into the same bowl she kept his blood and he saw a single drop of blood drip into the bottle.

Aamon's reaction was immediate and intense. His raven eyes went wide and then he screamed in rage and then he...simply wasn't there. And it wasn't only him. There was not a single demon left in the depot. They were all gone.

He stepped towards Paige and Visette and the opaque wall vanished. He watched Visette pull a stopper out of a pocket on her dress and set it firmly into the bottle. Then she slipped the bottle into her pocket.

Victor asked, "Is that it? Is Aamon in the bottle?"

She nodded. "He is, Hand of God."

Victor stepped close, took her face in his hands and kissed her on the lips and then stood back and laughed.

"You're welcome," Visette said.

Everyone gathered around her, and Elizabeth said, "Perhaps witchcraft is not bad after all."

"Tom pointed to the ceiling and said, "Uh, guys? We need to get out of here."

Victor saw he was right as more than half the roof was engulfed in flames and pieces were beginning to crash down to the floor. "Gather up your stuff quickly and let's vamanos."

Tank asked, "What about Jack and Colby's bodies?"

"No time," Victor said. "Lord's will be done."

Tank shook his head. "Man, getting guys to help you in the future is going to be harder if we keep getting them all killed."

Victor couldn't argue with that, so he didn't.

While he and his friends rushed from the burning building, he thought to himself, "Demon down. Reader next."

And he knew he was going to kill her. If it was the last thing he did on Earth.

Chapter Forty-Eight

They regrouped at the Riverside Inn. Tom was the only one who went straight home to bed due to the fact he was supposed to run a task force meeting at seven in the morning. The rest of them sat around a huge table with the news on the screen. The fire at the old train depot was all over the news. According to reports the fire burned so hot it completely incinerated everything inside and the stone walls collapsed in on themselves. The fire department said there were no reported casualties, though one firefighter was being treated for smoke inhalation.

Paige asked Victor, "The fire seems to have burned hotter than one would expect. Was that divine intervention?"

Victor waved one hand back and forth. "Maybe. I know I never have to worry about being arrested for Hand of God business. There's always a chance Uriel decided to help out and add some divine jet fuel to the fire." He then pointed to the bottle sitting in the center of the table. "And you're telling me Aamon is actually inside this thing?"

Visette nodded. "Not only him, but all the demons left

standing in the depot. Keep in mind, as I told you, it is not like they flew down into the bottle. They teleported to the spot where they thought you were hiding. Think of it like a pocket dimension Venus Fly Trap."

Hawkins shook his head in disbelief. "And now what do you do with it?"

Visette said, "I will drape it in a covering of tiny mirrors, then bury it."

"Where?" asked Victor.

"I think you not knowing is better. I will find a spot near running water then bury it deep. He will be trapped for eternity inside the bottle."

"Fair enough. I'd still like to know how Hawkins' granddad did it way back when. There's no mention he was working with a witch, is there?"

Hawkins said, "None at all. I'm guessing we'll never know."

Elizabeth yawned and said, "Fine. Demon is trapped. Day is saved. Time for bed. Let us go Cleatus."

Tank slapped the table with a large hand and said, "I can't think of a better way to celebrate." He stood up and said to the others, "The rest of you, get the hell out of here and go home."

Victor said, "Believe me, I know I could sleep for weeks. Let's all reconnect tomorrow and figure out what we're going to do about Sampson."

Victor, Paige, Visette and Hawkins walked out into the cold night air. Hawkins waved goodnight to Paige, got into his car and left. Victor walked Paige and Visette to their own car. Visette got in the passenger side and Paige turned to Victor before getting in. He shoved his hands in his pockets.

"It was a close thing tonight. You did good," he said.

Paige offered him a weary smile and said, "High praise from the Hand of God."

"Truth from a friend."

"Is this what your life is like all the time?"

He nodded. "Pretty much. Not quite always this intense, but kind of par for the course."

"I don't know how you do it," she said.

"Sister, it's one day at a time. That's all I can do."

She nodded agreement and then she did something that caught him completely by surprise. She stepped in close, grabbed the front of his coat in each hand, pulled him close and kissed him. Her lips were warm, and he returned the kiss. Then she broke it off, got in her car and drove away.

He stood there for a few more moments, cleared his mind and simply stared off into the darkness. He wasn't sure how long he stood there, but it started to snow and it broke the moment. Victor knew he needed to find Linda and figure things out. His life always seemed to be complicated and there was no doubt a large reason why was his own fault.

The wind picked up and the snow started to fall hard enough his beard was covered in seconds. From the fire of the train depot to the snow of a biker parking lot. If God was sending him a message, he wasn't sure what it was. Well, he knew one for sure: get the hell out of the snow.

Victor walked to his car, got in and drove to his room at the Derby City Mission. He spent part of the trip thinking about how close he came to finding out if he would go to Heaven or Hell. He spent the rest of the trip thinking about police detectives.

Bloody hell.

———

Paige woke up with the sunrise, the light bringing her out of a deep sleep. She thought when she went to bed the night before she would have bet she would never fall asleep. And she would have lost the bet, as she was dead to the world the moment her head hit the pillow.

She thought for a second and tried to catch the wisp of a dream she was having. She knew Victor was in it and so was Sampson. She could not be sure, but it felt like it was not a dream she would want to remember, and she let it go.

She got out of bed and took a long, hot shower and did her best to get the bounty hunter out of her head. She still wasn't sure why she'd kissed him the night before. It simply seemed like the thing to do. She knew he and Linda were a thing but wasn't sure how much of a thing. And Jay. He lay in a hospital bed, in a coma after trying to kill her. Paige believed he was being controlled, but if they made it through this, could their relationship ever return? For some reason, Victor gave her butterflies in the stomach. Men.

She was drying her hair when the phone rang. It was Mariah. She tossed the towel on the vanity and answered. "That was quick," Paige said.

"When you say rush job, it's a rush job. Besides, with the number of bodies piling up I wanted to be fast."

"I'm guessing you got a hit on the DNA?"

"I did. It matches a woman named Dorah Michaels. It was attached to a case in Montana. She was a person of interest in a murder when she simply dropped off the face of the Earth. They never knew if she was involved or another victim. I'll email you the information."

"Great work, Mariah. Thanks."

Paige put the phone down and finished drying her hair when her phone pinged alerting her to a new email and it was the one from Mariah. She thumbed through the file and got the gist of things. A man named Joseph Allen was found murdered in his home outside of Billings, Montana, having been shot several times.

Allen and Michaels were something of a thing at the time, and the week prior to the murder, he and Michaels were seen fighting. They were looking at her because several months before, Allen took out a life insurance policy naming her the beneficiary. When the cops interviewed her, she had a rock-solid alibi but there was always the possibility she hired someone.

Not long after the cops interviewed her, she disappeared and no trace of her was ever found; the murder remained unsolved. Paige knew if Michaels wanted Allen dead, she would have used her powers as a Reader to do the killing. Perhaps this was even her first time.

Paige thumbed to a picture of Michaels' DMV photo and there was a resemblance to the picture they had of Sampson. In Montana, she was a brunette, and she might have had some cosmetic surgery, but it was the same woman. Sampson and Michaels were the same woman. There was no doubt.

She went to the kitchen and sent Tom a text to call Mariah, get the details and to share it with the task force. She got out a bowl, poured some Honey Nut Cheerios, added some milk and sat at her kitchen table. She slowly ate her breakfast and thought about things.

The fact they now knew her real name was great, but it wasn't helpful in tracking her down here in Kentucky. And her defenses were too great for her to track her in the Collective Conscious. Linda, however, was a different matter.

When she finished the cereal, she rested her hands on the table, closed her eyes and tried to relax. She let her mind search the Collective Conscious for anyone thinking about Michaels, the Devil's Mark, inverted crucifix. Then on a whim, she added Victor McCain and it was there. Someone was thinking about Victor. And unlike most times when the image or thought came to her slowly, this time it was immediate. She latched on to the thought and realized they were thinking about him and what she would do when she saw him next.

Paige then saw an image start to appear and she concentrated until she saw the image as clearly as the person thinking it did: Dorah Michaels. The person was talking to Michaels and she saw they were also in a kitchen, but it was larger than hers. She sent a nudge for the person to reveal who they were. She saw a hand reach down and snag a police badge off her belt and glance at it. Linda Coffey.

Paige did her best to control her excitement. She sent another nudge: show me where you are. Paige then got another image as Linda glanced down at some mail on the kitchen counter and she read a name and an address:

Denver Sutton
    3116 Overlook Court
    Prospect, Kentucky 40059

She then lost the thread, but it didn't matter. She had an address. She knew where to find both Michaels and Coffey if they moved fast enough. She picked up the phone to call Tom and then hesitated. If she called in the cavalry, then things might go bad for Linda. She knew Michaels seemed to have found a way to maintain control of Linda and if they rolled up in several police cars, what would she force her to do?

Paige stood by the table. She felt her head swim. She could hear a faint voice. "My little Pigeon. You did well. You did well. Now finish this."

"What the bloody hell?" she said out loud. "Shepherd?" Shaking her head, she tried to clear those thoughts from her mind. Shepherd was dead. She saw his dead body. Fighting demons must be getting to her.

Back to reality, Paige, she said to herself. Reality? This felt like a horror film.

Getting her head back in the game, Paige realized she didn't want to take chances with Linda's career and life. Instead of calling Tom, she selected Victor's name and called him. Together, they would end this once and for all.

———

Victor drove like a mad man despite the snow on the roads. Overnight more than four inches of fresh snow had fallen and most of the roads, especially the seldom used ones, were still treacherous. Paige sat in the front passenger seat and Hawkins in the rear.

Victor asked Hawkins, "What does the Google satellite image show?"

When Paige called him to tell him she'd found Linda and Michaels, he snagged Hawkins and rushed to her place to pick her up. She gave him the address and his phone displayed the location of the house which was part of a new development outside of Prospect; a rich enclave of multi-million-dollar homes, some of which sat on a bluff above the Ohio River. Sutton's home was the first one built in the subdivision.

"Man, the house is huge and it sits literally on the bluff. His views of the Ohio River have to be spectacular."

"Let me guess," Victor said, "only one way in and out. Right?"

"You got it. He has a long driveway. If they're up there, we can use your car to block the road and they've got no chance to get out."

Paige said, "Victor, you and I need to talk about how we're going to use Mike. We don't have an Abet Stone for him. If we take him up there with us and she jumps into his mind, we will have a real problem."

"I'll be alright," Hawkins said.

Paige shook her head. "You can't guarantee that. She's found a way to get easily into people's minds and take up space there. If she gets into yours, with your skill set, it would be bad for anyone else around you."

Victor said, "Don't worry. I've already decided how we will use the good captain."

"Oh, really?" Hawkins said.

"Yes. Your idea of blocking the road is a good one. It looks like there's a good straight stretch. Once we get there, I'll block it with the Chevelle. Then you are going to set up with your sniper rifle. Feel free to use the trunk. I want you targeted on the driveway and if you see anyone drive down the road then I want you to put a bullet in their forehead, especially if it's Michaels. You will be able to take her out before she can find you in the Collective whatchamajiger."

"Collective Conscious," Paige said.

"Yeah. That," said Victor.

Hawkins was quiet for a moment then said, "Sounds like a plan. I won't lie, I'd rather be up there with you guys, but I get it. I don't want to risk her getting away."

"Good man," Victor said.

Fifteen minutes later, they found the entrance to the subdivision. It was new enough there were only four houses built so far and Sutton's house was all the way at the rear of the development. Victor found the street leading to his house and turned the Chevelle sideways to block the entrance.

The three of them piled out and Victor noticed how quiet the snow made everything. This far out into the country, there were no traffic noises, no kids playing, nothing to break the silence. The skies remained overcast, and the breeze was picking up. They were predicting more snow later in the afternoon.

Victor and Paige both wore boots as they planned to approach the house through a strand of trees off to one side of the road. They would be able to get close before actually making a move on the home. Victor took his katana and Glock. Paige had her Walther. This would either be a quick in and out or they wouldn't return at all.

Paige pointed to the driveway and the unbroken blanket of snow. "They were here this morning, and it means they are still here. They haven't left yet."

To Hawkins, Victor said, "Time to get ready, Captain."

Hawkins grunted and Victor watched as he set up his sniper rifle with practiced ease, using sandbags and wedges he brought along to give him a balanced shooting platform. When he was ready, he turned to Victor and Paige and simply said, "Happy hunting."

Victor fist bumped him and then he and Paige started making their way up the hill through the woods. He thought, *and through the woods to grandmother's house we go,* though he knew at the end of this walk there would be no sweet grandma with milk and cookies. Instead, he would find a viper and his girlfriend. The only question was what kind of shape she would be in.

The two of them made the walk in silence, both lost in their own thoughts. Victor was more than a little aware of the woman walking next to him and he felt the mix of feelings again. He pushed them aside. He needed to concentrate on the problem at hand, because if he didn't, then none of them would be around to worry about it.

They got even with the house, a two-story brick traditional with a three-car garage, and crouched down behind a huge pine tree, watching the house through a few breaks in the branches. Linda's cruiser and Michaels' Porsche were parked out front. There was a dead body lying on the ground next to the steps leading to the front door. From the DMV photo of Sutton Paige showed him before they left, it was clear he was no longer in the land of the living. Snow covered the body, but the man's head was turned towards them and the neat bullet hole right above his nose showed he had been shot. Damn.

Victor tapped Paige on the shoulder and motioned for them to move further using the woods as cover and she nodded her agreement. They made it even with the house and there were only two windows, one on each floor and both covered with curtains.

He whispered, "Looks as good a spot as any. Ready?"

"Yes. Let's do this."

"Damn straight. And remember, shoot her, don't talk to her. And if we see Linda, let me handle her."

Paige gave another nod and they sprinted to the side of the house. Victor was more than a little surprised they made it without anyone shooting at them. They pressed their backs to the house and then they inched their way to the first-floor window and glanced through the curtains. They saw a large dining room table and an archway that led to a huge kitchen.

Then he saw movement and Linda paced into and then out of view. She had her arms wrapped around herself, her head down, and he saw tears on her cheeks. Her clothes were wrinkled, and he saw blood stains on her shirt. He knew who it was who shot Sutton. Bloody hell.

Paige pointed towards the rear of the house and the two of

them moved that way. They stopped and glanced at the corner of the home. Paige's expression showed she'd seen the blood, too.

Victor said, "Linda shot Sutton."

"Yes, she did," Paige replied.

"Will she know she did it? Once we remove the mind control?"

"I think so. Hard for her not to. Caleb knew what he was being asked to do but couldn't stop himself. I'm guessing it will be the same for her."

"Son of a bitch," Victor seethed.

Paige laid a hand on his shoulder and said, "First things first. Let's get her free of Michaels. I may be able to do for her what I did for Caleb."

"Yeah, yeah, yeah. I hear ya. Let's do this. I don't think there's any point in being subtle. If this place is like most of these high-priced homes, then there will be a burglar alarm and it will announce any door we open."

"Fast and furious then?"

"Fast and furious. There's a patio door and if it's locked, I'll kick it in, and we go in. I'll take on Linda. Thankfully her gun wasn't on her hip when she walked by, but you can bet it's close to her. You take care of Michaels."

"Sounds like a plan."

They started towards the door when Paige grabbed his arm and pulled him to a stop. "Be careful," was all she said, taking him off guard by the fact she really did care.

He smiled at her. "Me? Not a chance."

And with that he rushed to the door and kicked it in and dove inside.

———

Paige slipped into the house right behind Victor, her robin's egg blue Walther in her hand. The patio door let them into a large family room and Victor took off to the right and an entrance to the dining room. She went straight ahead towards a hallway she knew had to lead to the kitchen.

She was almost to the hallway when she heard gunshots, two of them, and the breaking of glass as the shots hit the window in the dining room. In front of her Dorah Michaels turned into the hallway, saw her and then spun out of view away from the shooting. Paige cursed herself for not getting off a shot. She heard Michaels running towards the front door and she went out the patio door and around to the front.

When she got to the front, she saw Michaels running to her Porsche. Paige shot at Michaels and missed, but it forced Michaels to drop down behind her car. Paige took better aim and then shot out the front tire of her Porsche and then did the same thing for Linda's cruiser. Neither of them would be leaving any time soon.

Paige yelled, "Police. Show yourself with your hands up."

Michaels shouted, "Kiss my ass."

Then the woman made a break for the side of the house. Paige got off another shot and it hit Michaels and spun her around, but she kept her feet, turned the corner and was out of sight. Paige screamed in frustration, reversed course, and retraced her steps.

When she got to the rear of the house, she saw Michaels doing her best to run through the yard to a group of trees at the rear of the property. She slipped and skidded as she did so. At the same time, Linda Coffey came out the patio door and turned to face Paige, a gun in her hand. Linda began to raise the gun when Victor flew out the door in a flying tackle.

The two of them went down hard and Linda fought to get her gun hand up to shoot him, but Victor used his bulk to pin her arm to the ground. With one hand, he slipped the Abet Stone off his neck and placed it around hers. Immediately she stopped fighting him and her face broke into a look of horror.

"Victor," she screamed. "I shot you. My God, I shot you."

It was then Paige noticed the blood running from under his left coat sleeve and down onto his hand, which was now covered in blood and Victor's face was a few shades whiter.

Victor said, "It's only a flesh wound."

He rolled off Linda and gestured to Michaels running away. "Any chance you two can shoot her please?"

Paige said, "You're bleeding. You need an ambulance."

"What I bloody need, is a bullet put in that woman's skull," he snarled.

Before Paige could respond, Linda was up and after Michaels. Paige mumbled, "Dammit." And took off after the two women.

Paige saw Michaels look over her shoulder, the fear plain on her face. She slipped and fell to the ground, got up again and started to stumble away, whimpering the whole time. Linda, as if her anger made her impervious to the snowy ground, flew after her and closed the gap.

Michaels skidded to a stop and then turned around, frozen in her spot. Linda slowed to a walk, her gun up and pointed at Michael's chest. Paige heard Linda scream, "You bitch. You made me kill those people. You goddamned bloody bitch."

Before Paige could stop her, Linda pulled the trigger and shot Michaels. The round hit her in the right shoulder. Michaels fell backwards and disappeared. Paige ran up to where Linda stood and saw the bluff ended right where Michael's stood only moments before. She eased up to the edge and looked over. The Ohio River flowed by about a hundred feet below.

There was a shoreline of rocks and sand, but she did not

see a body on the shore. Michaels must have fallen into the river. She watched downstream, but the river was muddy, and she did not see a body.

She heard Linda crying and turned to the distraught woman. Her Abet Stone, which had been glowing orange, now faded to its natural color. Michaels tried to control the detective to the very end, but now her control was over.

Victor walked up behind them. He held his left arm straight down; blood continued to drip from his fingers. Linda saw the blood and took a step towards him, but then she hesitated. She stopped crying as an immense sadness settled on her features.

"Victor, I'm so, so sorry I shot you. I didn't have a choice," she said.

"I know, Linda. I know. It wasn't you who shot me. It was Michaels. It's over."

Linda shook her head and then moved a couple of steps closer to the edge of the bluff. "Yes it is. For me at least."

Paige instantly knew what Linda planned and she tried to jump into her mind, but the Abet Stone flared orange and blocked her from doing so. Linda glanced down at the stone and half smiled. "So that's what freed me."

Victor seemed to also know what Linda planned to do. "Look, Linda. We can work all this out. I need your help. After all, you shot me. You need to be the one to help me, okay?"

She shook her head. "Victor, I killed those women. All of them. I can't live with that. I just can't."

Victor lunged for her, but it was too late. Linda spun in one swift move and fell over the edge of the cliff. Victor fell to his knees and began to cry. Paige stepped up next to him and looked down. Unlike Michaels, Linda did not make it to the water, her body sprawled out on a large rock, her back broken and her life gone.

She felt tears in her own eyes and placed a hand on the shoulder of the Hand of God. She knew this would be hard for him to overcome. She knelt next to him, and silently put her arm around him. He leaned into her and cried while she held him.

Epilogue

Paige walked into the Raven and found Victor sitting at a table in the corner. In the month since being shot, his arm was healing up nicely. After all, as he pointed out, it wasn't the first time he'd been shot, and he knew to follow the doctor's instructions. He still wore an arm sling, but the doctors said he'd be out of it in a week.

He was nursing a bourbon and when the waitress came over, she asked for the same. Neither of them spoke until her drink was delivered. She raised her glass and said, "A toast."

He watched her wearily and said, "To?"

"To Linda and to an end to the Devil's Mark Killer."

Victor drew a deep breath and let it out and then raised his glass to hers.

"Did they believe you?" he asked.

"Yes, they did. No one wants to look too close at this one."

With the death of Linda Coffey, Paige told the chief of D's after the DNA results were in, Linda got a tip to where the suspect, Dorah Michaels, was staying and she contacted Paige to come as backup, but she tried to apprehend her on her own.

TONY ACREE & LYNN TINCHER

There was a struggle. Paige arrived in time to see Linda shoot Michaels and both of them fell over the edge. Linda unfortunately died and Michaels landed in the river. Despite a huge effort, her body was never found.

Paige made sure it was reported Linda died a hero. When it came to the bullet found inside Sutton which came from Linda's gun, Victor got his computer hacker friend, Kurt, to get into the LMPD system and delete the ballistics file on her gun so there would be no match.

Her bravery was all over the news stations for several days, then the next set of murders in the city moved the media's attention elsewhere. As for the brass, they were happy to have the case closed and buried.

Paige asked, "Where's Elizabeth?"

Victor shrugged his shoulders. "No clue. The day after Michaels was taken care of, she was gone. Tank says he doesn't know either. Something about heading home to take care of some old business."

"And Hawkins?"

"I think we will keep him around for a bit. He proved to be pretty handy."

She sipped her bourbon and then asked him, "And what about you? What's next for the Hand of God?"

"Brother Joshua says there's some kind of trouble going on in Atlanta and he wants me and Winston to go down and see what's what."

Paige had met Winston Reynolds the week before. A former NFL linebacker, Winston was every bit as formidable as Victor and she knew he was a great right-hand man for the kind of work the Hand of God was called to handle.

"What about Visette?" Victor asked.

Paige said, "She's good. I, well, I showed her a picture of Dorah Michaels. We'd hoped we found the last Reader. But no. Visette had met her before in Montana. We are still a Reader shy. I've got my work cut out for me."

Victor nodded in silence.

"Will I see you when you get back?" she asked.

He paused a few seconds before answering as he stared down at the brown liquid left in the bottom of his glass. "Here's the thing. The women I get involved with tend to end up either dead or damaged."

"I think you know I'm not like most women."

It made him laugh a bit. The first time since Linda's death.

"True that. Let's see how things are when I get back from Atlanta. Fair enough?"

"Fair enough," she said.

It was Burgers and Bluegrass night at the Raven and a bluegrass band kicked off the night with an old Irish tune. Victor sat down his bourbon, slipped off his sling with a slight wince and stood. He offered his hand and asked, "Care to join me?"

She took his hand and said, "I thought you'd never ask."

And the Reader and the Hand of God walked to a spot in front of the band and started to dance.

THE END

Tony's Acknowledgments

The release of the last Victor McCain novel, *Revenge,* was five years ago. Not long after it's release I suffered a major concussion and it took me a long time to regain my writing mojo.

What got me moving again was the chance to write a crossover novel with Lynn Tincher, the author of the Mind Bending series. Lynn, I can't thank you enough.

Added thanks to Starbucks Store # 2464 in Prospect, where I finished the book with the lifting of the pandemic restrictions. After my own family, I spend more time with my extended family at Starbucks than anyone else, and you guys are truly fam.

And thanks to you, dear reader, for patiently waiting for Victor McCain to once again come to life on the pages of a novel. I have my mojo back and you won't have to wait another five years for the next one.

Lynn's Acknowledgments

Special thanks to Tony Acree; without whom, this would not be possible.

About Tony Acree

Tony Acree is an award winning author, screenwriter and publisher. Tony lives near Goshen Kentucky with his wife, twin girls, two female dogs, a female cat, and the way the goldfish looks at him, he believes she's female too.

About Lynn Tincher

Lynn was born just outside of Louisville, Kentucky in the beautiful city of La Grange. One of her fondest memories of growing up was when a short story she wrote for an English class was read in front of the students at Oldham County High School. Since then, her love for writing blossomed. She studied Theater Arts at Eastern Kentucky University in hopes of becoming a Drama/English teacher. Lynn had several articles published in local magazines and online, but the thought of writing a novel always stuck with her.

Also by Tony Acree

Victor McCain Thrillers
The Hand of God

The Watchers

The Speaker

Revenge

Victor McCain Short Stories
Nightmare

Back to Hell

Lonnie, Me and the Hand of God (written with Marian Allen)

Samantha Tyler Thrillers
Vengeance

Absolution

Non-fiction

Tell Me More

Also by Lynn Tincher

Afterthoughts

Left in the Dark

Buried Deep

Where There is Light

Junna (coming soon)

Made in the USA
Columbia, SC
28 September 2023

23514618R00178